The Swap

The Swap

Antony Moore

DELTA TRADE PAPERBACKS

THE SWAP
A Delta Book

PUBLISHING HISTORY
Harvill Secker UK edition published July 2007
Delta Trade Paperback edition / September 2008

Published by Bantam Dell
A Division of Random House, Inc.
New York, New York

Library of Congress Cataloging-in-Publication Data
Moore, Antony.
The swap / Antony Moore.
p.   cm.
ISBN 978-0-385-34234-6 (trade pbk.)
1. Class reunions—Fiction.   2. Comic books, strips, etc.—Fiction.
3. Murder—Fiction.   I. Title.
PR6113.O5558S93   2008
823'.92—dc22   2008011048

Printed in the United States of America
Published simultaneously in Canada

www.bantamdell.com

BVG 10 9 8 7 6 5 4 3 2 1

For Stella and Conor

PROLOGUE

Cornwall, 1982

"*Superman One?*" The "odd boy" turned his face, never completely clean, toward the school building and Harvey watched his nose wrinkle as to a bad smell. "Why would I want that?"

Harvey gave a deep, exaggerated sigh; it wasn't as if he needed the deal.

"I don't know. Who cares? I'll swap with someone else. It's just not my sort of thing really. *Superman's* not so sharp, yeah? I like the *Silver Surfer.* This is so old, it's the first one . . . Kids' stuff really."

"So why would I swap?" The odd boy was plaintive, and Harvey sighed again. Did he need to explain? Because you don't have friends to play with; because you want to be in with me; because it breaks up the tedium of the school day; because this'll give you something to carry and show to people that won't make them laugh at you, that'll actually be halfway acceptable in the classroom between eight forty-five and nine o'clock when everyone is just killing time, usually by killing you. Any of these things would be easily said, except when you are twelve—even if you are sort of thinking them. So Harvey just shrugged and waved his hand. "Up to you, in't it?"

"And you want this?" The odd boy put his hand to the thin piece of plastic pipe that he was wearing round him like a bandolier.

"Not really. But I'll swap." Harvey had seen the odd boy slashing the grass with it as he walked up the track from the road toward the school, seen the way it lopped off the heads of the grasses, sending the seed bags spinning into the air. He liked that: neat, even balletic destruction. Every boy's idea of beauty.

"And if I say yes, that's it. I can't have it back?" The odd boy was being odder than usual and Harvey was losing interest fast. He wasn't a bully, but he wasn't a bloody nanny, either.

"Of course not. Once you swap, you swap; you can't undo it." He turned and began to make his way up the track that led to the back entrance to the school, a cart track really, overhung with great, untended cedars. "But forget it; it's not worth it really. Who cares?" That was an expression Harvey was growing into. He'd started saying it last year when it had sounded unnatural and he had always expected someone to say "Well, you do of course." But they never did, so he was growing into it. He felt that by next year, the start of his teens, it might suit him rather well. He had those sorts of feelings. And he sensed they set him apart: He kind of anticipated how things were going to be, he could see where he was going. Certainly he was different from classmates like Bleeder, the odd boy, who now trailed behind him up the path. Bleeder because of the nosebleeds and the scabs that always seemed to bedeck his body. Odd, for obvious reasons.

"No, hang on. I'm not saying I won't." Harvey heard the bleating need for a normal interaction in the odd boy's voice, the instant nostalgia for being treated with respect. He wondered vaguely if he'd done wrong. Mean to get his hopes up.

"Look, you fucking freak, do you want to swap or not? 'Cause if you do, let's get it over with. I don't want to be seen talking to you at school."

"OK, don't . . . don't . . ." The odd boy's voice made no real change as he took the verbal blow. This, after all, was what he was used to. "I just. I stole it like." He looked at Harvey, who had turned to regard him without sympathy, and for the first time their eyes met. "I stole it and it's difficult to give it to you."

Harvey ignored the bait; what did he care where he got it?

"So don't swap, then." He turned again and made, with some relief, for the farm gate that separated the school grounds from the surrounding fields. This was the last time he bothered with the deadbeats; he'd done it before, talked to freaks and got caught up in things that really didn't interest him. Sod it, it wasn't worth it. He was on his way out of this, out of small-town life and into the city. He'd been to London—admittedly with his auntie Kate—but he'd been there and it was where he was going. That was his future. All this rubbish, it didn't matter a damn.

"Here, here, let's do it." The odd boy was scrambling to get in front of him, brushing through the nettles that lined the path. Harvey wondered vaguely if his bare knees were stung. The odd boy gave no indication of pain and put his back to the gate, unwrapping the plastic tubing from his shoulder. "It's yours now. Don't tell where you got it from."

He held it out eagerly and Harvey gazed at it wonderingly: Why on earth would he want it? He actually shook his head but then caught the hope in the odd boy's eye and sighed again. God, it was ridiculous. He opened his satchel, a rather cool army surplus, canvas bag, on the flap of which he had painted the face of Donald Duck with a cigar in his beak. The painting was good. He pulled out the magazine, wrapped in the plastic sheath he put round all his comics.

"Sure?" he asked with heavy irony.

"Yeah, OK." The odd boy held out the length of plastic and Harvey took it but the boy did not let go.

"Give me the comic." His voice was taut for a moment and Harvey glanced up, surprised.

"Yeah, all right," he said. "I'll just take this plastic cover off. Only collectors use these." He tried to slip the liner away but the odd boy snatched it from him.

"No," he said. "I want it as you offered it to me." He let go of the plastic wire and held the comic against him tightly, as though ready to defend it from attack.

Harvey shook his head and raised his eyes with practiced disbelief. "You fucking freak," he said and, pushing the odd boy aside, clambered over the gate. He walked away, slashing the grasses to left and right, all the way up to the point where the wild world was tamed and blended into the edge of the rugby pitch. As he walked, the odd boy's eyes did not leave him. Clutched in his hands, the *Superman One* was pressed to his chest, tightly held, but also unwrinkled: guarded against harm.

CHAPTER ONE: London, the present

The sigh had become a feature of the man. And when he sighed it signified no special existential despair, only an acknowledgement of the fact that another day had come and the coffee that he was drinking was no better than it had been yesterday. He sat in unsplendid isolation at the counter of his shop, his back to the rows and rows of stands that ran away from him toward the front door. Each stand was thick with plastic, and in the harsh strip lighting it was hard to see that each piece of plastic contained a comic.

"All right, Harvey? Make us one, I'm freezing."

How long had it been from his own arrival until Josh tapped him playfully on one shoulder while walking the other way? The coffee cup was still warm in his hands. He looked up. "You're late." He hadn't actually checked the time but he liked to start each working day by registering a complaint, preferably to Josh.

"What's up? We open, are we?"

"Of course we are open. We keep business hours, or at least, I do."

"Well, the sign doesn't say Open." Josh went back to the door and turned a rather grubby picture of Thor, God of Thunder, saying Closed to an identical one of him saying Open. "You wonder why we don't get any customers, but you have to turn the sign round, Harvey." Giggling, Josh made his way behind the counter and through into the back room where they kept the coffee. "You might have been swamped with customers by now if you'd remembered that simple rule." Josh's voice was muffled by the sound of water being run into a kettle.

But not muffled enough.

"Fuck off." Harvey rose from his seat at the counter and moved to the front of the shop to avoid Josh's voice, which now began painfully to accompany music on Xfm from the back room. He opened the door and walked out into a February wind that made him lift his shoulders and narrow his eyes.

If only.

Some days it was worse than usual, the memories, the wondering. It had never left him. Ever since he moved from Cornwall, made his way to the big city, he'd sort of expected it to go, to withdraw into some back room of his mind, but every day it had seemed stronger. He breathed deep of the icy air and contemplated the empty street. Few customers here, no passing trade. The sigh was a part of him, as much as the hunch of the shoulder and the reach for the cigarettes from the inside pocket of his denim jacket. He struggled to light up in the hectic wind, failed, swore vaguely, and made his way back into the shop to sit once more behind the counter on one of the two high stools. After a few moments he stabbed out the butt with a hard vicious motion.

"Turn that shit down, will you, Josh!"

"OK, Harvey, OK. You don't need to get nasty." And Harvey put his head in his hands and felt the way his hair was disappearing, leaving him: abandoning ship.

"What I could have done." It was one-thirty and the Queen's Head was full. But they had been there for over an hour and had a prime seat. It was a pub without noticeable character or appeal. But it was located midway between one set of office blocks and another and had accepted the benefits of fortune

without complaint. It was also the closest place to get a drink to Inaction Comix.

"What might have been." Harvey was making a song of it, an ironic little play for Josh's benefit. What else could he do? He'd told the story too many times.

"Yeah." Josh's mind and his glasses were on the fruit machine and more specifically the T-shirt of the pretty blonde leaning against it. "Yeah, you could have been in Tahiti or something."

"New York." Harvey didn't like his fantasy to be made commonplace. No lottery winner's confusion for him. He knew what he'd have done. "A little coffeehouse downtown with murals on the walls, Spider-Man, the Fantastic Four, you know, classy but trashy, and I'd still have collected but just for fun."

"Yeah, cool. A Superman One would have got you that, no problem." Josh smiled hopefully at the blonde who turned away to her less desirable friend with a grimace. "You could have been a contender." He put on a comedy-Brando to cover his not unanticipated failure and tried to catch the friend's eye.

"Yeah, I could have been a contender"—Harvey pulled on his third pint—"but Bleeder is the contender now. He's out there somewhere with a Superman One. And good luck to him."

The blackboards above the bar described the almost risibly limited selection of foodstuffs that the pub had to offer. He examined them with the eyes of one who has read them before but seeks distractions.

"Maybe he's sold it, but maybe he chucked it away the day after you gave it to him." Josh found his attention caught, as it often was, by the topic of Harvey's loss.

"No, he hasn't sold it: They only come on the market every blue moon and it's always in the press when they do. I've sat and watched its value increase for twenty years. Every year I look in Overstreet and every year it's another few thousand dollars. A few thousand a year for twenty years ... So yeah, maybe he chucked it out with the trash. Or maybe he just likes reading it too much to part with it."

"What did you swap it for again?" Josh wasn't usually malicious; that's why Harvey liked him, or tolerated him at least. He picked up his pint and finished it in a long mouthful.

"Fuck off," Harvey said.

"So, have you decided about going to the reunion?" Josh was struggling to keep pace and his fourth pint was making him slur a little. Harvey had strict standards about alcohol consumption—don't get silly until the fifth pint—but he politely ignored Josh's faux pas.

"I've thrown the letter away," he said, making sure he enunciated clearly. "I just don't see the point really. What could I possibly say or do to interest those people?"

The letter had arrived in the Saturday post and Harvey had been expecting it. It offended everything in his nature that he was expecting it, indeed he had tried very hard not to expect it, which is a difficult trick to perform. Every year they came, and every year he attempted it. And every year the trick failed. When it arrived he had a debate with himself and this too was a repeat of one he'd been having for twenty years. The debate involved two levels. The first was the "I'm not going to go" level. The second was the "I'm not going to let my going or not going mean anything in a feeble, shallow way about where my life has got to" level. The letter was an invitation to a reunion at his old school in Cornwall, and at both levels he usually lost.

This year was particularly pressing as it was twenty years and would be a more formal affair. Twenty years since they had sat their O levels together in the drafty school hall, the same place they would hold the reunion. And now O levels were a historical relic, as meaningless when trying to impress the younger generation as boasting of your high score on Space Invaders.

"So tell them you run a comic shop." Josh managed to make it sound like a good thing to say.

"Mmm, you mean tell them exactly what I told them the last time I was down two years ago, and the year before that and five years ago, and ten?"

"Well, yeah."

Harvey sighed his sigh, and flicked cigarette ash into a metal tin on the ugly little table that the pub grudgingly allowed its customers to sit at. "Admit that in the years since I last saw them I've not got married, or had any children, or had a promotion, or inherited a fortune . . . That what I've done is exactly the same thing I was doing last time I went?"

"Well, tell them you've expanded."

"They'll see that for themselves."

"In the shop. Tell them you're doing really well and planning to open another branch, something like that."

"Lie to them?"

"Yeah."

"It's a thought." Harvey dropped the stub of his cigarette into the tin tray and watched it lying there smoking by itself. "But if I'm going to do that why not tell them I've won the lottery and am moving to New York to open a coffeehouse with superheroes on the walls? I mean, if I'm going to lie why not make it something exciting?"

Josh grinned to announce a joke: "Tell them you found a *Superman One*."

Harvey closed his eyes for a long moment. Then he sighed. The fact that he did it a lot didn't mean it was only a habit.

CHAPTER TWO

"The thing about reunions is that they bring out the old you."

"So don't go."

"But that's the point, I like the old me. I like the me that I was at school. Believe it or not, I was cool. In with the in crowd. Comics gave me that. That's why I've stuck with them. But whereas it was cool at school it kind of gets less and less cool as you get older. To the point where it will, very soon I suspect, become ridiculous. And then what do I do? Go for a job at a bank or somewhere, and they'll ask: 'Experience?' and I'll say: 'Adding up the cash register after selling a *Fantastic Four Number Six*.'"

"What condition?"

"Never mind."

"It's a big price difference. I mean if it was mint, then, to be honest, I would think any bank would be impressed." Josh spluttered into his drink. "And I guess for you it's especially poignant, going back."

"Why?"

"Because that was a time when you weren't bitter and twisted."

"What the fuck do you mean?" Harvey demanded, knowing exactly what he meant. "Who's bitter and twisted?"

"You are, about the *Superman One*. But you didn't know it was valuable then, so it's the one time in your life you weren't thinking about what you might have had."

Harvey looked for a while into the bottom of his glass. It was an occasional habit of Josh's to speak a devastating truth, unexpected and unlooked-for. Harvey had once taken, very briefly, to wearing a cape to work. It had been long and black with a red velvet lining. As he walked from the tube one morning he had caught sight of his reflection in a shop window and had tried hard to place what he saw. When he arrived, Josh was waiting outside the shop and Harvey had asked him what he thought. "You look like the Frog Prince," Josh had said simply. And Harvey, for all he had told him to go fuck himself, knew at once that he was right; and the cloak had been quietly put at the back of the cupboard against the unlikely event that he was ever invited to a fancy dress party. And Josh was right again: That time was special because he hadn't carried the burden that he always denied he carried now. That time did appear somehow blessed, and he always seemed to be looking for some way back to that. All roads for a long time had seemed to lead backward. So he told Josh to go fuck himself.

"So maybe you'll go back and you'll meet Bleeder there." Josh smiled encouragingly, making Harvey grimace, not least because it saddened him to think that his shop assistant knew this boy's playground nickname from his school days well enough to use it in conversation without pausing to think. They had had this conversation before, but not for a while, and Josh was suddenly animated. "I mean, he hasn't been back to any of the other reunions, has he? But this one is twenty years. People get more sentimental as they reach middle age, maybe he'll feel the time is right." He spoke with all the wisdom of the young and Harvey shook his head, wincing slightly at the words "middle age."

"I doubt it," he said. "You really don't listen, do you? Bleeder had a shit time at school; I've told you that. Every day of every term he had a shit time. Everyone took the piss, all the time. That's how it was. Why would he want to come back and see everybody again? He'd have to be mad."

"Well, why did you pick on him?" Josh blushed, making Harvey wonder, not for the first time, if perhaps he had suffered at school.

"Because he was odd. I've told you before. He was weird and everybody knew it. He didn't have any clothes other than these sort of weird mismatches from the charity shop. And his hair was cut short by his mum. And he talked funny, sort of high-pitched and freaky, like a kind of girlish voice. And he wasn't into anything. He didn't know music, or comics, or sport, and, of course, he didn't stand a chance with the girls 'cause of—well, all of the above. And to top it all he was ginger. And gingers are by definition fair game. In fact, in some parts of the world they are legally hunted." He sipped the last drops from his glass and noticed that Josh wasn't smiling. "Look, he took shit, OK? Every school has one and he was ours. I didn't like it, didn't do it much, didn't encourage it in others. If I thought about it, which I didn't very often, then I thought it was harsh. But it happened. And if it had happened to you would you go back for a get-together to see all those lovely people who made your life hell? No, of course you wouldn't. So that's why he's never there."

He spoke clearly and with confidence, but in his mind there was already forming a picture of Bleeder standing in the school hall where the reunions always happened. He was looking a bit downtrodden and sad and pathetic but Harvey was going up to him and shaking his hand. And Bleeder was smiling and saying there were no hard feelings and then he was telling Harvey: "Oh, that old comic, oh, no, we burned that years ago," and the two of them were having a laugh about those strange times and that strange day of the swap and that funny length of plastic that Bleeder was carrying and Harvey was saying "If only we had that comic now we'd both be rich" and they were laughing and shaking their heads over the inequities of fate and then it was over and Harvey was getting on with things, getting on with his whole life, in fact, without thinking about something as pathetic as this all the time.

That it was such a fully realized fantasy sweeping so swiftly through Harvey's mind is explained by the fact that it had done so many, many times before. "I'd love to see him," he said meditatively now, "just talk it over with him once. I've thought about phoning him a million times. Or phoning his mum anyway, getting a number for him, assuming he isn't still living at home." He sniggered before remembering that Josh lived with his mother. "Getting hold of him and just having a chat, you know. Seeing what he's up to, how he's doing . . ."

"Seeing if he's still got the *Superman One*. Seeing if you can have it back." Josh was not in a forgiving mood.

"No. Well, yeah, why not? Who knows what people keep, you know? Half the world doesn't know the value of what it's got in its attic. I've probably got a Rembrandt, or a rare stamp or some other junk. He might have a *Superman One*. I'd love to just check."

"And rip him off. Offer him fifty pence for it, say you want it back for sentimental reasons. And then flog it for a couple of hundred grand. Something like that?"

"Er, yeah." Harvey didn't like it when people he considered intellectually inferior to himself read his mind. "Something like that." And he laughed, but without much enthusiasm.

"Well, why don't you just ring him then? If his mum still lives in Cornwall why not just get her number from the directory and ring her up. For all you know he committed suicide as a result of your cruelty and you've been dreaming of ripping him off all these years for nothing."

This was so outrageously over the top that Harvey snorted with laughter and Josh was forced to join him. "It might happen," Josh said, trying to remain angry. "Anything might have happened in twenty years; you don't know."

"Yeah, he might have had twenty years of therapy and be

ready to forgive me. Maybe he'll even give me the comic to prove he's cured."

"So why don't you, you bloody git?"

"Why don't I ring him?" Harvey was sniggering in anticipation. "I'll tell you why, shall I? I don't ring him because I can't remember his fucking name. All I know is that he was Bleeder the odd boy." He laughed so loud he caused heads to turn in the pub and drowned out Josh's spluttery cackle. "Oh, Jesus," Harvey said, "I really ought to remember his name, after what we put him through."

CHAPTER THREE

On the journey down from London, Harvey again tried to remember Bleeder's name. He could see the pale, unhappy face before him but all he could think of was the odd boy. Bleeder the odd boy. It brought a vague and, in truth, fleeting feeling of guilt that he couldn't come up with any more than that. In the carriage of the 10:05 from Paddington to Penzance he prepared with what he considered military precision (but what was actually closer to civilian sloth). Lounging with a pen in one hand and a fake-leopard-skin-covered writing pad—one pound for two from Quidbusters, Lewisham—in the other, he planned his past. Josh's suggestion of lying had impressed him and, once he had decided to attend the reunion, he had spent some time toying with mysterious women friends, unexpected side careers, and even, for a dangerous moment, MI5. However, he had settled, as Josh had suggested, on a sense of heightened reality. Nothing too unlikely, just a mention of other departments at the shop; buying trips—actually to Bristol and Manchester—extended, more by implication than direct statement, to include New York and Vancouver; Josh multiplying, splitting amoebalike into a multitude of assistants; hints about cars, property. Harvey jingled the keys in his pocket and thought for a while about the house in Hampstead they might belong to. He really could picture it: nothing too flashy, one of those cottagey jobs up by the park. Was he married? No, that was too much. But he was involved. Kind of in love: Who wouldn't love her? But he wasn't sure he was ready. How do you ever know for sure? That was his problem. He actually chuckled out loud at the trickiness of the situation: How could a man in his position ever be really sure someone better wouldn't come along? She wanted kids, but, you know, he wanted to wait until he could see something of them, and that meant waiting till the pressure was off, and that could be a long wait. As the train entered a tunnel he found his own reflection looking back at him in the window. He saw the shaved head, where once dark hair had been tied back in a ponytail—shaved not to look like David Beckham so much as to stop him looking like his dad as it fell out of its own accord. He saw the stomach bulge underneath the black T-shirt with StanTheManLee written across it in green. He did the sigh. It was hard when people only saw you once every few years. How could that be anything but a punishment? The only consolation was that it was mutual. He thought for a moment about old Rob's battle with cancer and then hated it when he found himself smiling. Shit, that was not how he'd meant to end up. And that was the problem, of course: This was all about how you'd ended up, but he never felt like he'd ended anywhere really. He always felt, somehow, that he was about to begin.

And that took the guilt about forgetting Bleeder's name away. It was all so distant now, so meaningless. Why should he remember something from that far back? Who he used to be was disappearing into the image in the glass, as if he could see the person he had once been fleeting away from him in the racing landscape. What did it matter what Bleeder's real name was?

"**Charles Odd.**" **The man** in the smart suit—rather too smart for these surroundings—held out his hand, and Harvey shook it with wonder in his eyes.

"How are you?" Harvey felt the hand in his, firm and dry. The voice was strong, rich, without a trace of Cornwall in it.

How do we recognize people? It's an unanswered question.

Harvey had once read an article on psychology that said we plot the face like a computer scanner, remembering the tiniest nuances of singularity. Well, he had scanned this face long ago and it was fixed. He had sighted it from across the floor where he stood surrounded by most of the old crowd: Jack, who had got into heroin for a while after college but now was clean and living in Wales with his "old lady"; Rob, who played lower-league football for three years after school and then did a bit of coaching and now, following cancer treatment, worked in a sports shop in Ealing ... ("We should get together, H, I'd like to see your shop ...." Slight panic there, partly at the idea of some-one witnessing the reality of his carefully constructed fantasy life, and partly at being called H again—a name that was so cool it hurt at school, but which now made him think of that twat out of Steps); Susan, who used to go out with Jack but who was now married to a man in the navy who was away a lot (Harvey noticed Jack look at her with a mixture of nostalgia and possibility); and Steve, who'd stayed in town, stayed in lit-tle old St. Ives all this time, and ran a beach shop. That had led to the usual humorous remarks: "Not far to come, then, Steve?"; "Well, you've spread your wings, you must have flown at least two hundred yards," et cetera, jokes which were gen-uinely funny at that first get-together, fifteen years ago, which was a less formal affair when everyone was still optimistic, and when the town seemed like a deadly snare rather than some-thing troublingly like what they were looking for.

And the man whose face he'd scanned all those years ago had come over and smiled. "It's Harvey, isn't it? H? I'm sure I remember that face." And Harvey had swallowed, like a child meeting a policeman, and had grinned and felt a ludicrous blush spread over his cheeks. "Er, yeah, and I know you ..."

"Charles Odd. I was in your class, actually, though I don't think we moved in the same circles, did we?" He laughed. "It's good to see you, though. How's things?"

Harvey wanted to scream. Indeed, he felt some sort of cry

welling up inside and had to actively repress it. Bleeder. Bleeder Odd: not just odd but Odd. Fuck, he should have remembered that. Bleeder was here. Exactly as he had dreamed it. As he had seen it in his mind's eye. Except here he was dapper and smiling, not the shuffling, miserable deadbeat that Harvey had created. But here he was. A man he had thought about every day of his adult life. And never without regret and desire, pity and self-pity, guilt and bitterness, avarice and anger. Here was that face: the pinched eyes grown clear; the long, pointed nose, drawn back by the fleshing of the cheeks; the narrow, frightened mouth, full-lipped and open to show perfect teeth in an almost constant smile. All the singularity altered, yet recognition was instant and indubitable. Harvey tried to focus on psychology. He couldn't take much else in.

"This is my first time back in St. Ives for ages," the clear voice said as if telling him something small and of little interest, not something he had wondered about for twenty years. "I don't get down much and I'm not so sure about reunions, it's a funny business, isn't it, meeting up like this? But this time I happened to be here anyway so I thought I'd drop in." He glanced round with polite interest at the school assembly hall, taking in the long passageway that ran off it where the boys' toilets were: toilets in which Harvey knew for a fact Bleeder had been beaten senseless more times than he could remember. Harvey felt he was inhabiting a dream. Like fantasizing all your life about meeting Lou Reed and when you finally do finding that he chats about soft furnishings. Harvey hadn't really ever fixed in his mind what he and Bleeder would talk about, except of course for the *Superman One*. But he had assumed it would be significant, emotional, meaningful; that it would matter. Now here he was, here was Bleeder, and he just happened to be here and was exhibiting every sign of finding it a bit dull and of preparing to leave. "Have you been before?" Bleeder asked politely.

"Er, yeah, yeah, once or twice." Looking for you. Only looking for you.

"And are they always like this?"

"Like what?"

"Well . . . a bit sad?"

"Mmm. I guess so." Harvey could feel the top of his head beginning to lift, as if his brain was about to make its own way out of the situation. He put his hand up and scratched hard.

"So, what are you up to now?" This was a question that he and the old crowd had actively and specifically banned when they came back for that first ever get-together. It was sort of a joke, so now they said it with irony and it actually meant "This is boring, let's move on" sort of thing. But now Harvey said it and realized that it was The Question; it was what he had wanted to ask every day for two decades.

"Oh, I do a bit of work in the City." Bleeder smiled. "Maths was always my thing, I guess." No it wasn't, you didn't have a thing. You never had a thing.

"Yeah, I remember."

"So I set up a little company a while ago and it worked out quite well. I sold out last year, but I still do some consultancy work, a few days a week, here and in New York. It keeps me busy, without the stress." He smiled again and Harvey found himself smiling back. He reached desperately for his pockets and remembered that it was no-smoking this year for the first time. He also remembered his leopard-skin notebook from Quidbusters; might Bleeder have one, too?

"Really, the City, cool. So finance, huh? Interesting." It wasn't quite what he'd planned to say, but it was as good as anything else.

"Yes, mostly at Reiser and Watts." Bleeder produced a card and handed it to him. "Do you know them?"

"Um, no, I just . . ."

". . . or perhaps you're not in finance?"

"No, no, not finance."

"OK." Bleeder glanced round the room as if looking for someone more interesting to talk to. "So, what are you in?"

"Comics." Harvey found his cigarettes and got the packet out. If he couldn't smoke he could damn well fiddle with the box a bit. Attached to the packet, as if melded by his bodily emissions, was one of his own cards, with a picture of Betty Boop on it and his address. He passed it to Bleeder.

Bleeder was laughing. Bleeder was laughing at him. The realization of how far this was from the fantasy picture he had painted was enough to make him want to join in.

"Comics?" Bleeder was gazing at the card.

"Yeah, funny really." Harvey tried to smile. "I just sort of carried on being interested after school."

"Jesus, yes, you were the comic king, weren't you? Always swapping and bartering. You were a real wheeler-dealer. You should have ended up in the City really." He laughed again and Harvey felt his scalp give another skip. Always swapping? Christ, do you really have no idea?

"Er, yeah, so I just sort of stuck with it. Stick to what you're good at." He made a vague phrase, for no reason discernible to him. "I've got a shop, in London, in Old Street." He should have added something about departments and assistants and foreign trips, but somehow it got lost.

"Right." Bleeder nodded and gave a longer, more searching glance around the room. "Well, I guess if you like something . . ."

"Exactly." And Harvey saw his chance. He could just ask. So much buildup, twenty years of buildup, was making it harder than it needed to be. He could simply ask straight out and be done with it. It would be over. Unexpectedly an enormous rush of adrenaline shot up his spine and sealed his mouth shut. If I ask it will be over. If I ask I will have to hear an answer. He looked down and saw that the cigarette packet was trembling in his hand, trembling so much that the cellophane wrapper that he had left round the box was making little crinkling sounds. He raised his head and took a deep breath.

"Oh, there he is." Bleeder was looking past him at a crowd gathered in the corner where the bar was. "I've got to have a word." And before Harvey could stop him, before another word could escape him, Bleeder had moved off into the crowd. Harvey found he was panting as if he had been running. And he wanted to run, to race after Bleeder, grab him by the shoulders. He had been so close to a new life, a new start. As he stood breathing heavily and pushing the cigarette packet in and out of the cellophane, he looked at the group by the bar. Bleeder had joined it and was talking to an old man Harvey didn't recognize. Could he just go over? Demand that they continue the conversation? But he needed Bleeder alone. Perhaps he could drag him bodily outside. Who was that he was talking to? What could be more important than this conversation?

Rob and Steve came over.

"Bleeeeeder!" Rob hissed. "Having a nice chat, H?"

"Mmm, well, yeah . . ." Harvey was still gazing after Bleeder, as if watching a departing unicorn. "Who is that?" he asked. "Talking to him, the old bloke?"

"That's Mr. Simes," both Steve and Rob answered together. "Taught me physics," Steve added, "but also took maths. Top-stream maths. Not our class. Out of our league. Swot division. Hey, did Bleeder have your comic? The one that's going to make you rich?" Sometimes Harvey regretted his openness with his friends.

"Er, no. Don't think so . . . Was Bleeder in the top stream?" He moved the conversation on quickly to a point that caused him genuine surprise. "I thought he was, well—"

"Just there to be kicked?" Rob finished for him. "He was; he liked being kicked. But occasionally, just for a change, he did maths. Not much of a change really. I'm not sure I wouldn't have preferred the beatings myself. Touch and go."

"Simes liked the maths swots," Steve added. "Bleeder was probably his pet. Kept him in a basket in the corner, fed him on bones."

Harvey realized they were sniggering and forced a smile. "How old are you again?" he asked. This was another regular phrase, again getting less funny as the years passed.

"Yeah, but he's Bleeder, H," Steve said, grinning. "He's Bleeeeeeder."

"I know." Harvey found a sharp note in his voice as he said it. "I am fully aware of that."

"Uh-oh, sense of humor failure. You need a drink, mate." Rob patted him on the back and moved off toward the bar, which consisted of a long table with many plastic cups full of warm white wine on it.

"We all need a drink." Steve followed Rob down the room, leaving Harvey watching Bleeder with Zen-like focus. The old man he was talking to was hunched in a suit that could only belong to a retired teacher, gray and stained by a thousand chalk accidents. Mr. Simes. Harvey tried to remember if he had been taught by Mr. Simes at all. Perhaps he could go over and join in the conversation, mention algebra, for instance, or fractions. He didn't remember much else from maths and he didn't think he'd ever had Mr. Simes. Once he would have known without having to think. Bleeder was animated now, waving his arms. People in the group were glancing round; looks of vague surprise that anyone could talk excitedly about anything at a reunion seemed to flicker across polite smiles.

What is he doing? Harvey wondered. What is going on?

But whatever it was ended, and Bleeder at once moved away toward the door. Harvey saw that the old man was tempted to follow him. He made a move in the same direction as Bleeder's departing back, but then stopped as if uncertain. At that moment one of the group by the bar came over to the teacher. "So, still doing sums for a living, Simmo?" he asked loudly and got a small laugh from the crowd. Harvey shook his head; he'd done all the get-the-teacher-back stuff years ago. He turned and saw Bleeder stopped in the doorway—he was having to squeeze past someone that Harvey didn't recognize but wished he did. She was redheaded and nicely rounded with a clever, pretty face covered in freckles. She wore a long patchworked dress and her hair was tied back under purple silk. He noticed that much as he moved quickly to follow Bleeder. And as he passed her the woman spoke: "I'm sorry, am I in the right place? I'm looking for Class of 1986."

"Er, yeah." Harvey liked her voice, it was sort of husky and mellow at the same time, like Mariella Frostrup after a Lemsip. "It's in here; are you a graduate?"

"No, not me." She smiled and he liked that, too. "My husband"—*damn*—"is Jeff Cooper, I don't know if you know him?" Harvey did. Big heavy fucker with a tattoo, liked rugby—of course—one of Bleeder's most persistent tormentors in the old days.

"Yeah. I think he's down by the bar."

"That would be Jeff." And her voice carried just enough weariness and even disgust for Harvey to feel suddenly happier. He glanced out into the hallway and found Bleeder was still there, looking at the inevitable stand of old photographs: always the same pictures.

"I'm not sure it'll be much fun if you weren't at Trehendricks," Harvey said kindly. "It's a bit of a sad bunch getting nostalgic. I can't say I go for it myself," he added quickly.

"Oh, I don't know." She smiled again. "I think there's something rather sweet about doing it. Our past is who we are, isn't it?" Harvey nodded thoughtfully; it certainly was for him. There were times when he thought that was all he was.

"Mmm, scary thought," he said. She smiled dutifully and he wished he'd said something more intelligent, so he tried again: "I guess I'm never sure whether I'm trying to get away from all this or get back to it, you know?" He wasn't sure what he meant actually, but she reacted and looked him in the eye for a moment.

"Yes, I do. And I feel very much like that a lot of the time.

Recently, especially . . ." She looked over Harvey's shoulder into the hall, without enthusiasm. Harvey turned and found that Jeff Cooper was standing just behind him.

"Chatting up my wife, Briscow?" He stabbed Harvey in both ribs with his fingers. Harvey managed not to squeal.

"Trying to," he said through his wince, "but you're interrupting."

Cooper laughed at that. "Cheeky fucker," he said and attempted another dig, but Harvey blocked with his elbows.

"He was very kindly helping me," she said, giving Harvey a rueful, almost fraternal smile.

"Yes, you left her stranded in the hallway, Jeff," said Harvey, "and I was being gallant, in case you know what that means. The least you can do now is introduce us."

"If you like." Cooper moved gracelessly round and took his wife by the arm. "Maisie, this is Harvey Briscow; Harvey Briscow, Maisie Cooper, my lovely missis. And now I'm removing her so she can meet somebody interesting." He guffawed and began to move away but found she wasn't coming with him.

"I have already met someone interesting," said Maisie Cooper deliberately, "and I thank him for his help."

"No problem at all," Harvey muttered and was appalled to find himself blushing again. He moved quickly on into the foyer, and she allowed herself to be steered off by her husband. Not looking back, Harvey took several deep breaths and gazed for a long moment at a photograph of a 1980s hockey team. It was only after he had realized just how unrewarding this was that he noticed Bleeder had gone.

"Shit." Without any noticeable change in mood, Harvey knew what he wanted to do: needed to do really. He ran out of the two sets of double doors that fronted the school and into driving rain.

CHAPTER FOUR

The school had allowed the weekend visitors to park their cars along the forecourt and the drive that led down to the road. One of these cars was revving and its lights were on in the gathering afternoon gloom. Harvey ran to the car, heedless of the fact that he had left his coat behind in the foyer, and tapped on the window. Bleeder leaned across and wound down the window. "Hello," he said. "Need a lift?"

"Yeah," Harvey had to shout against the wind, "thanks." He grabbed the door of what he realized was one of the nicest cars he'd ever entered, and climbed aboard.

"Thanks," he said again. "I came without a coat. It was all right earlier."

"Yes. Cornish weather." Negotiating the driveway, Bleeder seemed to have other things on his mind. They sat in silence for a few moments until the car had pulled out of a difficult blind turn and onto the main road. Then came traffic lights, which were red.

"Which way are you heading?" Bleeder broke the silence and Harvey waved his hand vaguely.

"Oh, into town. I just wanted to get out of there really. It's a bit . . . I don't know."

"Yes, there are better ways to spend an afternoon." Again, Harvey was astounded by the change from boy to man. He was articulate, precise, engaging, competent. All the things he hadn't been at school.

"I guess for you it's very hard." Harvey only realized he'd said this aloud as he heard it echo to the backbeat of the rain.

"Me, why?"

"Well, I guess you had a rough time here. At school, I mean. I mean, didn't you? I seem to remember you getting a bit of stick and stuff . . ." A bit of stick.

Bleeder smiled, he actually grinned. "Did I? Yes, I suppose I did, though I was hardly aware of it at the time. I had other things going on in my life." He put this last sentence in slightly ironic parentheses and then added with even greater emphasis: "I had issues."

"Right, yeah. Well, I guess we all do at that age."

"Do we?" Bleeder looked across at him with genuine interest. "Did you?"

"Er, well, yes, I guess."

"What were your issues?" *Jesus.* Harvey had the strange sensation of suddenly wanting to get out of a conversation he had been waiting twenty years to have. "Um. Well, you know, teenage stuff and home was, you know, tricky."

"Yes? Can you say more about that?"

Christ. "No, no, not really . . . I mean, it's kind of my stuff, I guess, water under the bridge and so on." What was he supposed to say?

"OK. I can understand that." Bleeder was nodding. "But it can help to talk that stuff through a little bit, engage with it and let it sort of unpick itself, don't you think?"

"Oh, sure, yeah, I talk about it a lot. I just don't really want to now."

"Sure, that's fine."

"Thanks." Harvey found himself literally mopping his brow with his sleeve, though whether it was rain or sweat he wasn't sure. He went on quickly, "I mean, so, you know, what's up with you being here? I mean, you said inside that you just happened to be passing. But—I don't know why—I don't get the impression you pass through town that much or that often."

"No, I don't." They were driving down the main road to St. Ives, and suddenly caught a glimpse of the sea. The rain was blowing from that direction, buffeting the driver's side of the car as they passed the lines of hotels and guesthouses, mostly empty so early in the year and poignant with that special decay of a resort town in winter. "I'm only here now to sort out Mother."

"Sort her out?" Harvey was dying for a cigarette but didn't like to ask if he could light up in this extraordinarily civilized car. The seats were deep cream leather, the dashboard a riot of technology, set, with the typical obscenity of the engineer, in wood-look surround. It was warm and Harvey could sense underchair heating, which, after the rain, made him feel just a bit as if he had wet his pants.

"Move her. She's reached an age when she can no longer rattle about in the old house. Do you remember my old house?" He shot a glance across at Harvey and Harvey ducked. He did remember the house. He had been inside only once, but had bicycled past it many times. Indeed he and his friends sometimes used to ride past and sing at the same time. And what they sang was: "Bleeder Odd, super-bore, looks like a spastic and his mum's a whore." To the tune of "Jesus Christ Superstar," of course. Sometimes they had sung it twenty times or more before Mrs. Odd—"Old Mrs. Odd" as she was even then—had run out screaming at them, her hair always a mess of tangles, her clothes weirdly smart but filthy. Screamed words of such obscenity that secretly Harvey had been terrified. But he had laughed and ridden off, yelling insults with the rest. So yes, he knew the house. It stood alone, a white, child-architect's square box, in the land that was slowly being colonized by the new estates spreading out from St. Ives, not far from the school. And with that, he realized that Bleeder was driving directly away from his own destination.

"Yeah, I remember the house, and—er, sorry, am I taking you out of your way?"

"It's OK. I'm glad to have a look at the place again. It's so long since I was down and I only got here last night. Meetings going on till lunchtime, then a long drive. Pretty crap day, actually."

"Right, right." Something was itching in Harvey's brain. Something was niggling.

"You say you're moving your mother," he said deliberately.

"Yes. The social services have found her a place in sheltered accommodation. Three rooms, private bathroom, but part of a community. It's up near St. Ia's Church, so it's a lot closer to town. She can't manage the bus so well now."

Harvey flapped his hand at this extraneous information as at a mosquito. "So you must be throwing out a lot of stuff?"

"Oh, God, yes." Bleeder shook his head. "She's been there forever. You would not believe some of the stuff . . ." He stopped, as though reminded of something. "There's so much stuff."

"Must be. I wonder . . ." Harvey stopped.

"It's amazing what you accumulate. Over the years. It's amazing what you manage to keep. Bits and pieces."

Harvey looked across at Bleeder, who was speaking slowly and with an uneasy precision.

"Lots of things from your school days, sort of thing? Stuff from when we were kids?"

"Oh, stuff from forever. From way back, before I was born, things of my dad's. She's been packing for weeks with someone from the social services helping her. They've thrown loads out, but there's still boxes and boxes. I'm supposed to be going through it, things the social services woman thought might be mine . . ."

"They've thrown loads out," Harvey repeated slowly.

"Yes, gave it to Oxfam and the other thrift shops, I think, what was salvageable. But a lot of it just went to the dump."

"But your stuff," Harvey was staring at Bleeder intently, "you haven't gone through it all yet?"

"No, I haven't started. Couldn't face it last night and today I had the reunion. Tomorrow we might get a bit done but Mum's going to see her sister, Auntie Flo, who lives in Padstow, and she insists she's got to go through everything herself. So it'll be tomorrow night and then all day Monday." He sighed. "I'm not sure I can even be bothered really. Maybe it's just better to get rid of everything, you know. I haven't needed any of this stuff for twenty years. Why would I suddenly need it now?"

"Right." Harvey nodded hard. They had driven well past the turn to his parents' house. The long row of shops that led them into the town center had been passed without him really noticing at all, and they were now following the road that skirted the center itself and led out along the harbor wall and up to rejoin the coast road beyond. "It's funny," he said, "but talking about old stuff, I was wondering if you remembered something."

"Oh?"

"Yeah. It's nothing really, just a memory that came back to me just now." Harvey felt his voice beginning to rise as if in panic. He coughed and cleared his throat. "Excuse me. It's just, ages ago, back at school, you know, there was a day: We were walking up to school and we swapped something, I think. Yeah, that's it, we did a swap. Do you remember at all? We exchanged something."

"A swap?"

"Yeah, yeah. I remember it because I swapped a comic, I think. That was it, wasn't it? I swapped a comic with you. Do you remember that?" The twenty years of thinking about this moment hadn't misled him; it was just as hard as he'd ever imagined it might be.

"A swap? A comic?" Bleeder was narrowing his eyes as he turned left and followed the road away from the harbor toward the hill that led out of town. "A swap. I do remember something. You gave me a comic."

"Yeah, some crappy comic." Harvey was very sure it was sweat that he was feeling now and wished he could turn the wet-pants device off. "You wanted it and I let you have it. Something like that. Remember?"

"I do. I sort of do." The road was busy as people drove out of town from shopping and there was a traffic jam up the hill toward the lights. Bleeder brought the car to a halt. "I wanted your comic and you let me have it. It was a swap." His voice was far away from the car and the traffic, even from the rain and the wind.

"It's just . . . It's funny, I was just then wondering what happened to it. The comic, I mean. 'Cause I run a comic shop, as I told you, and I was just thinking: I wonder what happened to that old comic. I don't even remember what it was, what kind. But I do remember swapping. I wonder if it might be with your stuff, the stuff you're going to go through on Monday."

"Yes, a comic. I do remember, but it was so long ago. We did a swap; you swapped a comic. What did I swap?"

"If you are going through your old things, I just wondered, if you found it you might let me have it back. 'Cause comics are kind of my thing. You never know, it might be worth a few quid now. I might buy it from you for a couple of pounds, just for nostalgic reasons, yeah?" Harvey laughed a weird and, to his ear, raspingly unattractive laugh, a skull's laugh. He was gazing out of the windscreen now, staring forward, watching the raindrops splash and splinter the red lights and then be swept aside over and over again.

"I'll—I'll think. I'll have a think." The lights changed and Bleeder engaged the engine. "I'll have a think, but it may be gone. It's probably gone." He pulled forward as the queue began to move. "Where am I dropping you, by the way? I can't remember where you—"

"Oh, actually, anywhere's fine. I need to go to the shops and so on. Thanks." The car came to an immediate halt, bringing a horn's cry of outrage from behind.

"So, there you are," Bleeder said.

"Oh, right, yeah, cheers." Harvey, surprised by the suddenness of his arrival, fumbled with his seat belt and tried to open the door. The horn sounded again and Bleeder reached across him to grab the handle. "You have to push it like this." His voice was as clear and precise as when they first met, but when Harvey looked for a moment into his eyes they were wild and staring, as if Bleeder had seen something terrible, something unthinkable. And the hand that opened the door for him, Harvey couldn't help noticing, was trembling.

CHAPTER FIVE

The road was eerily familiar. Tired bare trees led the eye from the end of a row of cheap prefabs directly past the house, as though the planners had intentionally wanted it not to be noticed. Harvey could see their point. The estate had encroached a little more, perhaps. A few extra buildings, but indistinguishable from those that had marked the end of the estate in his day. There were even some boys riding their bikes up and down the road, using the curb as a minijump to perform wheel spins. The boys gave Harvey a look-over and passed some inaudible but apparently hilarious remark, and then carried on. None of them was singing. Harvey was glad of that.

The house itself sat with its same grim disinterest back from the road behind a garden that had the look of somewhere that had been beaten up. It was as though someone had stepped into the matted nature and slashed about them with a scythe until there was a semblance of desolate order. Harvey stood uncertain outside the peeling white gate in the peeling white fence and looked at the windows. There were net curtains at all four of them, gray net curtains. Then he walked, whistling casually—until he realized he was whistling "Jesus Christ Superstar," at which he stopped abruptly—along the road past the house. He assumed Bleeder must be out, for no handsome silver car adorned the road in front. "If I had a car like that I wouldn't leave it here," Harvey muttered to himself, and then realized the implications of that. "Shit, what if he's parked down on the main road and is even now watching me through the netties." Harvey himself had parked his father's car ("Now don't go scratching me paintwork, I know you"; "Piss off, Dad") about half a mile down the main road from the town. Now he stomped on through the estate, past the boys who stopped their play to stand and stare at him, their mouths agape. "Bloody inbreds," he said. But he said it very, very quietly.

Last night had been a long one. He had returned home early, his mind so full of Bleeder and the conversation in the car that he had forgotten the dangers of family life. It was only as he crossed the threshold and heard that oh, so familiar phrase—"Is that you, dear?"—filled with hope and joy and eagerness, that he had realized his peril.

"Yes, it's me, Mum. Who else is it going to be?" Funny how fourteen is still lurking in even the most full-grown of men: The words had come as naturally as breathing. He had attempted the surly stalk upstairs to his room. But what had worked in youth seemed to have lost its power. Maturity had emasculated him. That, or his mother had grown braver with age.

"Come in and have a chat while I make you something to eat. Your father's in the garden and we can have fresh salad with the stew. There's football on later, your father said, and we might get the Scrabble out. Could we play and watch at the same time? I know how you men like to watch football and not be disturbed . . ." and on and on. And it was either use the absolute sanction, the "Fuck off, you old cow" option, or come on the Reds and double-word scores. Harvey had done the sigh and accepted that you couldn't go for the absolute on your second night in town: second of four. So he had gone in and listened to his mother's voice talking about her church meetings and her friend's bad leg and the tourist who drowned in the bay and the bad weather and anything else that floated into her mind. And while she spoke he sat and went over and over the conversation with Bleeder, picking it clean of meaning, stripping it, trying to tear his way to an answer he could accept. At some point his father had come in clutching a handful of spring onions and started being boisterous. "Come along, come along, where's my dinner, woman? I'm back from the hunt and ready to eat."

"Oh, yes, you must be starving, darling, and Harvey is, too, aren't you, dear? Two big hungry bears..." Harvey had sat smoking at the breakfast bar, into which, if he looked closely, he could see "Johnny Flame" carved in his own childish hand. He tried not to look closely.

"Starving, are you? Good man. Need a bit of real cooking. Not that rubbish you eat in those fancy restaurants, eh? None of that nouvelle cuisine? Shite cuisine I call it."

"Donald!"

"Well, it is. Not enough on a plate to feed an Ethiopian. Real food, that's what we want, eh, Harvey?"

"Mmm." Harvey wondered vaguely if perhaps one day, a long time ago, someone had laughed at one of his father's jokes, someone other than his mother, of course, who was now tittering distractedly. Harvey wondered if it might be possible to find that person and punish them in some way. After all, the past did piece itself together sometimes. Pieces that seemed un-linkable, knots that seemed unpickable... sometimes the past can surprise us. And so back to Bleeder.

After Scrabble ("I'm sure 'quark' is a word, dear, but I've never heard of it so we can't count it: That's our house rule, re-member..."), and after *Match of the Day* ("They're overpaid and should respect the referee!"), when he was finally allowed to get away and up the stairs into the one true sanctuary he had ever known, Harvey lay very still in his bedroom and blew smoke at the ceiling. What had Bleeder said? "I'll think, but it's probably gone," something like that. What did "probably" mean? Well, it meant it might be gone. And that would be all right. As he smoked, Harvey had nodded to himself, unsurprised by this fact. If it had definitely gone—sent off years ago to some kids' charity, or burned on the bonfire or whatever—

then that was OK. On the other hand, if it had only been given away in the last couple of days . . . that wasn't OK. Where would it have been given to? Oxfam, Bleeder had said. Could he go trawling round the secondhand shops of St. Ives hunting for a comic? Did charity shops even sell comics? He'd been in enough but couldn't remember ever seeing any. What if the charity shop owner knew enough to inquire about a first edition? What if the headline in the local paper a week from now was "Charity Shop Owner Strikes It Rich (and Opens Superhero-Themed Coffee Shop in Downtown New York)"? That very definitely wouldn't be all right. But Bleeder's stuff hadn't been gone through yet. That was the point. That was, in fact, a very key point. Harvey had sat up and looked around his room for a while. It was a room unchanged since his childhood and that, of course, was typical in families like his. What was less typical and slightly more troubling was that it bore a close resemblance to his current rooms in London. The old bedroom posters were of *Batman* and *Spider-Man* rather than *Darkman* and *Tomb Raider*, but they weren't posters he would find unacceptable in his grown-up world. He sometimes tried to argue that this was because he had always had good and adult taste. It was an argument entirely with himself, and was another that he rarely felt any confidence of winning.

Sleep had not come that night, not until the morning was advancing. This was unusual. Harvey was normally a good sleeper, beer having a pleasantly narcotic effect. But this time there was a reason for insomnia. Deep in his heart he already knew that he was going to rob Bleeder's house. He couldn't pin down when that decision was made. It was as if he had always known it. Perhaps it had formed as an inevitable somewhere in those twenty years of waiting. You can't care this much about something so particular for this long without some sort of action, however ineffectual, becoming necessary. Harvey knew that he owed it, as it were, to the next quarter of a century, to do everything he could do. It was as simple as that: His future self depended on it.

Which didn't make it easy, of course. As he strode rapidly away from Bleeder's house, he thought of how impossible crime could seem. He sometimes liked to think of himself as a bit of an outlaw: the tin under his bed with the lump of Black in it; the car with the "applied for" sticker in place of a tax disc; the "adult graphic novel" section of his bookshelves. But somehow this had nothing to do with breaking and entering. The house looked so solid. The walls and windows such tangible, physical proofs of right and wrong. It was as if, for a moment, as he walked purposefully away in the wrong direction, he could see the very tablets of the Old Testament re-formed and reconstituted into solid whitewashed walls.

CHAPTER SIX

Breaking a window with a brick is actually quite difficult.

After a swift walk through the estate, intended to give the impression that he was late and going somewhere important, Harvey had made his way round to the cul-de-sac that ran along the bottom of Bleeder's garden. The road had no houses on it and came to an end in a thicket of half-grown trees and burned-out cars, with only a muddy track running off it. Harvey recognized the track as the one he used to walk up to school. At other times he might have stopped for a brief bout of nostalgia, characterized by the words "Thank Christ I don't have to do that anymore." But today's business was too serious for such indulgences. From the path, Mrs. Odd's back garden looked worse than her front. No wild threshing had happened here. Thick nettles and brambles were intertwined with long grass and piles of rubble. Bits of unknowable things emerged from bushes. This was comforting to Harvey. Clearly no one had been up Mrs. Odd's garden for a very long time.

After traversing the hedge and the jungle of the under-growth with only a scratched hand and a slightly twisted ankle sustained in an encounter with a deflated but still smiling Spacehopper, Harvey had found himself standing, SAS-style, to one side of the kitchen window, as if about to burst in shoot-ing. Glancing down and observing his beer gut heaving in a way that looked frankly unhealthy, he forced himself to breathe more easily. He was in the garden of an old friend; it was hardly a capital offense. The brick in his hand was less easy to explain.

He tried tapping at the window, just to check that the Odds weren't having a quiet afternoon in, and then with the mixed air of fear and interested experimentation, he walked to a safe distance and slung the brick at the central glass panel in the kitchen door. Plan A was that there would be an explosion of glass and a nice brick-shaped hole would appear for him to put his hand through. Luckily, Plan B was to run like a deer as soon as he threw it because, in the event, the pane merely split in an ugly and deafening crack up the middle and the brick landed at his heels.

After a pause for thought, spent standing on one foot ready to flee at the slightest sound, Harvey returned from his position in the undergrowth, removed his denim jacket, wrapped the brick in it, and began to bash away at the cracked pane. This proved more productive as well as oddly satisfying, and within a minute he had made a neat hole for his hand to pass inside. After admiring his handiwork for a while, Harvey dragged himself into the danger of the moment, reached inside, and fumbled for a latch. That it was reachable was entirely a matter of good fortune, but reachable it was. And with a troubling sense of this action being both easy and impossible, Harvey found himself opening the door of a stranger's house and stepping inside.

He had been inside the house only once before and it had been a mess. The first impression now was that things hadn't changed. Piles of damp newspapers stood incongruously around the sink, and the sink itself had a brown discoloration, a soiling that laid a faint patina of disgust over his insurgent terror. But as he moved on through the cooking area, he realized that, in fact, things had a certain order. Boxes stood open with old and nasty frying pans emerging from them; plates were stacked in reasonably matching piles; knives and long-handled spoons protruded from a carrier bag. The hand of the social services could be seen in the way the base shell of the kitchen was appearing from its years of darkness.

As Harvey moved, mouselike, toward the hall he was aware of an almost overwhelming need to defecate. Into his mind flickered a complete story, pictured, perhaps predictably, in comic-strip form: of him rushing upstairs to the toilet, relieving himself, and then finding that the flush was broken. "The police were able to trace the intruder using DNA samples found at the crime scene..." Harvey gave a low gasp of fear that was also, unexpectedly, a sort of hysterical giggle and forced himself to run upstairs.

His parents would love this. That was the thought that beset him as he crept, a faint fat shadow, along a landing lit only by the most meager light from the bedroom windows. Ever since he brought home a presentation book of Brooke Bond Tea cards belonging to his best friend's sister when he was nine, he had been perceived as potentially criminal. "It was only to be expected," he could almost hear his father saying. "We always had our suspicions." There was something rather satisfying about fulfilling so exactly his parents' worst fears. Perhaps he should become homosexual as well, and start supporting Chelsea.

He found Bleeder's room without difficulty. It too seemed like his own, unchanged from boyhood. But here the lack of progress seemed less the product of sentimental mothering and more of a generalized neglect. Nothing appeared to have changed in the Odd house for a very long time indeed. Ownership of the bedroom was confirmed by the poster of Abba hanging above the bed. He knew that poster: *Arrival*. White jumpsuits and cowboy boots. In the seventies you could buy it for fifty pence from any newsagent in the land. It was a poster that would have been out of date by the time Bleeder was ten. It was the sort of poster only someone who had really given up trying would have had. He stood for a moment transfixed. He'd forgotten how tasty Agnetha was. Had Bleeder even realized that? Harvey doubted it. He did the sigh, or a sort of panicky version of it, and moved to the one large cardboard box that stood in the middle of the otherwise stripped room.

The box had been sealed neatly with long strips of masking tape, and for a moment Harvey felt an odd impropriety in undoing such careful handiwork. That this was an inappropriate concern in a burglar who had already broken a window struck him forcibly and he began tentatively picking at the strips with his fingernails. This took some time. The tape had been layered in thick gouts, one strip on top of another, and Harvey's fingernails were bitten almost comically short. After some ineffectual picking and swearing, he ran back downstairs and returned armed with a long-handled kitchen knife. Panting, but prepared, he slashed the masking tape with inexpert precision. The *Superman One* was not inside. What was inside was a very motley collection of items. Maths textbooks; some electronic devices of unknown use; a hair dryer (when did Bleeder Odd ever wash his hair?); a Dennis Wheatley novel; a picture of Victoria Principal; a packet of condoms (when did Bleeder Odd, etc.); three pairs of shoes; a nasty and possibly unsanitary pink teddy bear; and at the very bottom of the box, under some tight-waisted knitwear with stars up the front, a pile of comics.

Harvey's heart had started beating too quickly for a man of his girth who is sitting down as he reverently removed the comics one by one. But they were just the typical frayed remnants of a boy's collection, like so many he had been sent for valuation over the years at the shop. No rare first editions, nothing special at all. He read a few pages of an *Iron Man* that he hadn't looked at for years, not really being much of an *Iron Man* fan, and then remembered his predicament and stood up fast.

When upright he found that some of his fear had lifted. The fact that his mission seemed to have failed had removed some of the terror of discovery, as if the criminality had somehow slipped out of his actions now that there was nothing to steal. With great care he put everything back in the box in the right order and then did his best to reseal the tape. That done he made his way back onto the landing. Logic said he should leave now—surely Bleeder's room was the likeliest place to look—but his future self, the one who had come to him in the restless night and said it was better to be arrested, even go to prison, than to live with uncertainty any longer, was back with him. "I will make you come back here again if you don't finish this today," it told him. "I will send you to reburgle the same house again tomorrow. And just think how much more difficult that will be." With an irrational desire to punch his own future, Harvey made his way to the next room. It was clearly Mrs. Odd's bedroom and was as yet unpacked. It smelled strongly of feces and talcum powder, reminding Harvey of a great-aunt from his youth who had been both fashionable and incontinent. The idea of Mrs. Odd keeping the comic he'd swapped with her son in 1982 in her bedside cabinet was pushing reason beyond any natural limit, future self or no future self. But he looked anyway. It wasn't in there. There were lots of light-bulbs and a packet of lemon jelly.

Harvey followed his own absence of logic carefully through each room in turn, and once started he was thorough. He looked under beds and inside bathroom cabinets. He opened four more cardboard boxes using the red-handled kitchen knife. None of them contained anything of any interest, or not at least to a burglar. There was a *Dukes of Hazzard* baseball cap that Harvey found rather captivating. As he made his way to the stairs it occurred to him that he might find some other object of value: What would he do then? He was surprised but pleased to find that the idea of stealing anything else held no interest for him. Perhaps he wasn't a criminal after all. Perhaps he was merely reclaiming something that belonged to him. Perhaps it was really his to retrieve . . . "My preciousssss," Harvey hissed and giggled loudly as he made his way back downstairs.

On the ground floor he followed the same procedure. Most of the fear had now passed, to be replaced by a sort of jumpy boredom. All the boxes contained unpleasant objects that he really had no wish to see, including an extraordinary amount of counterpanes. Did she collect counterpanes? And why were so many of them orange candlewick with tassels? Was this some sort of recognized fetish? It might be worth checking on the Internet. And when finally he stood in front of the last box in the sitting room, surrounded by damp-smelling bed linen, Harvey realized that he was done. Somewhere he could sense his future self throwing up his hands and smiling: "Fair do's, you've tried, I'll give you that." And he would continue to run a perfectly pleasant little comic shop on Old Street rather than a superhero-themed coffeehouse in Gramercy Park, and that was OK. Maybe it was actually for the best. With a last, almost affectionate glance round the old place (as he now thought of it), Harvey strolled out into the hallway and made for the kitchen. As he did so he was struck by a thought. He hadn't been down to the front door itself. Maybe there was a cupboard there, something like that. So he turned and walked back down the hall, with a sense almost of wanting to prolong what had really been a rather pleasing exercise: a completely new experience— and those were rare in his life these days, perhaps too rare; perhaps he should do things like this more often.

Turning over the idea of robbing people's houses now and again just to keep his adrenaline levels up, Harvey approached the front door in a mood of benign affection for crime and for criminals as a group. And it was then that he noticed the wooden door on his left and realized with complete suddenness that the house had a cellar. Frozen for a moment, he stood caught between impulses. He had been ready to leave, to turn and stroll nonchalantly out into the garden and fight his way back through the jungle. His first instinct now was to continue with that plan. Who would keep a comic in a cellar? It was probably just a damp hole full of old tools or bits of coal. And he didn't, he really didn't, want to go in a cellar right now. All his insouciance left him in a rush. What if someone came in while he was down there? What if he got locked in forever?

What if Bleeder Odd was the psychopath that any comic-strip writer would make him and came back and found Harvey in his basement? The basement where he kept his victims locked in metal cages, hanging upside down. What if Bleeder Odd had never left St. Ives and had been living in the basement all this time just waiting for this moment...? Harvey took several deep breaths. "I know, I know," he muttered to his future self, and, opening the door, he stepped inside.

CHAPTER SEVEN

Well, this was more like it. The darkness was all-embracing and all-disorientating. Even with the tenuous light from the hallway, Harvey's senses were befuddled by the absolute blackness. This surely was what a burglar was meant to feel like. Again it was his parents' faces that swam into Harvey's mind. When he was small his father had liked to tell him tales of how pirates would hide in the local caves and some would get lost in the darkness and never be found. The child Harvey had been frightened by these stories and had questioned their validity. "Oh, yes, it's quite true, dear," his mother had told him when he asked. "Only wicked pirates go in dark caves, wicked pirates and naughty boys, of course." It had been a source of resentment over many years that he had been frightened in this way. And even now he was able to feel a certain annoyance that his first thought on being in this dark place was that pirates might come and get him. He fumbled along the wall for a light switch, trying to keep his mounting terror within rational boundaries. Surely there had to be a light switch? If there wasn't, then his future self would have to just accept that he'd done his best. Or to put it another way, his future self could go fuck himself.

Still clutching the kitchen knife in one hand, Harvey patted the other along the wall, aware of soft things brushing his fingers that he hoped were spiders' webs (rather than pirates' beards, for instance). After a few edgy moments his fingers discovered an old-fashioned switch and pushed it down. This drowned him in light and switched his fears of the dark to panic as to what this display might do if seen from outside. Moving quickly onto the little square landing at the head of the stairway, Harvey pulled the door almost closed behind him.

Stepping forward, he immediately banged his head on the first of a series of low beams that ran down at about ear height. Ducking and peering before him, he concentrated on making his way down the damp and splintered steps. What if they couldn't support his weight? What if the Odds found him in the morning, dead in the cellar? Or what if they never came down here? What if they shut up the house and Mrs. Odd moved to St. Ia's and he was never found? What then? Harvey wasn't sure what then, so he just tested each step with his toe while hanging on very tightly to an equally uncertain wooden rail that ran down the wall on his left side. The rail wobbled slightly in his hand and he had a nightmarish vision of the house simply waiting to collapse under the weight of abuse that it had suffered over the years: the Odd years. Perhaps his violation was the last straw, perhaps the house itself would take its revenge. Like in *The Haunting* (graphic novel edition). It seemed to take an age to turn the corner on the stairway and to find his way down into the cellar proper. And he was almost at the bottom and on the cellar floor itself before he dared to raise his eyes from the steps and survey its contents. There was not a lot down there. Clearly it had never been much used. But this was not the thought that came first to Harvey. What was down there was quite enough. In front of him there stood one large cardboard box. Like the others upstairs, it had clearly been sealed, but the masking tape had been shredded from its top. This should have caught Harvey's attention, but it was mostly fixed on what was beside the box. At first he thought it was a mannequin, some ageing tailor's dummy abandoned on the floor. It was the great circle of darkness around it that told him he was wrong. She was lying on her back, her mouth and eyes open, and at her throat was a long, curved opening.

Harvey took all this in very slowly. Moving uncertainly, as if wearing roller skates, he stepped forward into the black pool around her and squatted down beside Mrs. Odd. Laying down the kitchen knife, he put one hand on the slimy surface of the floor and reached out to feel her neck. There was no pulse, and he knew in some distant place inside that it was ridiculous to think there might be. For a moment he just stayed there next to her, looking at the purpled mouth of the wound and wondering where he had seen something like it. Into his mind came the thought of a sex show he once attended in Amsterdam: The opening in her neck was like some pornographic display put on for his titillation; as if she was posing like this for him. And then he was unexpectedly and violently sick.

The sound of his vomiting filled the damp silence of the cellar and came back to him in a muffled echo. It was the sound that roused him and made him stand. For a moment he stood erect, drool running down his chin, feeling as a physical sensation the rising of the panic that was coming, hearing it like the sound of an approaching train. In the moments before its arrival he looked around again, not at the body but at the cardboard box. It was with only a vague, distant aftershock that he saw, tucked inside the open flap, a mint-condition *Superman One*. It was still wrapped in its plastic casing. He moved carefully around the thing that lay on the ground, and picked up the comic. He remembered this cover, he remembered buying it, remembered the day of the swap, when he had haggled this away for a strip of plastic. The comic looked perfect, untouched. He examined the wrapper carefully and as he did so noticed that where he touched it his fingers left vivid crimson smears on the clear plastic. And that is when the panic arrived.

Dropping this thing he had thought about every day of his adult life as if it were rubbish, as if it meant nothing at all, he ran for it. Where in descent he had tried every step carefully, on his return he simply flew over them. He charged up the stairs, his feet battering a terrible beat on the exposed wood. He ran headlong along the passageway toward the kitchen, desperate, as if life depended on it, to breathe some air that was not touched by what he had seen. He charged through the kitchen and overturned the box of unsanitary saucepans. They came down with all the sound of Armageddon and he heard himself sob with terror. Hurling the back door open he ran into the jungle. He didn't stumble this time. It was as if he was floating over the uneven ground, as if fear had lifted him free of the normal inconveniences of the everyday. Through the nettles he fled, into the bushes and the brambles, down the little ditch at the end of the garden and into the cul-de-sac. He turned instinctively toward the road, toward aid and civilization, but then some other instinct, not as deep but equally compelling, made him pause, turn, and race the other way. Up the track he ran, the bare boughs of the heavy cedars bringing an early twilight, past the long grasses that lined the path. Over the gate of the school, a vault that used up what little youth he had left, across the rugby pitch, stumbling now in the thick, clogging mud; over the gravel path they used to follow from classes to the gym; and over the low front fence onto the main St. Ives road. Without looking he sprinted across and onto the grass verge on the other side. Wheezing now and with cramp in his side he stumbled on for several minutes and then, hearing a car approaching behind him, threw himself, with a final act of will, into a gap in the hedgerow and lay there prostrate among the leaves, gasping like a landed trout.

CHAPTER EIGHT

Only when he felt the solid floor beneath him did Harvey raise his eyes from the steps and survey the scene once more. The body was gazing at him with unflinching accusation and he nodded a sort of greeting. "All right?" He didn't actually say it out loud, but he came close. For a nightmarish moment he imagined her replying, "Hello, Harvey"; he could hear it in his head, her thick Cornish vowels: "Hello, Harvey." He tried to focus on the fact that she was no great loss to the species. Callousness and insensitivity had seen him through a number of difficult situations in his life; he could see no obvious reason why they shouldn't work here.

He had sat for a long time in the wet grass by the roadside. When he could stand upright again he had run at a lumbering and heart-attacking pace back to his father's car. And then he had driven for a while, following the road toward Truro—Cornwall's only city, and a place of great grandeur and metropolitan grace to the boy Harvey. As he drove he found he went that way as if by instinct, seeking—as he had learned to do so well in London—the safety of the urban environment, the blissful anonymity of crowds. He had wanted to be away from little places, the narrow places of his past, from funny little culs-de-sac with burned-out cars, from new estates where a stranger was watched by half-feral children, and from cellars where steps led down to unimaginable horror. And thankfully there was traffic on the Truro road. The red Ford Fiesta Fling that his father had unwisely but not untypically selected as his mode of transport blended so completely into the background roar that Harvey had felt he was already away, felt he could drive on for miles and never be found, never go back, finally sever those links with a past he never wanted in one swift chop of his hand. But then he had seen the knife.

It had crept back into his vision like some glimpsed terror in the corner of the eye, its red plastic handle so bright and clean against the deep black crimson of the blood. Driving had done what it sometimes did for Harvey, for whom learning to drive and the advent of maturity were linked: It had made him think like a grown-up. He had broken into a house; he had picked up a knife; he had left fingerprints; he had left the knife with his fingerprints on it next to the body of an old woman whose throat had been cut; his fingerprints were on her throat. He was in trouble. And he knew what was necessary for him to do. Where the road for Truro turns off from the dual carriageway there is a roundabout. Harvey went round it twice. As he whirled, a hundred uncertainties flashed before him from which appeared two clear paths, two exits from his spinning motion: he could take the Truro road, drive straight to the police station, tell all, and it would be over. Or he could drive back the way he had come and try to fix things, to make it all right. Twice he went round and then he took the St. Ives road.

He was tired now, and his back and knees were singing. He had been cleaning for some time. A bucket, rubber gloves, a duster, and a bottle of Zest he had found under the sink in the kitchen, and with these tools he had begun methodically to remove all traces of himself from the house. The trail he had followed previously he now went over again, wiping himself away. It struck him that in some ways this was what he'd been trying to do ever since he left St. Ives twenty years ago: eradicate his traces from the place, and its from him. He was topless, having used his T-shirt to wrap around his hands as he entered the house, and this was now tied round his neck, giving him the air of a portly

Romany. The measured calm of the seasoned housebreaker that he had affected earlier was long gone and every whisper had become a hunting, every sigh a haunting. By the time he made his furtive way down into the cellar he felt like a sweaty Orestes.

He had left the basement till last because he knew his nerve would not hold for long. Now, as he stood and faced the worst, his breath came heavy through bared teeth, his mouth open in a strange grimace that he knew would stay when this was over: an expression he had never made before had entered his range. When would he use it again? The taste of beer that wasn't quite right? Josh's morning aroma? A racist joke? To what use would he put this new look that he found on his face? He closed his eyes for a moment, then grabbed his sponge cleaner from the bucket and, bending, eradicated his own footprints in the blood. Then he started on the rather neat round pool of sick, which seemed to be keeping itself to itself like a little snobbish pizza. Mixing water with the blood softened it and it ran about his feet in a swirling pattern, creating pretty ice-cream sundaes on the floor. Pizza and ice-cream: his favorite. But the blood running around was bad. It was soaking his trainers. He needed to stand on something so he could clean one set of footprints without creating another. He looked around . . . What could he use? With the makings of a ghoulish grin, he glanced at the cardboard box: He could use the *Superman One*, of course he could. Perfect. He could use this priceless treasure of which he had dreamed for so long to soak up the blood. The *Superman One* would save him from disaster. Cackling, he stepped across to the cardboard box but then stood nonplussed. The *Superman One* was gone.

Harvey struggled with this for a moment. He looked behind the cardboard box. Then he looked in the box at the other stuff that was inside: curtains with pictures of trains on them, a long length of Matchbox car track, shoes (there were more shoes in this house than Harvey had ever seen before), various boxes of old plastic toys, an orange counterpane . . . Because he couldn't take anything out of the box without covering it in blood, Harvey leaned right over and almost disappeared into the box as he hunted. But it wasn't there. However much he scrabbled in the illogic of the situation, he could find no trace of it. Rising, he stood briefly in thought. If it wasn't here—and he had definitely dropped it here—then . . . then what? Mechanically he continued to clean, at the last moment remembering to run his duster over Mrs. Odd's neck. "It means, of course, that someone has taken it." Harvey spoke out loud as he picked up the red-handled kitchen knife from where it lay beside the body and sat down on the bottom step to remove his bloodsoaked shoes. These he wrapped neatly in the T-shirt from around his neck. Then, walking carefully in his socks, he made his way back up the stairs. He gave one last look down as he stood on the little landing step. Had he erased all his prints? His head ached and his knees felt as though he had been praying for days. He nodded; he couldn't think of anywhere else that he had put his hands. He mounted the final flight of steps, switched off the light, and padded carefully over the damp carpet and into the kitchen. There he emptied his bucket and washed it out. He rubbed the kitchen knife over and over with the duster and returned it to the plastic bag. Putting the sponge cleaner and the dusters in the bundle with his shoes, he took off the rubber gloves and put them carefully back under the sink. Then he stepped out into the garden, pulling the door closed behind him using his T-shirt to hold the handle.

The night smelled of the country and of the sea. He stood for a moment in his socks, almost too weary to walk back into the nettles and prickles of the garden, and looked up. A faint blue still sat at the corners of the evening and the stars were dim, as if politely waiting for this last vestige of day to fade before they made their entrance. He breathed deeply of the clean air and was about to step into the jungle when behind him he heard a sound, just faintly, of a door closing. So he didn't step into the jungle. He ran like fuck.

CHAPTER NINE

"Is that you, dear?" The voice seemed to come from a dream of another world, another life that he had once had.

"No, it's your secret lover." His own voice, too, sounded uncanny.

His mother chirruped happily, "Come and have a chat, Harvey. I'm just brewing a pot of tea."

"Yeah, I'll be down in a minute." He ran to the stairs. Denim jacket, buttoned over bare flesh, was not a suitable sight for his mother. Nor were his sodden socks. Nor was the bloody bundle he carried in his arms.

"Don't just disappear, will you, darling? We want to see you."

"No, Mum, I'll just grab a quick shower." That used to work.

"Oh, good idea, love, I'll put the immersion on, although you may have to wait for it to heat up completely but if you're only in there for a few minutes you might be all right, I'm not sure if your father . . ."

Harvey left this nuisance to continue by itself and headed for his room. The bundle he put into a carrier bag and placed beside his bed. Then he sat on the edge of the bed and put his head in his hands. "Jesus fucking Christ," he said very slowly. Carefully he removed the jacket and laid that on the floor. He took off his socks and put them in the carrier bag and then slid it under the bed. After a few moments he made his way to the bathroom and ran the shower. It was cold but he stood under it anyway and scrubbed himself, picking and picking at his fingernails. When he was clean he went back to the bedroom, shut the door, and lit a cigarette: the first since the nightmare had begun. Never in human history had that particular mixture of carcinogenic material and nicotine tasted so good. He dragged the smoke into his lungs as if it were feeding him, as if it were nourishment. Eventually he moved to the chest of drawers and found another black T-shirt, distinguishable from the first only to a trained expert in comic imagery, and got dressed.

"So, what have you been up to today? Nothing dodgy, I hope." His father was in jocular mood and Harvey was not sure that he could cope.

"No, just having a bit of a look around."

"Well, yes, you've probably forgotten the place, you haven't been down for so long."

"Mmm." Harvey had the newspaper and was pretending to read it, but as usual with his father this didn't seem to reduce the unwanted conversational gambits.

"I hope you have left my car as you found it?" Harvey ignored this altogether, so his father moved on to more general topics. "Did you see the new development by the seafront? Twenty-two new flats they're putting in. It's going to be wonderful for the area." Like most country people, Harvey's parents approved enthusiastically of anything that would uglify their area or ruin the environment.

"Oh, yes, they'll be right on the sea, perfect," his mother joined in. "It'll do the town so much good."

"Mmm." The newspaper was a local one and led its front page with a Boy Scout jamboree. Harvey couldn't help feeling that tomorrow's edition might be rather more eye-catching.

"So, you just wandered about, did you? Didn't see any of your disreputable friends, I hope?"

"Donald! I'm sure Harvey's friends aren't disreputable, or . . . well . . . not all of them."

"That Jack Cranshaw is very disreputable, was when he was young and still is. Got into drugs and all sorts, didn't he, Harvey?"

"Er, yeah, I guess."

"Totally worthless sort of character. Now he comes down every few months and sponges off his parents. He should be a parent himself by now and instead he's living like a feckless teenager with some girl in Wales." Like most country people, Harvey's parents were also fascists. Harvey did the sigh and found it oddly satisfying. However unpleasant sitting talking to his parents might be, at least he wasn't cleaning dried blood off a carpet with a corpse in the cellar and possibly a psychopathic killer in the house. And frankly, this was a comfort. That sound had stayed with him. Had he really heard it? The garden had been dark . . . and he had been about dark business. Perhaps he had imagined the click of a door closing. Perhaps the breeze through the kitchen door . . . but there had been no breeze. He shifted uneasily in his chair and reached for his cigarettes.

"Another one? You keep Marlboro going on your own, you do." Harvey didn't bother to look up.

"Piss off, Dad."

"You'll kill yourself with them."

"Your father's right, Harvey. I was reading a piece in the Mail about it. There are so many ways to stop now. Lots of different methods, it's really not that difficult."

"He doesn't want to stop. If he wanted to stop he'd stop tomorrow. It's not hard, a bit of willpower is all you need. But he doesn't want to stop. He wants to kill himself—"

"No, Donald, don't say that. But, Harvey, they make a sort of thing you can put on your arm. It's like a sort of plaster and it feels like smoke going into your arm, it's quite reasonably priced—"

"Right. Thank you." Harvey put the paper down and stood up.

"Oh, are you going out, dear?"

"Yes." Harvey surprised himself. "I wasn't, but obviously I have to if I'm going to get any chance of peace or nonlunatic conversation."

"Oh, charming!" His mother chuckled. "Well, take your jacket. It's not as warm as it was. It's not as warm down here as it is in London."

"That's right, Mum, you have a different climate in Cornwall."

"He hasn't got a proper jacket. Denim isn't a proper jacket. How is that a jacket? It's not waterproof, it doesn't have a lining. It doesn't even cover your backside. It's not a jacket. If you want a jacket, Harvey, borrow one of mine. There's one on the peg. That'll keep you warm when you're out gallivanting . . ."

"Thanks, Dad. If I want to look like a reject from a special-needs charity bazaar, I'll definitely take you up on it." Harvey picked up his cigarettes, left the room, put on his denim jacket, and ventured back out into the night.

"Bye, dear, don't be too late back." He could hear the voice still calling to itself as he walked away down the road.

CHAPTER TEN

Harvey's reactions were concerning him. There was a feeling of studied calm to how he had behaved since his return home. He had sat on his bed and he had sat in the armchair. He hadn't shivered, or experienced panic attacks. Could it really be as easy as this to commit crimes? Perhaps it was. Perhaps the idea he had always had of criminals as abandoned creatures, living on the fringes of the civilized world, was quite misplaced. Perhaps they were just like him: popping out to do terrible deeds in the afternoon and getting home again in time for macaroni and cheese and *Star Trek: Voyager*.

He walked out from his parents' house onto Trelawney Road, close to where Mrs. Odd would have moved to if she had lived. She and his parents would have been near neighbors: something about keeping all the strange people in one place came into his mind but he ignored it and walked on. The hill ran down toward the town center and from there he could see the whole sweep of the bay, from Porthminster Point out to the north of the town, along St. Ives's own beachfront to the harbor and then away to The Island to the south. For all that he felt St. Ives represented repression, misery, bourgeois values, and empty traditionalism, it still held a certain picturesque charm. He had been away long enough to recognize that. The town nestled neatly as if held with a mother's love in the two arms of the bay. And it had held him. He was aware for a moment of just how safe this place had always felt. That's why he had wanted to leave it, of course. But now? Did it still feel that way?

Harvey walked down Church Road, past the church where he had gone as a child to Sunday school and where he had first learned to smoke; past the little car park with the great white wall where he had once sprayed the Batman logo in gold paint; and down onto the high street where he and Rob and Jack used to go shoplifting on a Saturday afternoon. "My life of crime," Harvey muttered. It was odd to think, now that he had time to think, that the most criminal thing he had ever done had happened in safe little St. Ives. And it had happened this afternoon. What he needed, he realized, was a drink. Several drinks.

St. Ives had a lot of pubs. Most made their money in the summer, but they all stayed open throughout the year. In theory, there was a wide selection to choose from, but like most people in their hometown Harvey could only really think of going into a handful. And all carried baggage. There was the Lifeboat on the harbor front where tonight there would be a jukebox and on Fridays a local band; that was where he had first thrown up into a public toilet and first dragged self-consciously on a joint. There was the Golden Lion, which would be quieter but might contain one or two hard lads with shaven heads and tattoos; that was where he and Rob had fought and won against two rugby players from the rival secondary school. Or there was the Blue Bar, which would be the quietest of all with a bit of folk music playing on CD; and that was where he had taken Jill Penhaligon on the night her parents were away at a funeral, so there was somewhere to go back to, for the first time. And all these memories were tied up with the places and meant that he needed to get the choice right. And although a part of him felt that distractions were just what he needed or that toughing it out might be the best option, he went to the Blue Bar because a larger part knew that he needed to think and to feel safe and to be cared for by the gentler ghosts he would find there.

———

The lounge bar of the Blue Bar had been redecorated since he was last there, the walls painted in a pale lime green and the floor laid to stripped pine. The walls were enlivened by pictures by a local artist, which featured beach scenes where there was a lot of blue for the sky and a lot of blue for the sea and a tiny strip of yellow in the middle for the sand. They were not like any Cornish beach Harvey had ever seen. He found them depressing. The Blue Bar had always been more of a wine bar than a pub and there had been a time, around the age of sixteen, when Harvey had considered wine bars the height of sophistication. On a damp night in February it was almost deserted and just seemed rather hopeless and displaced. The bare whitewood tables and chairs had the appearance of a set of deck chairs laid out on some forgotten liner. He ordered a pint of Guinness from a bored student and found a corner. What he wanted was peace, and he had found it. It crossed his mind that it was possible to have too much peace, because his thoughts began at once to crowd in. He might be arrested tonight. When he returned home his mother might be in tears and his father nodding knowingly. There might be a brief explanation, a reading of rights . . . things from *The Bill*. And then he might get in the back of a car and be taken to a cell to spend the night. And the next night and the next. This was real. He could be arrested for concealing a murder . . . was that a crime? Harvey felt there was probably a more official term for it but that was basically it. He had concealed a murder. And not some drunk-driving or a hit-and-run but a real, old-school, Agatha Christie, body-in-the-library, suspicious-vicar sort of murder. Like most comic fans, Harvey was not drawn to real drama. He contemplated the enormity of what had happened for several minutes with the aid of his Irish assistant. He would, he realized, need to get very drunk indeed. So he rose quickly to get a second pint, and it was then that he saw her.

"Oh, hello." Maisie Cooper smiled at him and he wondered

how she could have been so near to him without him sensing her presence.

"Er, hi. Where did you spring from?"

"Oh, I just got here. It's nice to see you again."

"Oh, right, you too. You on your own?" Harvey tried to keep the hope out of his voice.

"No, Jeff's gone for a pee and the others are on their way. We've all been somewhere else, the Lion, I think, but we're doing the rounds."

How did she manage to convey in these simple words just how grim this itinerary had been and just how much better it would have been if Harvey had been with her? He did not know but he certainly believed he heard all of it in her voice. He caught the student's eye. "What are you having?"

"Oh, it's OK, you were enjoying a bit of peace, by the look of it, and now you're going to be disturbed."

"That's all right. I'm happy to be disturbed by you." How clumsy and crap was that? He blushed at his own ineptitude and then blushed more to find himself blushing.

She smiled at him. "OK, I'll have a white wine, thanks."

"Right." She understood his embarrassment. She was someone who understood things. He immediately felt that was what he most needed right now. At which point the pub door opened and half his past fell through it.

"Bollocks, you can have a double or nothing, you slacker . . . H!"

"H!"

"H, H, H, H, H, H, H, H, H!" It became a chant.

"Er, all right, lads." Harvey felt, strangely, that while he wished he hadn't spent the afternoon wading around in blood it was still perhaps preferable to having spent it with his friends.

"Where've you been, man?" Steve threw his arm around Harvey's shoulder and, reeling, almost carried them both to the floor.

"Avoiding you." Harvey disentangled himself. "How many have you had?"

"Not enough. We're on the doubles tonight, Harvey boy. Pints and doubles only. We are getting pissed!" This last was shouted at great volume and was greeted with a cheer from the other twenty or so reunionists who had poured in behind the vanguard. "We are drinking the town dry!" Steve yelled again and then leaned himself heavily on the bar. "Bar, beerman," he called.

"Steve's getting going well." Rob joined Harvey and Maisie Cooper. "I don't think he gets out that much these days, what with the third baby. So he's letting his hair down."

"Yeah. That's not all . . ." Harvey wished he could have made the quiet moment with Maisie mean something before they all arrived, but there hadn't been time.

"And we've had quite an afternoon," Rob went on, slurring himself a little. "And guess who we had a drink with earlier? Only Bleeder Odd. I drank with Bleeder Odd; I can die a happy man."

"You saw Bleeder?"

"Yeah. He was in the Bell, wearing a suit and chatting on his mobile phone, for all the world as if he was a real human being. So we all bought him a pint. I think we owed him a few, you know what I mean? When we left he had about twenty pints in front of him on the table. So now we've made up for all the years of misery." He chuckled happily.

"At it again, Briscow? You can't leave my wife alone, can you?" Jeff Cooper, appearing through the crowd, was smiling slightly less than the last time he made this joke. "I thought that was you skulking in the corner when we came in. Only a sad bastard drinks on his own, mate. And you are a bit of a sad bastard, aren't you? Look at you, you look like a fucking weirdo. Why don't you grow a decent amount of hair and buy some clothes that aren't designed for teenagers?"

"Er, yeah, OK, Dad." Harvey reached for his drink but found

he hadn't got one. For once this was a good thing, as it meant he could focus on that rather than on Jeff.

"Pint of Guinness and a white wine when you've a minute, mate," he called and turned to his little group. "Drinks?"

They sat in the corner, Harvey and Maisie and Rob and Steve, who came to join them. Jeff had a chair at the table and no one took it, but he spent most of the evening in the door-way with the rugger buggers, as Harvey had always known them, shouting and at times singing in a fashion that Harvey could only feel was not conducive to marital bliss. Mostly, though, he was unaware of Jeff or of anyone else but her. Steve and Rob were debating politics and football and beer and music, and it was a conversation he could have recited by heart before they began it. So he talked to Maisie Cooper. It struck him as funny, when he had time to think of it afterward, that when the evening started he would have said that nothing short of an earthquake could drive the thought of that afternoon from his head, yet for long periods it hardly entered his mind, so complete was his immersion in her. What did they talk about? As he walked home, Harvey asked himself that but found no obvious answer. Or none that could account for how good it had felt to do the talking. And the listening. She was interesting; she knew about stuff. And not just beer and sport and music but about people and ideas, stuff that he used to think was important but which somehow got lost in the comic shop and the growing older and not really getting what he wanted or even knowing what that was. When occasionally Rob or Steve had tried to join their conversation, usually when the other of them had staggered to the bar or the toilet, she had been kind and open but had made it clear, to Harvey at least, that she preferred to return to the one-to-one as soon as possible. Once or twice Harvey had caught in Steve's or Rob's eye an inquiring look, familiar from another century, but he had ignored it. Let them think what they wanted; he had no answer to those looks because he had no idea what was happening. As he wandered, cold but smiling, back up Trelawney Road at nearly midnight, it struck him that life-changing days come along only very rarely. There seemed at that moment a good chance that this might be one, for two entirely unrelated reasons. It made him smile and, because he had been on the whisky for a nightcap, it made him sing. So he ended the evening singing a plaintive, if somewhat uncertain, solo of "Reeling in the Years" by Steely Dan (it had been playing in the pub), when only a few hours earlier he would have laid pretty long odds against ever singing again.

CHAPTER ELEVEN

"Haaarvey! Time to rise and shine. You've got a party to go to today."

Fumbling in the dark for cigarettes, Harvey heard the voice and closed his eyes very tight. Everything was wrong. His mouth felt as though someone had come in during the night and used it as a toilet: There was unknown but malodorous matter at the back of his throat, yet a sort of slimy, unnatural wetness on his tongue. His head seemed to have been re-molded so that it now came to a point in the blinding pain between his eyeballs. His belly lay about him, jellified and sagging to the sides, forming a ring around his prone form. From hours too early to consider, his father had been busily walking along the passage outside his room making a noise. This was a familiar practice and was one of a number of reasons why Harvey very rarely went home for holidays. Today, Donald Briscow had been calling. "Do you know where that drill is, Ann? I need that particular one. I want to put a screw in the bedroom, for the picture. I've been meaning to fix that picture for ages . . ." And his mother had been calling in reply and then there had been the banging and slamming of a drill being found and then, of course, there had been the drilling, protracted and extended. And then there had been more calling and his mother had come along to admire the picture . . . Harvey, lying now on his back, lit a cigarette, opening his eyes to tiny slits and then closing them again very quickly.

"You won't want to miss it, dear, it's your last day."

He tried to remember his dreams. They had been filled not with pretty, attentive women in wine bars finding him fascinating, but with dark passageways and shadows. He had been running, he remembered, running into . . . that was it, into his own shop. But the lights were off and he could hardly see. There was a sense of unease. Something was wrong. There were people there who shouldn't be there. Something terrible had happened. And then it all came back in a rush. "Shit." The air was cold on his bare arms and he tucked himself tightly under the quilt, doing his best not to burn more holes in the cover, which already showed its history as a drunken smoker's blanket. For a few minutes all he wanted to do was crawl deeper into the dark, warm, somewhat smelly cave he had made for himself, just stay there until it went away. But then a rush of adrenaline forced him to sit up, cry out as the point at the front of his head collided with the day, and then scramble upright. He needed to know what was going on. Never before in his life had he prayed so hard for so little. All he wanted in life right now was for absolutely nothing to happen.

The human brain collects and stores information in extraordinary abundance just on the off chance that it might be useful. Harvey would not have said that he knew when the *St. Ives Chronicle* was delivered to his parents' house each morning. Indeed, he would have said he had always actively avoided knowing anything at all about St. Ives's shambolically amateurish local paper. Yet at ten A.M. prompt he was waiting on the mat, and he was not disappointed. Horrified but not disappointed. The murder was splashed across all three columns of the front page and showed all the grammatical errors and inaccurate speculation of the late, replacement front-page lead. Harvey wondered vaguely what they would have led with if they hadn't got this in time. His mind played wistfully with coffee mornings and new church roofs. The story was supported by a rather fuzzy photograph of Bleeder's house looking eerily like every crime scene Harvey had ever seen on TV. The police had been called to the house at six-thirty P.M. by the deceased's son, Charles Odd. His mother had been killed with a kitchen knife. There were signs of breaking and entering and police were seeking an intruder. They had not yet established any motive for the crime. The killer had made elaborate efforts to cover his tracks, but the police were able to say that some evidence had been found at the crime scene . . . Jesus. Harvey clutched the paper to him and felt a wave of nausea sweep across his hangover and carry it up to a higher level. He doubled over and clutched on to the wall, then straightened up, eyes squeezed shut, breathing hard.

"Here, don't scrunch up my paper." Donald Briscow strode out into the hall and took the Chronicle from him, pulled a face, and straightened it out carefully. "Some of us want to know what's going on in the world." Harvey willed his breathing under control.

"Ann! Ann! Look at this." Briscow senior was appalled. "*England Slump in Pakistan* . . . outrageous." He ambled off muttering and Harvey leaned against the wall, letting the wave pass, letting it flow back in lesser form, letting it slacken and ebb away.

"I've cooked you a fry-up, Harvey. Sausage, bacon, kidneys, and some black pudding we had left over from last week. Come along in and eat up, it'll do you good and get you ready for the party."

Harvey made his way into the kitchen and sat very carefully at the table. His mother placed this butcher's shop in front of him and he contemplated it with Mrs. Odd's throat in his mind. "There's been a murder, Harvey."

"Yes, the Pakistanis are murdering us." His father came and joined Harvey at the table.

"I'll get you a cuppa, Donald. Yes, someone Odd up by the new estates near Trehendricks. I don't mean odd, I mean Odd, it's spelled O-D-D, you see? Killed by an intruder. Isn't that awful?" Harvey's mother smacked her lips excitedly. "You'd think we were in London."

"Yes, you bring trouble with you, don't you, Harvey? If you are going to do things like this I wish you'd do it up in the city, not down here." Mr. Briscow was chuckling.

"Oh, dear, that's not funny," said Mrs. Briscow, chuckling also. "This poor woman killed in her own bed . . ."

"In bed?" Harvey, who was still contemplating his breakfast, roused himself for a moment.

"Well, wherever she was."

"In the cellar." Mr. Briscow had the paper. "He cut her throat in the cellar. Now that's plain evil. I don't know how you can say he shouldn't be put down for that, Harvey. Killed like an animal, that's what should happen to him. It would stop this sort of thing from happening all the time. But oh, no, the bleeding hearts want to give him counseling and let him out after twenty minutes so he can do it again. These people are evil, Harvey, and they should be put out of their misery."

"Oh, Christ." Harvey put an undercooked lamb's kidney in his mouth and tried to chew. It tasted simply of meat; he could feel the blood leaking onto his tongue. A grimace filled with exhaustion crossed his face. He hadn't realized how tired he was.

"What's wrong with that, Harvey?" His mother was scandalized. "That's lovely, healthy food, that is. You should eat that up, it's what you need."

"Yes, none of this vegetarian rubbish you get up in London. Alfalfa sprouts and soya beans? They're not sprouts and they're not beans. Should be done under the trade descriptions act. Simple as that."

Harvey focused for a rare moment on what his parents were saying. He had sometimes tried to picture London as they viewed it: a place of constant violence, where no one ate any-thing but tiny portions of vegetables before going off to watch pornography and take drugs. It actually wasn't that far from his experience of it. He tried to smile and then grimaced again as it made his head hurt. He put a piece of black pudding in his mouth and then, realizing too late that this was a more serious proposition than he had expected, he started to chew.

"It says the son, Charles Odd (thirty-five)—why do they have to tell us how old people are all the time? What do we care how old he is?—went to Trehendricks . . . Well, Harvey, that would mean he was in your year." Mr. Briscow looked at his son with genuine interest for the first time Harvey could re-member, and Mrs. Briscow jumped up and whipped round to check the facts over his shoulder.

"So it would. Charles Odd, Harvey, you must have known him. Now let me think, do we know a Charles . . . Was there a Charles in your football team? No, that was a Christopher, wasn't it? Charles? Charles? Do you know him, Harvey? You must!"

Overwhelmed by the experience of the black pudding and troubled by his parents' enthusiasm, Harvey nodded. "Yeah," he managed, still struggling with stray pieces of skin between his teeth. "I knew him but I never really hung round with him at all. But, yeah. I saw him at the reunion on Saturday—"

"You saw him at the reunion!" Both parents pounced like hungry seagulls on this titbit of news. "You saw him on Saturday and on Sunday his mother was killed," Mrs. Briscow said triumphantly. Harvey frowned.

"So what?" he demanded. "Everyone there saw him. It's no crime to have seen him."

"Don't get defensive, Harvey. You'll only cast further suspi-cion on yourself."

"Piss off, Dad."

"If you did it you may as well come clean."

"Look, you may find that funny—"

"But, Harvey, perhaps the police will want to interview you." Mrs. Briscow's eyes were shining.

"Why the fuck . . . ?"

"Harvey!"

"Language, boy, you're not in London now."

"Why the fuck would the police want to interview me? I saw him briefly at the reunion. We hardly exchanged two words. Why the fuck . . . ?"

"You spoke to him! Harvey, I thought you said you didn't know him. You spoke to him and the next day his mother is killed."

"Jesus Christ . . ." Harvey felt suddenly that this would never end. Why had he come to this awful reunion in this crappy little town to be with these ghastly people who asked him impossible questions at breakfast and fed him terrible meats that tasted of death? He shuddered bodily.

"Eat your breakfast, dear. It'll do you good and get you ready for the party. Now, tell us about Charles Odd. What did you talk about at the reunion?"

Harvey filled his mouth with black pudding. It seemed the easiest way to stop himself from crying out loud.

CHAPTER TWELVE

The worst aspect of growing older was when habits became traditions. The lunch party had become another one: After
every reunion they went to Steve's and stood around in his sitting room, drinking too early and feeling uncomfortable. This
unease was usually added to for Harvey by the fact that Steve
had two children, now risen to three, and he had no gift with
children. Even though his interests were, by his own admis-
sion, almost exclusively juvenile, he did not enjoy sharing
them with, well . . . juveniles. And he hated fucking *Pokémon* and
that always created a clash. Today, however, he hardly gave the
kids a thought. Indeed, he felt quite ready to pretend to be a
train, or build something out of toilet rolls or even watch
Japanese pocket animals if it was required of him. He was feeling a powerful and passionate desire for normality. He wanted
to be bored.

Looking back on the party afterward, Harvey found it very
hard to fix his emotional reactions. He had arrived with so
much to think about, more really than he had ever had before,
but he spent much of the early period talking about sex with
men less knowledgeable in that area than himself—and such
men are not easily found. How this happened was not altogether clear. He had arrived seeking boredom and the absence
of incident and at first had found it in abundance. But then
someone had mentioned the murder. A discussion of Bleeder

and his mother had begun and Harvey had suddenly felt a desperate need to stop it, as if between them the reunionists were about to solve the crime and point the finger at him. So he had mentioned, pretty much at random, that it might be a sex killing: that perhaps the local press was being delicate to spare Bleeder's feelings. This led to a general expression of doubt that anyone would wish to seek sexual congress with old Mrs. Odd. And Harvey, whether through the desire to move the conversation into other areas or through some obscure gallantry, felt compelled to defend the old as potential sex targets. This had led to the suggestion, from Steve, that perhaps Harvey liked "a bit of scrag-end." From here the conversation had taken a personal turn and Harvey had found himself becoming red in the face and defensive. "I do not have any interest in screwing old ladies, you fucking arsehole" were the exact words he was speaking into a silent room populated by, among others, two children aged six and three and a babe-in-arms, when Maisie Cooper arrived. There was a long silence penetrated by sniggering from the men grouped around Harvey.

"Well, that's good to know, Harvey." Jeff Cooper had also arrived. "But your mother must be devastated."

Many smokers feel angry about the bans and prohibitions around their habit. But Harvey had always rather welcomed them. Being part of a segregated minority, being oppressed, was something he had quietly dreamed of through most of his adult life. Nothing too harsh, of course, not racism or lack of human rights, but the minor grievances of being a smoker in a nonsmoking world suited him rather well. And for this reason he felt an unfair but real animus against Steve for being liberal and open-minded enough to have ashtrays all around his sitting room. What was the matter with him? Didn't he care about his children? No one in London would dream of behaving in such a decadent manner. What Harvey craved was to get out into the peace of the garden, turn his jacket up against the cold, perhaps moan a little, certainly do the sigh, and have a long miserable smoke. Instead, he was cornered by a bunch of men discussing sexual fetishism. "And what about vacuum cleaners?" Rob was saying. "Who discovered that one, that's what I'd like to know," when she came over and joined them. "Hello, Maisie," Rob broke off to greet her. "We are just talking about having sex with household implements," he added helpfully, "in case you have any interests in that area."

There was a collective leer in which Harvey steadfastly refused to join.

Maisie smiled. "No, I prefer garden tools, to be honest. Have you seen the garden, Harvey?"

"Er, no," Harvey lied loudly to cover the sound of melodramatic intakes of breath from the circle around him.

"Be gentle with him, Maisie. He's new at this; he may not be ready for the lawn mower. Stick to the shears . . ."

He followed her out through the open French windows.

The day had taken a turn toward rain and a light spittle darkened his denim jacket. They walked round the side of the house and found some shelter under a denuded willow tree. She took a cigarette from him and he had to cup his hands round hers to make a windbreak. For a moment it was as if he was holding her hands in his own, as if he was sheltering her. "Thanks." She looked at him and he dropped his eyes to concentrate on lighting his own cigarette. Then he looked up and met her gaze. He shivered. He had not seen her outside before; the wind was flicking her autumnal hair out from its neatness and into a wilder frame for her face. It was like watching her lose her civilization for a second, watching her animalize. He groaned. "God, you're lovely." It was the first time he had said anything of the kind and she looked troubled by it, but he did not take it back.

"Thanks, but you shouldn't say that."

He wondered if he had spoken too much or too soon, but

really he didn't care. It was not a day for worrying about the niceties. "Does he tell you that? Jeff, I mean. He should tell you every hour. If you were mine I'd tell you every hour." Looking back on that evening, Harvey found it hard to imagine that he had actually said these words to another human being. He was forced to wonder if perhaps being involved in a major crime had somehow achieved an alchemical reaction in him: transformed him into the dashing and irresistible lover he had always dreamed of being. If so, it was a terrible price, but he was not at this moment sorry to pay it.

"No, he doesn't tell me that, and nor should you." She said it as a criticism but he heard the longing in it and felt his stomach turn over. He was suddenly aware how much he wanted her. It was hard to remember anything that he had ever wanted so much. Except, of course, the *Superman One*. He pulled a face and turned away to look into a different emotion: He could see again the plastic cover, and it was stained with bloody fingerprints. "It's funny, I came down here with Jeff on sufferance. I thought I was going to absolutely hate it."

"And you don't?" He hadn't cleaned the fingerprints off because it wasn't there. He could feel the nausea again, the sudden certainty that things weren't going to be all right.

"Not completely, no. Not completely."

Harvey turned back but found she was not looking at him. She had turned, too, so they had been standing for a moment back-to-back. He knew that this was a moment. But it was a terribly wrong moment. If he said the right thing to her now he might get what he had just realized he wanted more than anything else. Even that. Especially that. Shit. There had been blood all over his hands. He could feel it on his fingers, feel that sticky, runny, KFC quality it had as he cleaned up. He shook his head from side to side, uncaring of the hangover that still hung like a net curtain around his skull, like that gray net curtain. Fuck, fuck, fuck. "Oh, Christ, Maisie, I don't know what to do." It came out unexpectedly, as a sort of strangled cry, and he could feel an actual sob in it. He was almost crying and he never cried, or only at E.T., never at real stuff, and now he was going to cry in front of a woman he was desperate to impress. "Oh, Jesus Christ." But, completely unexpectedly, the horror of blood and death worked wonderfully in his favor. Because within a second, she was in his arms.

"Oh, Harvey," she responded. And even Harvey himself could see that he might have had a better name at that moment, and he could also see that what he had lacked all these years in his dealings with women was depth and that he had just acquired a massive amount of it, quite by chance and overnight.

"Oh, God, you're wonderful." He was also old enough to know that, whatever the circumstances, in moments like this absolute abandonment was the only right course of action. So he lost himself in her extraordinary hair. She smelled like warm honey and he thanked a god he had never believed in that he'd had a shower that morning. After that, he just forgot everything and let her claw herself tight against him as if he might be a buffer against all the torments of the world. And perhaps he pulled her tight for exactly matching reasons. So they clung for a long moment in each other's arms like fighters who have thrown their swords away and put all the trust they have simply in their shields. And that is where Jeff Cooper found them, of course, when he came looking for his wife.

It was an ugly scene, not improved by the fact that all Harvey's friends came out of the French windows and peeped round the side of the house to watch. Jeff went for Harvey with real violence and Harvey, to his shame, forgot his protective role and ran for it. He ran about the garden like a large, ungainly Labrador, dodging round trees and at one point using the shed as a barrier: him going one way round, Jeff the other.

"You fucking, miserable bastard." Jeff had a way of speaking that was low and mean when he was angry, even when he was moving fast, and Harvey heard in it the sound of his own suffering. He was aware of how silent everything else was. Why wasn't anyone saying "Come on, Jeff, leave it, he's not worth it...," that sort of thing? Why wasn't she saying anything? But all seemed rendered mute by the vehemence, the unarguability, of Jeff's anger. With a sudden realization, Harvey knew that Jeff had wanted to do this for a long time; that though they had pretended to friendship at times because Harvey had been popular at school through the comics, and Jeff through the rugby, really they had hated each other, sneering beneath the banter, disrespecting each other's route to cool. And now Jeff had found the mother and father of all excuses for doing what he'd been longing to do. If Harvey had had time to consider he would probably have been on Jeff's side. He actually had quite strict morals about men stealing their friends' wives; it was like not buying your round, or shagging women who were really pissed. However, he did not have time to give it much thought because he was busy in flight. There was, briefly, time for him to think what an extraordinary few days he was having and to wonder if perhaps everything dramatic and life-changing that ever happened to him was going to happen over one long weekend. And then, with a horrid inevitability, he was caught.

It happened as he hurtled back past the willow tree. He had formulated the vague plan that he would run down the side of the house and into the front garden and away down the road. So he had dashed behind the shed again to mislead Jeff and once he was out of sight, Harvey had come at speed, panting hard, down the lawn under the willow boughs (and it isn't easy to run fast doubled over, but he attempted it) and out the other side. However, Jeff, who was a flanker and used to chasing things, had not been completely fooled and appeared very quickly from the shed diversion. He then made the simple maneuver of running close to the wall of the house, thus avoiding the tree altogether, and because he didn't need to double up, caught Harvey just as he was emerging from its protection. He

hit him hard in the stomach and Harvey, who was already gasping like an asthmatic at an orgy, felt as if he had suddenly been
placed in a bubble with no air inside at all, a bubble vacuum
that would lift up into the sky and float him away from this terrible scene. As he doubled over, Jeff hit him again full in the
face, catching him in the right eye, but Harvey hardly felt this
second blow. Everything in him was trying to remember how
to breathe. As he crashed to earth, the grass tickled his nose and
he was momentarily back on the roadside near Bleeder's house;
he had put bloody fingers on the comic and the comic had van-
ished. How do things vanish? Like this, perhaps . . . In the bubble he was drifting on the air; the ground felt pillowy soft, as if
he might sink down into it. Perhaps the bubble would go
down, not up, sucked and swallowed by the world. He knew
that he had been kicked and that after that, perhaps spurred by
the thought that two murders were too many for one reunion,
the other party-goers had been galvanized into action and had
dragged Jeff away. Distantly, he could hear her saying "I hate
you, it's over . . ."; stuff like that. For a moment, he wondered if
she was talking to him, and then he knew she wasn't and felt
glad.

CHAPTER THIRTEEN

Steve's spare bedroom had an alien cleanliness that Harvey found restful. There were white built-in wardrobes with gold knobs. There was a matching dressing table with fancy ornamentation around the legs, which Harvey characterized, after a moment's thought, as Barbie-style. The walls were of pale peach and enlivened with pastel artworks involving mice in Victorian clothing. One of the old crowd, Jessica, who had married Bob from Bristol who was in property and couldn't hold his drink, had trained as a nurse. She was kind and gentle and tenderly put her hands on his face, on his belly, and on his side where he'd been kicked. Harvey got a partial erection despite himself and hoped it didn't show. Then she left him alone for a while and he lay on his back looking at the pale pink ceiling. It occurred to him that perhaps this was how people coped in wartime: So many troubling things happened to them in such a short space of time that their brains began to blend one into the next. The mind sort of stopped bothering to process them and just let things happen. That was how he felt: as if he had passed some watershed beyond which nothing really mattered, a place of Zen peace. The last thing Nurse Jessica asked him as she left was "Are you all right?" and he murmured some noncommittal acknowledgement. But in truth he wasn't at all sure if he was all right or not. The feeling of being in a bubble and floating had remained after he got his breath back. He had a sense of potential pain. At some point his eye, his belly, and his side were really, really going to hurt. But for now he was becalmed, drifting in a pink and peach sea, and he floated into a deep and untroubled sleep.

It was Steve who woke him after about two hours. "All right, H?" He was standing by the bed looking worried, and Harvey wondered for a moment what the cause of his concern was. Perhaps it was something to do with that god-awful drilling that his dad had been doing under the bed, which seemed to have cut him open from the side. Then the dream lifted and he raised himself up and yelped. Shit. Three quite distinct reasons for extreme concern flew simultaneously into his brain, driving out the dream entirely.

"Shit. Steve, where the fuck is Bleeder?"

"Eh?"

"Shit. I mean, where the fuck is Maisie?"

"She's gone. She left after the fight. Jeff went, too. I think they were breaking up." Steve sat on the edge of the bed. "I hope this doesn't mean you won't come down again, H. I hope this hasn't spoiled our parties for you. We look forward to them, really do . . ."

"What? Look, Steve, when did she go? Where did she go? I should have . . . done something."

"What, like get yourself even more kicked?" Steve chuckled vaguely. "Don't worry, Maisie can look after herself. They'll have gone home to thrash it out. How are you feeling?"

"Me? Oh, peachy." Harvey took a line through the wallpaper. "Really pinky peachy, Steve. How are you, mate?"

"Oh, I'm all right. But you are a stupid cunt."

"Eh?"

"Trying to get off with Jeff Cooper's bird? You must be completely bloody bonkers. Ten out of ten for guts, mate, but minus five for sense. He was going to kill you if we hadn't pulled him off."

"Yeah, I know." Harvey ferreted for his cigarettes and, seeing that his jacket was on the white and gold chair by the bed, reached over and yelped again. "I must get the name of your decorator," he muttered, moving much more slowly. "So, what's happening now downstairs? Any other dramas?"

"Well, yes and no really. That's why I came up."

"What?" Harvey looked at him with some desperation; surely there couldn't possibly be anything else.

"Well, it's just . . . well, I thought you must have heard, from what you said when I came in . . ."

"What?"

Steve lowered his voice. "Bleeder's here."

"He's what?"

"Bleeder Odd, you know, Charles Odd as he insists he's called. He's downstairs."

"But his mum just got murdered." Having fumbled in his jacket pocket, Harvey had managed to light an extremely squashed cigarette, which now stuck to his dry bottom lip as he opened his mouth to gape at Steve.

"I know. Fuck knows why he's come."

"Did you invite him?" Harvey grabbed a decorative pot-pourri from the dressing table to use as an ashtray.

"Yeah, we bumped into him yesterday lunchtime, on the piss-up. I was a bit smashed even then and I'm afraid I was a bit rude to him."

"Why, what did you say?"

"I said I was sorry he couldn't be allowed to join us last night because he was too odd, but if he'd like to come round today we would be more than happy to receive him. Something like that."

"Sweet." Harvey buried his head in his hands and very nearly burned himself. His lungs hurt as he dragged on his cigarette and he grimaced but did not remove it from his mouth.

"It's just, I thought because you knew him better than the

rest of us, you might like to come downstairs. It's a bit awkward having him here, to be honest. I don't know what to talk to him about."

"What do you mean I knew him better? I've never known him any better than—oh, hi, Blee—Charles." Bleeder had entered the room and was striding toward the bed.

"Oh, all right, mate?" Steve leapt to his feet and made for the door at speed, passing Bleeder on the way. He attempted a halfhearted slap on the back, missed, and moved off. "Leave you to it for a bit, H. Come down when you are feeling better, yeah?"

"No, hang on, wait a sec, I am feeling better . . ." But he was gone and the door was closed. Bleeder came and stood directly over Harvey and looked down at him.

Harvey looked up and attempted a smile. "You all right?" he asked weakly.

"Mmm. Yes, I am, actually."

"Right. Good." Shit. "So, I, er . . . heard about your mum."

"Yes?"

"Harsh."

"Yes."

Harvey hadn't intended to say "harsh." He had been meaning to say something else but the image of Mrs. Odd's throat had returned again to his mind. He didn't want to discuss this. There hadn't been a lot of time for cogitation since the previous evening, but Harvey knew that the murderer must have got into the house without breaking and entering. There had certainly been no sign of damage when he arrived. The most obvious suspect for the killer therefore was now standing a little too close to the edge of the bed. Harvey inched away under the covers.

"I mean, bad one," he added. "You must be in shock and stuff. I'm surprised you came to the party really."

"I needed to get out of the house."

"Oh, right, yeah." Harvey could understand that. It was that sort of house.

"Do the police know anything?" It was a perfectly natural question and there was no reason why he should blush and shift about furtively when he asked it. But he did.

"They are seeking a killer." Bleeder had a sort of faraway voice today with an arch note in it, and Harvey recognized it from their past. Even though he was wearing a suit and tie and his hair looked like it cost more to cut than Harvey had spent on his last holiday, the old Bleeder seemed once more present. "They are compiling their evidence."

Was "compiling" the right word? Harvey wasn't sure. "You sound odd," he said, and then rushed on, "Or rather, not odd so much as troubled. You must be troubled. You've a lot to be troubled about really, I suppose. I sometimes wish someone would murder my parents, but of course in truth I'd be very . . . troubled."

"Yes. It has come as a shock." For a moment the new Bleeder, the Charles as Harvey now thought of him, returned. "It has been quite a shock." And he sat down on the edge of the bed exactly as Steve had done. Harvey felt very differently about this new arrival in what was, when all was said and done, his personal space. He shifted a little further across the mattress.

"I hear you had a fight."

"Um, yeah. Bit of one. Not really a fight as such, just a bit of a wrestling match, sort of thing. With Jeff Cooper."

"You were kissing his wife."

"Well, not kissing as such. Rather sort of . . ."

"Wrestling?" The new Charles was back and smiling. "You're obviously a bit of a wrestling fan."

"No, not really, I just . . . it's been a funny few days."

"Mmm. Yes, it has." Bleeder frowned for a moment. "I wish to God I hadn't come down here. It's years since I was here and I don't know why I came back."

"No . . . God knows why any of us do. I guess one has to

come back occasionally, but yeah, I can see how you might have preferred not to be here when this happened." Harvey looked at him closely, but Bleeder just nodded.

"Mmm? Yes. Yes, that's true. I wish I'd stayed in London. There isn't much point in going back..." Bleeder seemed to see something in the gold-rimmed mirror on the dressing table that worried him, for he shook his head and turned to face Harvey again.

"My mother was not an easy woman," he said suddenly.

Well, of course, that wasn't what the rumors had always said about her, but Harvey didn't mention this. Instead, he simply shook his head and leaned across for the makeshift ashtray. His side spasmed again and he groaned. Bleeder seemed not to hear. "In many ways we were distant from each other. She had problems; her mind was not right. It took me some time to realize that. And to get away from her, to really leave St. Ives. Do you know, I think it took me years really."

"And now you're back," Harvey added helpfully.

"Yes. Yes, I'm back. But she's gone." He paused for a long time. "I want to know now," he said suddenly. "I think now I want to know everything."

Harvey had managed to light another cigarette from the collapsing butt of the first. This one was equally flat and with bits of tobacco falling out of the end. He felt panic rising in him.

"You want to know?" he said. "Want to know what? And anyway, why ask me? What am I to do with anything? I don't know anything." He was glad Bleeder was not a policeman at this point, because even to his own ear he sounded guilty as hell.

"You were there," said Bleeder simply. "So you must know."

"I was not. I don't know what you mean...How do you know I was there? Where were you? That's what I'd like to know: Where were you?" Harvey could hear his own voice rising to a pitch of terror unlike anything he'd heard before. He had thought he knew himself, knew his voice, yet here in extremis was a stranger suddenly shouting from inside his head.

At that point the door opened and Nurse Jessica returned. "Feeling any better, are we?" she caroled sweetly. "Steve said you were awake. He's rung your parents, H. He thought you could do with a lift home. Your dad is coming for you."

"Oh, right, right, yeah." Harvey called his voice back to itself, as though calling a ferret from a rabbit hole. Even as he said it, even as he forced the panic down by an act of will, he was able to feel a faint regret that his father was coming. Why couldn't he have been out? He could handle his mother.

Bleeder had stood up and was gazing unseeing out of the window.

"Let's, er . . . you know. We can talk again, Charles." Harvey hauled himself up and allowed Jessica to help him, even though he could manage, really. She smelled of soap and had such gentle hands . . . Bleeder did not reply. "I guess I'll just . . . you know, downstairs. Better say my good-byes and—you know . . ." Harvey, once upright, moved quickly toward the door and then caught sight of himself in the oval mirror. "Jesus, look at that." He studied the beginnings of a black eye. "I look like a real bruiser." Trying to control the pride that was replacing the panic, he moved to the door. "So, er, see you then, Charles, yeah?"

"Yes. Yes, see you, H . . . Harvey. We must have another talk. I'm sure we will . . . talk."

"Er, yeah." Harvey grabbed the door handle and ran.

"A fight?" Mrs. Briscow looked at Harvey with her deepest disapproval. "You go to a party and you get into a fight?"

The alcohol and the bruises from earlier in the afternoon were beginning to take their toll. All Harvey really wanted was to go back to sleep. "Look, actually it was just a bit of horseplay and I don't think it needs any more discussion." The eye was coming up nicely and Harvey was examining it in the hallway mirror. He had attempted to tell his father that he had fallen down the stairs, but unfortunately Steve had already explained over the phone.

"Lying and fighting, I don't know which is worse."

Harvey pulled a face and watched himself pull it. Was that really how he looked when he did that? He did it again a couple of times. Jesus, he looked fifty when he did that.

"You should surely be too old for putting us through this, Harvey." His mother's voice dragged him unhappily away from the mirror.

"Oh, yes, sorry, Mum. I get punched in the face and kicked in the kidneys but you are the ones that really suffer, aren't you? I mean, Jesus, how inconsiderate of me."

"Kicked in the kidneys! I thought you said it was just some horseplay. I should take you down to the doctor's: You might be bleeding inside."

"I'm not bleeding inside. I may be crying inside but don't trouble yourselves about that; I wouldn't."

"Don't be soft, lad." His father was now reading the paper. "If you get into a fight you must accept the consequences; no good blubbing about it afterward."

"Thanks, Dad. What a loss you were to the caring professions."

"Your father was an ambulance driver in the army," his mother reminded him.

"Yes, I know, Mum, we've met before, if you remember. The point is that I am alive and I suggest we break out the champagne rather than behaving as if I am nine years old and have misbehaved myself. Now, I am going up to my room and I am going to stay there for a long time. I have had a shock and what I need is rest. I do not want to be disturbed. If there are any drills needing to be found, or little chores to be performed outside my door, I would ask you both very kindly to delay them until I get out of this lazar house first thing tomorrow. OK?"

"First thing, is it?" Mr. Briscow's eyes shone. "I'll see you first thing then, son."

"Oh, shit." Harvey shook his head and felt the exhaustion more strongly than before.

"And no more rubbish under your bed, please." His mother had returned to the kitchen and was humming happily, having delivered this directive. Harvey was halfway up the stairs before it reached his brain. He walked carefully down again.

"Sorry?"

"I found that bag of clothes under your bed, covered in muck. I dread to think what you get up to sometimes. I put the whole lot through the washing machine twice, including your plimsolls. They are as good as new now."

"Er, right. OK. Thanks, Mum." And he crept up to bed at half past eight, exactly as if he was nine years old. It had been a very long day and for once, for once only, it felt good.

CHAPTER FOURTEEN

Why do parents like waiting at railway stations? If there is anything to say it can be said in the car, or before leaving the house even. Yet here were Harvey's parents hanging about with him on the Penzance platform in an awkward and unnatural silence, waiting for a train that was ten minutes delayed. "You can go if you want, you know. I'll be all right." I'm thirty-five, for Christ's sake. But he couldn't say that because he had a rule: Never leave under a cloud. You don't want your last face-to-face words to your parents until next Christmas to be unkind ones.

"No, we'll stay, darling. We want to see you off. We see you so rarely, we have to take every minute we can." His mother's sentimentality was kicking in and he thought he could detect actual tears imminent.

"Yeah, OK, it's nice to have some company actually." Not yours, of course, but . . .

"You could lose a bit of weight, Harvey." His father was not, as Harvey had learned to his cost in the past, afflicted by his own concerns around departures. He remembered vividly the day he went off to university, his first real leaving home, and his father's last words to him: "You can't do much worse there than you did at school, can you?" Half his journey had been ruined thinking about it: What kind of valediction was that when the only child leaves home forever? Shouldn't there be some rite of passage, some passing on of wisdom from father to son, not just a wanton insult? Where was the ceremony? Where was the passion? Jesus.

"Piss off." Rules, after all, are there for the breaking.

"Now, Harvey, don't be rude to your father."

"He said I was fat."

"No, he didn't, he said you could lose some weight. That's a different—"

"He is fat."

"Look, will you piss off. You're not exactly the glamorous granddad yourself."

"He's not a granddad, Harvey. I'd so love him to be, but he isn't . . ."

"Oh, for fuck's sake, I don't believe you are going to start on that now . . ."

And so the leave-taking descended into abuse as, in truth, it almost always did, rules or no rules.

Harvey had been looking forward to the journey home. His father had roused him at half past six by coughing outside his bedroom door and padding up and down the landing. Harvey, who rarely arose before nine, was feeling the pace a little. The journey, he felt, could be restful. A time for clear and considered thought. He needed to draw a line under everything that had happened. Get some distance, literally and figuratively. Move on. But instead, almost at once, he found himself thinking in circles. And they were circles of guilt. "I should have gone to the police at once"; "I should have found out where she was staying and telephoned her"; "I should have stayed and talked it all through with Bleeder." This last was the most wretched cycle of all. If he had just had a little courage he might have found out how much Bleeder knew. Instead, he had left himself open to hope and fear in equal measure. For all his efforts on his future self's behalf he had let him down after all and he felt bad about that. What if I never know? That was one of the fears assailing him. It was perfectly possible that there would be no coverage of a murder in Cornwall in the national press. He would find it hard to ring his parents more than once a week without causing major suspicion in their minds. There was the possibility that he would never hear anything further about the murder of Mrs. Odd. And that was a good thing, of course, except that he knew his sleep patterns were going to suffer.

The journey from Penzance to London is of nearly six hours' duration and there is a limit to how much of the English countryside any man can take. Harvey had a book in his bag, a biography of a seventies rock star. But somehow groupies and drug binges seemed a bit shallow and unexciting; compared to the last few days at the seaside they sounded like a rest cure. So, to stifle the anxiety attacks that were threatening to send him heaving to the tiny train toilet, he drank beer from outrageously overpriced tins of Watneys, warm and sticky, but good for the memory. He started soon after he boarded at ten-fifteen and was still sipping from his last can when he arrived at Paddington at four-thirty. By that time he had forgotten pretty much everything.

Although he had taken very little to the reunion, he still found his rucksack heavy and unwieldy. Stumbling a little and slipping on the polished platform surface, he considered abandoning the bag in a passing luggage trolley. However, with a quick snatch of "Should I Stay or Should I Go" by the Clash, which happened to be in his mind, he decided instead to keep the bag. It was his, after all. People were looking at him, he realized, as he made his way toward the Underground, and he smiled benignly. "Hello," he called kindly. "I didn't do it, in case you are wondering. I am entirely innocent. Well, no . . ." he corrected himself, "not innocent entirely, not guilty or anything. I broke a window, for Christ's sake." He swung the bag up from his trailing hand onto his shoulder, buffeting an old lady who was following behind him. "Ha, shouldn't stand so close. 'Don't Stand So Close to Me.' " He sang a bar or two of Sting as he turned round again to give her a smile, but she had gone. "Bye. Shit." He stumbled again and headed for a bench. "I must sit down." He sat for a few moments, aware of two things. One was that he had cured the circling thoughts in his mind; they had definitely disappeared; however, it now seemed that everything else was going round and round. The other was that the station was prettified by a sort of plastic facsimile of a traditional English pub, which opened off to one side of the concourse. Harvey had the idea that he had drunk there before and decided that he should revisit those days. This spirit of nostalgia got him through two further pints before he felt ready to go. "Cheerio," he said to a slightly smelly but very friendly man he had met in the pub. "Have one more on me." He handed the man a fiver and received an expansive smile.

"Ta, gov."

Then, smiling in a way intended to take in the rest of the pub's patrons and, in truth, the entire human race, he made his way to the Underground.

It was as he was buying a ticket that he became aware that he wanted to go to his shop rather than head for home. He wanted to look at what, if the hard truth was faced, was his only real achievement in life. He wanted to run his hands over it. Feel that he really was back in town. With a brief burst of "Mack the Knife," he headed for the barriers. Josh had been left in charge for the four days Harvey had been away and Josh was not to be trusted. He was not managerial material. A good manager should check his stock. A good manager put job before home life. So instead of taking the Bakerloo Line to Charing Cross, Harvey took the Circle Line to Moorgate and walked up Old Street to Inaction Comix through a light drizzle. The shop was in darkness and he took a while getting out his keys. As on most of the shops in the area a metal awning had been sealed shut from top to bottom over the windows and door, and Harvey spent a long time trying to get the key into the lock at the bottom of the door guard before realizing that he was using his house keys. Giggling and with a long, ultimately explosive fart, he found the right key. Grunting with satisfaction he opened the padlock and slid the metal up. He had always liked the way the metal grille folded in on itself and tonight he did it twice before unlocking the door, turning a switch, and blinking in the painful glare of the strip lights. Carefully he shut the door behind him and looked around.

All seemed to be well. No one had stolen the stock or set fire to the cash register. Nor were there any signs of flooding or insect invasion. Giggling again, Harvey found his way past the counter and into the back room. It was not uncommon for him, when drunk, to sleep on the long grubby gray couch that took up most of one wall. He seriously considered his condition now. Was he drunk enough to stay the night? It was always a bit of a toss-up. It meant instant rest, which suddenly seemed terribly compelling, but it also meant waking up cold, fully clothed, on a couch, usually with Josh standing over him looking considerate. Like so much in life there were pros and cons. He picked up the heap of mail that Josh had dumped on his desk, most of it bills, and sat down on the couch. It was very comfortable. No, he didn't want to come and look at a fifteen-year-old boy's comic collection; no, he didn't want a TV license; no, he didn't need another four credit cards; no, he wasn't the winner of a million-pound prize draw. Josh had done very little to sort the mail, mostly because he knew he wasn't allowed to open it and this rankled. But to prevent it slipping off the desk and onto the floor he had piled it in size order with the larger items at the bottom. This meant that the hard-backed A4 brown envelope that provided the foundation for the whole pile was last. Harvey was yawning and feeling really that in fact a lot of decisions just made themselves. He leaned back against the tobacco-scented cushions and tore the end off this last envelope, then, with a slight struggle, extracted its contents. After that he sat and looked at what he had got for a long time. It was a mint-condition copy of a *Superman One* in a plastic slip protector. And on the front of the plastic protector were a number of red, smudged fingerprints.

Harvey held it for minutes that seemed to be sucking at him, as if time was draining the alcohol and the faith out of him. Then he got up and walked unsteadily to his desk. He found the keys on the top and this time got the right one at once. Unlocking the bottom drawer where the petty cash was kept and lifting out the black metal tin inside, Harvey put the *Superman One* underneath it and then replaced the tin and closed and locked the drawer. Then he walked backward to the sofa, unconsciously enacting an exact reversal of his previous movements, and fell heavily onto its untender mercy. He lay for a long moment awake but without thought, without response. Blank. And then he sank, blissfully, into total darkness.

CHAPTER FIFTEEN

"You left the door unlocked . . ." Josh's voice seemed to be coming from the locked drawer at the bottom of Harvey's desk, which unexpectedly was buried under some brambles in Bleeder's garden. ". . . all night with the shutter up." There was amazement in his tone, mingled with a sort of grudging respect. "I can't believe you did that." Harvey untangled himself from his T-shirt, which had become rucked round his neck, pushed off the cushion that was smothering him, shook off the dream that was still circling round his head, and sat up. Then he groaned. At everything.

"Leave that!" he said suddenly as Josh, attempting to perch on the edge of the desk, moved the pile of opened mail. "I'll deal with that." He rubbed his hand over his face to clear the dreams that had invaded the deep, dark wonderful nothingness of his drunken slumber and then, pushing himself up like an old man, ran bowlegged to the toilet. Josh heard what seemed to be a river cascading through the shop. It took a while before the flush went and the sound of taps replaced it. Harvey reemerged, drying his face on the filthy hand towel that they kept in the equally filthy staff bathroom. "That's a first even for you," Josh continued as if Harvey had not left him, "all night. Anyone could have wandered in and stolen the stock or done you in. How lucky are you?"

"Lucky?" Harvey emerged for a moment from the towel, his face pink overlaying gray beneath the stubble, his whole head gleaming with droplets. He considered the word for a moment as if examining a rare Japanese Hentai. "How lucky am I?"

"Well, you could have been mugged."

"Yes. I could." He made his way back to the sofa and sat down to light a cigarette.

"What happened, by the way?"

"Eh?"

"Your eye. You get in a fight, yeah? Or fell down or something?"

"Oh, yeah, bit of argy-bargy, nothing really."

"Right. Bad one." Josh put on his best bedside manner. "Want a McBreakfast?"

"Yeah, OK." Harvey realized that Josh was right; he did need a McBreakfast.

"Big Breakfast?"

"Yeah."

"How many?"

"Two."

"Sure?"

"Yeah . . . No. Three."

"Right. Can I take a fiver from petty cash? I'm a bit boracic?"

"Yeah, yeah, OK." Harvey was searching for his matches, which had fallen off the end of the sofa during the night. The difficult part was getting his hand down to the floor without bending over because bending over made the blood, and more important the pain, rush to the front of his head. Josh tinkered for a moment with his keys and then began to pull open the bottom drawer of the desk. His progress was impeded by Harvey, who rugby-tackled him from the side and hurled him bodily to the floor.

"What in fuck . . . ?"

"Shit. Sorry." Harvey got up, shut the drawer, and then rubbed his shoulder. "Shit, that hurt." He looked down to where Josh lay on his back. Somewhat distractedly he reached out to help him up. "Sorry, just, er, playing."

"You nearly broke my bloody back, you fucking idiot." Josh got up slowly and tested his limbs for damage. "You could have killed me."

"Yeah, sorry."

"What the fuck's the matter with you? Just 'cause you get in one fight in Cornwall you start acting all . . . twatish . . ."

Twatish? Harvey stifled an inopportune giggle, which started in the pool of hysteria he could feel somewhere down at the bottom of his stomach. "Sorry, Josh. Look . . ." He felt in his pockets and found a tenner. "Look, get us both some breakfast, all right? Get yourself some pancakes and syrup, that's your favorite. And a thick shake." But Josh was not to be mollified. He refused to go at first, but then grabbed the money and without a word stalked off, slamming the shop door behind him. As soon as he'd gone Harvey went at once to the bottom drawer. There was just a chance, if he prayed really hard, if he called in all the favors he had ever done a benevolent Maker, that it would turn out to have been just a drunken hallucination. That was the best plan he could think of at the moment. He knew it wasn't a good plan and that it had very little chance of success. And sure enough the *Superman One* was lying neatly under the money box. He took it out and looked hard at it for several minutes. None of his old desire was left. He felt no pleasure in it, no wish to open the packaging, no interest in its contents. It represented nothing but suffering and misery. And mystery. While drunken sleep rarely fulfills the same purpose as good sober rest, it had allowed some things to clarify. What Harvey now felt for certain, as he had only vaguely guessed before, was that he was being set up. Somehow, someone was trying to get at him. He felt the rising panic, the anxiety attack coming; he felt his head throbbing, his mouth felt like a sawdust floor, and he could taste vomit somewhere in the background of his palate. As he held the bloodstained comic in his hands he realized something more: Whoever it was was succeeding. Never in his life had he felt as got-at as he did right

now. What was he to do with the evidence? He had read Edgar
Allan Poe but had always considered him a fool. Hiding something in plain view was all right in novels, but if he left a real
Superman One on the mantelpiece Josh would wet his pants. He
might perhaps have burned it, although if Josh came back to
find him setting fire to priceless comics at ten-thirty in the
morning that might be the end. Harvey wasn't sure that the end
hadn't come anyway, because when Josh did return he refused
to speak and took his pancakes and syrup off to the counter
where he sat making disgusting slurping sounds. Having returned the *Superman One* to the petty-cash drawer, Harvey went
and fetched his three Big Breakfasts without complaint from
the counter where they had been dumped. In truth, the silent
treatment was just what he needed.

In his mind he ran over the facts. People knew that he wanted
the *Superman One*. He had told his story many times. His old
school friends knew. Josh knew. It seemed for a moment as
though everyone must know. Except his parents, of course. He
never told them anything. And people told other people: For a
while, part of Harvey's resentment about the *Superman One* was
that it had become the most interesting thing about him. When
people talked about him they would often mention it. Indeed,
in his darker moments, he had imagined being referred to as
"that bore who lost the comic" or "that weird guy who could
have been rich . . . remember him?" So other people at the reunion must have known how significant his meeting with
Bleeder really was. Not many people had mentioned it, of
course. But that was because people were like that. They were
polite or they were discreet or, most often of all in his experience, they weren't really interested enough to bother. Of
course, one of those someone elses might have been rather
more interested than he knew. Just because he had dreamed of
the *Superman One* for so many years didn't mean that he had

some special claim on it. Anyone who fancied two hundred grand might have popped round to Bleeder's house to try their luck. Harvey pictured the scene . . . for some reason Jeff Cooper was cast in the role of burglar. Mrs. Odd comes in from her shopping trip just as Jeff is getting the comic out of the box in the basement. Mrs. Odd hears a noise; she creeps along the hallway to the cellar door ("Don't do it, Mrs. Odd"); she peeps inside—but of course you can't see into the cellar from the top step, so she moves silently down step by step ("Go back, Mrs. Odd," but she goes on), down and down; Jeff has a knife from the kitchen for opening the box; it is a big carving knife with a red plastic handle. He snatches it up as he hears a creak from the stairs ("Don't do it, Jeff"); she runs at him, trying to stop him; they wrestle; he turns her round and cuts her throat ("Oh, my God, what have I done?"). Then in a panic he runs out of the house, dropping the knife, or maybe washing it first . . . and he must be really bloody, too . . . Well, anyway, he runs out but then realizes that in his fright he has left the comic behind. He returns, planning to collect it, but as he is about to enter he sees Harvey Briscow, his old enemy and sexual rival, fucking about in the garden. He hatches a cruel—nay, wicked—plan. He waits somewhere outside—in a bush or whatever—then when he sees Harvey run panic-stricken out of the house, having left lots of incriminating fingerprints, he sneaks back in and steals the Superman One, little knowing that Harvey will also return and helpfully clean up all the evidence for him. Perfect. Fiendishly simple. Harvey nodded with great confidence. Jeff did it. But then he spoke aloud: "So why the fuck did he send me this?"

Well, it sort of almost made sense. Harvey was reunited with the sofa. He rolled flat on it again and lay in his favorite position, on his back, blowing smoke up in neat streams toward the ceiling. The problem with being in the comic business was that it made you a narrative idealist. Comics, unlike the modern novel or the postmodern artwork, had a linear and complete logic. However complex the plot, in the end the good guys won and the bad guys got caught, usually by the good guys, often with the good guys wearing muscle-defining bodysuits and cool capes and masks. You can't be exposed to that sort of storyline too many times without starting to expect some sort of logical outcomes and neat resolutions—involving capes at the very least—in your own life. So it was that Harvey's daydream, up till now sensible and well reasoned, did not end at that point. Instead, a whole story developed from it in which Harvey returned to Cornwall, followed the trail of clues to their obvious denouement, captured Jeff, gave him two black eyes, handed him over to the local police, and got off with his wife. This last section went on for a very long time and Harvey was at the point of rolling over onto his stomach when Josh came in.

"Phone," he said and went out again.

Harvey struggled with his erection for a moment and then managed to stand upright. Had he slept again? He looked at his watch and found that it was ten past twelve. Jesus, it was lunchtime. He discovered that he still had some bits of McPattie in his teeth and—when he put his hand to his head—in his ear. He was picking at these as he made his way through into the shop. "Thanks, Josh," he said pointedly, but got no response. Harvey picked up. "Hello?"

"Harvey? It's Maisie Cooper." And his heart did a twist.

"Hi, Maisie," he said, and he said it in tones of such hon-eyed sweetness that his erection reasserted itself, presumably assuming that sex must be on the cards. Josh also gave him a grudging glance of interest. Harvey hadn't had women ringing him for a while, and Josh loved gossip. Wait until he hears she's married to my old school friend and that he gave me the black eye, Harvey thought. If that doesn't make things up between us nothing will. He turned his attention to the phone.

CHAPTER SIXTEEN

"Can you talk?"

"Er, yeah." Harvey glanced at Josh, who had acquired a packet of Wine Gums. He hadn't had them when he came back with the McBreakfasts and Harvey wondered vaguely how he had managed to go out and buy them without leaving the shop unattended. "Yeah, no problem."

"Look, this isn't an easy conversation for me to start. But I figured you didn't have my number . . ." Would Josh really just wander off and leave the shop? "Harvey?"

"Yes. I mean, no, I didn't. If I had I would have called you."

"So when I didn't hear from you after that ridiculous fight . . . God, fighting like two schoolboys, how pathetic was that? I assume you're OK?"

Leaving the shop unattended was strictly forbidden. "Oh, yeah, yeah, I'm fine. I guess I didn't exactly shine in the hero stakes but I did get a black eye."

"Oh, please! The very idea of Jeff attacking you . . . I suppose that reunion just put him back in the playground. Not that he ever moved very far from it in the first place."

"Yeah, well, he was obviously angry. I mean, I was hugging you." OK, he had left the shop unlocked all night but that was different. Drunkenness had always been an acceptable excuse for bad behavior in Harvey's world, but Josh was stone-cold sober.

"Yes, you were, and I think we need to talk about that." He'd have had to go all the way to the newsagent's. That was further than McDonald's.

"Right, yeah."

"I can tell that you don't want to talk about it. Men never do want to talk about things."

Ten minutes, minimum. "Mmm? Well, it is hard, like you said."

"Yes, it is. But I think we should be clear about what happened and where we are now. For the record, Jeff and I have broken up. I've left him."

Fifteen if that girl Shanaz was serving. Josh always went all red and giggly and hung around wasting time when she was there.

"Right. Bad one." He thought for a moment. "Or rather, good one. Look, where are you?"

"I'm here. I've come up to stay with my old school friend Lisa. It's strange, this all seems to be about school somehow, about going back..." Fifteen minutes, they might have been cleaned out. Harvey looked round the shop critically. What if half his stock was missing? He was mentally checking the racks when he realized there was a pause to fill.

"You're in London?"

"Yes."

"Cool. Let's go out."

"You want to go out?"

"Hell, yeah. Of course I do."

"I've just told you I'm not sure what is going on. I've arrived five minutes ago. I don't know where I am or what I'm doing. I think maybe I want to just be on my own for a while, think things through."

"Yeah, right. You must be confused. So maybe a drink or something, yeah? Make you feel better." Everything looked all right.

"Harvey, are you listening to me? I'm totally confused. I don't know what I'm going to do."

"Oh, OK. No problem, maybe a meal, yeah? Pizza?"

"Jesus. You don't let up, do you? All right, maybe a drink..."

"Cool, OK." The thought of drink made Harvey feel slightly queasy, but he knew himself well enough to know that by the evening this feeling would have been mysteriously replaced by a sort of gray thirst, as if only beer or spirits could unfur his tongue.

"Where shall we meet? I'm in Croydon and I feel like I've moved to another planet."

Jesus. "Er, OK, can you get to earth? Maybe we could meet in town, yeah?"

"OK, where?"

Harvey focused at last. Shit, where do you take a beautiful woman you want to get off with but who wants to talk about life? Especially when you've slept in your clothes, have Satan's hangover, and are very possibly about to be accused of murder? Harvey thought for a moment: "I'll meet you at the Boot." Perfect.

After giving fulsome directions, Harvey rang off and confronted Josh. "Where did you get those Wine Gums?"

Josh regarded him with a cold eye. "Mary gave them to me."

"Mary gave them to you?" Harvey felt a wave of remorse. Mary was a mad Scotswoman who lived in one of the covered alleys opening off Old Street. Occasionally when business was especially good they would give her a pound from the till and then watch her go to the off-license across the road (where she got a discount) to buy a can of Tennants Super. She would always open it in the doorway and then raise it in a toast to them and to Inaction Comix. They liked that. And in return, because she was, like many street people, heart-wrenchingly generous, she would bring them things. One day she brought them a very battered *Beano* that she had found in a dustbin, and they had considered it seriously and told her that if only it had been in mint condition it would have been worth a fortune.

"You let Mary buy you sweets?"

"She found them in the street and thought I might like them." Mary liked Josh better than Harvey, whom she regarded as a representative of the ruling classes. Mary was very class-conscious.

"And you are eating them? You are eating sweets that a tramp found in the gutter?"

"Yes." Josh selected a red one and put it ostentatiously in his mouth. "Want one?"

"Yeah, all right."

And all was forgiven.

"So, she's left him and she wants you to come out tonight." Josh's excitement was pretty to behold. Unlike other single straight people of Harvey's acquaintance, Josh rarely seemed jealous or bitter when Harvey achieved romantic success. Rather, a sort of focused fascination came over him, and he achieved a look similar to the one that came into his eye when he was reading *Vampirella*. Harvey had wondered before whether this was due to genuine kindness, a desire for an example to follow in his own life, or just plain weirdness. He had settled—mostly for malicious reasons—on the last of these. "And he hit you for snogging her?"

"Yeah, kind of. He sort of chased me round and then he punched me in the face."

"Shit!"

"I know."

"Real danger. Shit. Total action adventure. What else happened?" They had finished the wine gums and they had made Harvey thirsty. One of the good things about running a comic shop was that you rarely got a rush, so you could focus on these things.

"I need a drink."

"Water is what you need." Josh fetched him a pint glass, stolen from the Queen's Head, filled with gray tap water.

"Was that glass clean?"

"Course. So what else happened?"

"Well, he kicked me in the kidneys and then the others pulled him off. He's a big bastard, mind, a rugby player. I could have been killed."

"Right. Shit." Josh's glasses were shining with interest. "So hospital, yeah, or not?"

"No. I just went to bed for a bit and then Bleeder arrived so I had to go."

One of the reasons that Harvey had been satisfied with the silent treatment from Josh was that it meant he had been able to delay this moment until he was capable of dealing with it. He took a long pull on his glass of water, grimacing at the mixed tastes of dust, very, very old beer, and London tap water. He decided, in the brief moments that he had to think, that this last was probably the least appealing of the three flavors.

"Bleeder!" Josh's voice when excited would sometimes move up an octave, as if he was transported back to a prepubescent state. It did so now. "Bleeder was there?"

"Yeah. Yeah, he was at the reunion and then he came along to the party. We had a chat."

"A chat! You chatted to Bleeder!" Harvey had to like Josh. For all his many and various failings as a friend and an employee, he was a very good audience.

"Yeah. We talked twice, actually . . ."

"And . . . was there . . . ? Did he . . . ?" Harvey, despite himself, burst out laughing.

"I'm not telling," he said and reached for his cigarettes. "But watch this space." And with that, and with a plaintive and desperate shop assistant trailing him back into his office, he returned to the couch and, after a heartening cigarette, slept once more.

CHAPTER SEVENTEEN

She was late. Which did not surprise Harvey, and he sipped his Scotch without rancor. It was not an easy bar to find and Croydon was a long way from it. As he drank, Harvey could feel the hangover that he had woken with and the horrified realization, and the daylight sleep that he had had since, and the second awakening and the second horrified realization, all sort of hanging around waiting for the Scotch to kick into it and wake it all up and make it play. Meanwhile, he surveyed his favorite bar with a brand of Martian affection. It was on another planet: Planet Gaelic, perhaps. The walls had pictures of hurling teams and the floor was covered in genuinely filthy sawdust. The barman was drunk and everyone else was keeping him company. There is, of course, a very good reason why people go to pretend, plastic "Oirish" bars in London, and that is so that they don't have to drink in the real thing. But for Harvey, the Boot represented an authenticity that he had long had to accept was never going to emerge from his own disordered and misplaced identity. He had even, at one time, toyed with an Irish accent but had sounded offensive. So he just tried to look Irish, which wasn't too hard because coming from Cornwall he was pale and dark and miserable to begin with, and soon he would be drunk to complete the picture. He had never tried to get off with anyone sober and he doubted it was possible. While alcohol may inhibit the sex drive, without it the act would become entirely impossible: something mythological that only happened in ancient civilizations, before the Internet.

While he waited, Harvey considered his options. There was the possibility that he could tell Maisie Cooper everything that had happened in Cornwall. While not particularly drawn to confidences, Harvey could see how sharing his problem might help; certainly it might stop his brain revolving in his skull, just to speak it out loud. However, there was also the possibility that she would insist he go to the police and that would lead to irreconcilable differences much too early in the relationship. She might also suspect him, and again, starting a romance with one party thinking the other is a murderer, while not a situation he had been in before, seemed unlikely to succeed. So he decided to do nothing at all. It was a decision he made often in his life, but rarely found wanting. This choice was still fresh in his mind when she walked in. She was wearing a long, orange, caftanesque thing with beads and tassles. Her hair was tied up in a scarf and she had on Dr. Martens boots. Harvey was not sure he had ever seen anything so lovely. Very hippy-dippy, he thought, very gorgeous.

"Hello." He grinned and felt the truth of the smile; it was one of those smiles that sort of take over from inside. He turned away to stop the smile from spilling all over her.

"Hello you." She put her hand on his arm and he realized too late that he might have kissed her. "Interesting spot." She was looking round and Harvey could hear that she meant it. She wasn't being sarcastic like most of his friends would be— "Interesting spot!"—she really was interested. "Drink?" "Just a mineral water, thanks. Lisa and I sat up till nearly three, drinking wine and just talking everything through." Harvey nodded understandingly while acknowledging internally that if he drank mineral water every time he stayed up and got pissed, well . . . he'd probably be a lot better off.

"It was one of those talks where you work stuff through. Do

the big stuff, you know? And I guess I realized that I had been unhappy with Jeff for a long time."

Harvey turned to the bar and ordered her some water, which came with a look of sympathy from the barman, and another Scotch for himself. If they were just going to get straight into it he needed to get another one under his belt fast.

"I'm not sure I can really remember why I married him in the first place. It was as if someone else did that and I woke up and had to face the consequences. Do you understand what I mean by that?"

Harvey nodded vigorously; he knew so well what she meant that it seemed to cover the majority of things that had ever happened in his life.

"I mean," she went on, "I believe one must take responsibility for one's decisions and Jeff was one of my decisions and I guess he did get me out of Bath, which is where I grew up, got me away from there, at least as far as Bristol."

"How far is that?" Harvey sipped his whisky and wished he'd ordered a double so he could concentrate better.

"About twenty miles," she admitted ruefully, "but at least it was somewhere else. I guess it was the beginning of leaving. It took me a long time to take the next step."

Harvey realized he knew next to nothing about her.

"You don't have kids, do you?" He was suddenly worried at that thought. What might he be taking on? For taking her on was what he discovered he wanted. The thought of letting this voice, this presence, go, of returning to Josh and the pub at lunchtime every day without this to think about, was already moving outside his range of acceptable options. He was surprised by how fast that had happened. Perhaps because most of the rest of his life seemed to have been crammed into the last few days, he was speeding up.

"No. Jeff didn't want them and I was never sure. I guess I never really felt that I was there for good. Do you ever feel like you are always halfway out the door?"

"Yeah, my entire life, actually. I'm always going somewhere else, always about to leave. It's not very Zen, is it?"

"No." She smiled. "It's not very Zen, and I think it's time to stop, for me anyway. Whatever I do now has got to be what I really choose to do. I don't know yet what that is, but it has to be right."

"Yeah." Harvey nodded thoughtfully. "I know what you mean."

"Do you?" She looked at him very closely and he hid in his glass. "One of the things Lisa and I talked about was you, and I realized that I don't really know who you are, Harvey. I don't know what's going on for you at all. You were just this man who wasn't my husband, who was kind and listened . . . It all seemed so unlikely somehow, so far away from everything. All those strange people in Cornwall. Jeff and I just falling apart. And you were there and you listened. You're a really good listener." She put her hand on his arm again. "I'm really grateful for that. But now I've come back to some kind of reality and I guess I'm thinking . . ."

Harvey didn't want to know what she was thinking. He didn't like the way she was talking at all. He had taken it for granted that meeting for a drink was a beginning; it only now occurred to him that she might see it as an end.

"I'm thinking that to rush into anything right now would be crazy . . ." She was continuing slowly to speak words Harvey had not prepared himself for. Usually he would have done; he had enough experience of romantic disappointment to know the importance of preemption, but there hadn't been time. He'd been too drunk or too preoccupied or too hungover, or too busy cleaning up bucketloads of blood and sick. He had just had to take Maisie for granted. He shook his head wildly now.

"Wait, wait!" he shouted, and gained a bleary but penetrating glance from two aged Irishmen in the corner who were

discussing the Eurovision Song Contest. "Don't do this. I need your help. I really do need your help."

He hadn't planned to say that but it was a good thing to say. If he'd said I love you, or I need you, or I know we belong together, as he would normally have done, she would have been shocked and slightly scared because they'd just met, and she would have been polite in a really sweet and intractable way. He had just met her but he suddenly felt he could read her a little bit. Unlike him, he saw now, Maisie had thought this through to quite an extensive degree. Surprise was really the only possible way of preventing her smiling kindly at him.

"What do you mean?" She went off script and gazed at him, startled by his vehemence. "What's the matter?"

"Um..."

"Because while you have been very kind, and you were there when I needed someone, there are so many things I have to work through..."

"I'm in trouble," he cried wildly. "I am in real trouble and I need your help."

"What kind of trouble?" She was still looking at him as if trying to see inside his face. This time he met her gaze.

"Murder," he said sternly. The rest of the pub returned to its own affairs. Murder was a private matter at the Boot.

Maisie narrowed her eyes. "What do you mean?" she asked, but he could tell that she knew at once exactly what he meant.

CHAPTER EIGHTEEN

So he changed his mind and told her. He told her about
the swap and the *Superman One* and she was confused and disbe-
lieving: "No one would pay that much for a comic." And he
told her about Bleeder and she shook her head and whispered,
"That is so cruel." So he told her about Jeff and Bleeder, at
which she nodded with exactly the same expression on her
face. And he told her about Mrs. Odd and the house and how he
used to cycle past it (although he didn't mention the singing).
Then, after another Scotch, this one a double, he told her about
the last six days. And as he was telling her, as the words were
spilling out in a stream driven partly by the need just to hear
them in the air, and partly by the need to keep her there, keep
her eyes so intently on his, and partly by the Scotch, he became
aware of what he was doing. He was giving her his life in exchange for a few more minutes of hers. She could quite easily
walk out and call the police from the call box outside the Boot
(Actually, she couldn't, as it had been vandalized. It usually
was; it was that sort of pub. But that wasn't really the point) and
he might well go to jail forever. But he was risking that really
just because he didn't want her to tell him that it was too soon
to get involved. He wanted her to kiss him and accept the inevitability of his higher drama, and take him back to her place
to meet her flatmate, the kindly Lisa, and he wanted to kiss her
back and borrow her toothbrush. He didn't want to be told he
was very nice and it was she who was missing out. So he gam-
bled on scale. Compared to his predicament, her own marital

dilemmas should appear in shadow. He was asking her to shake herself, admit that really what she was going to say didn't matter, what mattered was the big picture, life and death. And when he had finished telling her, telling her all the detail: the scrubbing brush, the duster, the knife, the brambles—although not about finding the comic—she did. She took the hand he held out to her, and when he pulled her against him she didn't resist. She smelled again like warm honey mixed with dew on grass, and he got a difficult and embarrassing erection almost at once. And she believed him, that was the point. She didn't mention the police or look at him sideways or carefully take her hand away in case she was touching the fingers of a killer. She let him hold her in his arms, his denim jacket open so she was resting against his chest. And she made a sort of "phew, eee" sound, as though he had told her something way too big to take in at once, that would need more mulling over and discussion. And it was then that he knew he had done right, that the gamble had paid off. It was only afterward that he realized her understanding and his desire for her were one and the same thing: that really the gamble had been a sure thing from the start.

But he didn't tell her about finding the comic or about the bottom drawer of his desk. Even in the catharsis of confession it is necessary to be cautious. One step at a time. One set of overwhelmingly troubling revelations at a time. The comic could wait until he had some sense of what it meant and where it came from, some sense of what it was doing in the events of that terrible afternoon and what it was doing in his petty-cash drawer.

After a period of sitting in friendly silence, she lifted her head from his shoulder and looked hard into his face. Momentarily he was aware of how bloodshot his eyes might be and of his breath, which was probably a bit whisky-based . . .

and then he saw her eyes, how deep green they were, and he just stayed with that. "You know," she said thoughtfully, "you've had quite a week." She put her hand to his right eye and touched the black bruising around it. Harvey nodded.

"I know." He stopped nodding and shook his head. "I am quite keen for it to be over, actually. I don't think I was cut out for anything like this."

She smiled. "Really?"

"Oh, I don't mean this, I mean, you know ... all this ... mess."

"Mmm. I can understand that." She stopped and turned her head away to look around the bar, as if it was a source of inspiration. "But I think a bit of mess is probably what I need just at the moment. Mess kind of makes things seem more sane. You know?" Harvey nodded understandingly but with no sense at all of what she meant. He was simply desperate for order. "With Jeff," she went on, "I think everything had become too ... I don't know, too neat I guess, too worked-out. We had nothing left to find out."

"Oh, right." She had looked away and Harvey wanted very much to have those eyes again locked with his own, even though he suspected they still made him blush. "Yeah, I guess long-term relationships can do that," he added, "make you get lost ... if you see what I mean." He wasn't used to this. He hadn't had a long-term relationship for eight years and then it had been a mess from start to finish. He shook his head again and felt the tiredness inside it.

"So, you don't believe in the long term, Harvey?" She smiled and allowed the eyes to return to his. Like serpent's eyes, he thought, like the jeweled serpents in *Tomb Raider*, with emeralds for eyes. It took a moment before he realized what she had said.

"Oh, I do sometimes. It's just, I guess there has to be something special there to start with, yeah?"

"Mmm." She nodded and smiled again, and this time the

emeralds went soft and turned into forest pools like the ones in *Swamp Thing*. "Yes, I think that's right. And Jeff and I were never special. We had fun sometimes and we helped each other sometimes, but we were never special." She, too, shook her head, sat up on her chair, and sipped her water for the first time for a while. "But that seems somehow . . . I don't know, earlier today I would have said it was all that mattered in the world. Now here I am thinking it's a small thing that can wait. What is it the footballers always say: 'It's put things in perspective'? Jeff always takes the piss . . . took the piss . . . when they said that on *Match of the Day*. But actually it's a good line. You've put things in perspective. I feel released from a circle of thinking that I realize has obsessed me for . . . Christ, for years. Am I right with Jeff? Should I carry on? Should I move on? Can you make right what wasn't fully there from the start? Can new shoots grow in barren ground . . . ? And on and on and on. And now here I am in a strange bar, in a town I hardly know, with a man I just met, and everything else seems like such small beer. You know? Small beer. And I need a drink. This is water, Harvey. You can't expect to tell me all this on water. You should have guessed I would need alcohol." She laughed and made for the bar. "I'll get you another, shall I? A double, was it?" Jesus. Harvey shook his head again, hard from side to side, and said, "Er, yeah, cheers." He was getting drunk and he had given his life away. This was not the sort of date he had envisaged. However, he did seem to be making progress. You never knew; that was going to be his new motto in life, assuming he had a life: When it came to matters of the heart it was all just up in the air.

"But there is one thing I don't understand." She was back opposite him across the table, and was catching up on the whisky. Not that she had had as many as he had, but she was less used to it. He could tell that from the way she had been giggling, and she had taken her orange head scarf out of her hair and put it round his neck. Her hair was streaked with reds and auburns, a cascade of interlacing colors. While Harvey was old enough to realize that this was achieved with a great deal of time, effort, and money, he was still young enough to find it irresistible.

"Well, actually, there are lots of things. Like why you were so bloody silly in the first place." She laughed again, but with a serious look at the end of it. "I mean, going to steal a comic . . . and then going back . . . but that's just—it doesn't make sense." They were back on the murder and Harvey felt, unexpectedly, on safer ground. Murder might be a new subject to him, but he still felt more at home with it than he did with relationships. If there had been time this might have worried him; as it was, he had far too many other things to think about.

"What do you mean? Or rather, which bit of what you don't understand don't you understand especially?"

"The murderer." She sipped her Scotch and ginger. "How did he do it? I mean, I can see your bit of the whole thing, crazy though it seems, but I don't get him really."

"Right, right . . . Why not?"

"Well, you say when you went to the house all the boxes were sealed. You opened them with the kitchen knife, even the one in Bleed—I mean, Charles Odd's room."

"Yeah, so?" Harvey knew what she was going to say.

"So, why did the murderer go to the cellar first? I mean, if he was after the comic why didn't he search the house first, just like you did? I mean, you would start in Charles's room, wouldn't you? Indeed, you did start there. And so would anyone else, it's the obvious place. I can't see how he could have been after the comic. The comic must be a red herring. It was probably thrown out years ago. Either Charles Odd did it, which still seems the obvious option, or someone else did it for some other reason. Maybe someone else just decided to burgle the place or something . . . Or maybe someone just hated Mrs. Odd . . ." She stopped, and Harvey admired the way her nose wrinkled when she was thinking.

"It doesn't make any sense actually," he said. "My thinking is, if Blee—Charles Odd didn't do it, then someone else that he spoke to at the reunion did. Maybe he told this other person more than he told me. Maybe he told him where the comic was packed. Maybe he did find it and ran off with it. That was the motive for the murder. Maybe Charl—Bleeder, sod it, knew where it was but didn't tell me. Maybe talking to me triggered some memory of where it was . . . You can't have too many co-incidences without seeing a pattern. It was the reunion, he was there for the first time, his mother was moving house, all her stuff was in boxes, she got killed. Add that shit up, as Dr. Dre would say, it has to make some sort of sense."

"Yes, and then along comes Harvey Briscow. Are you saying you are not a part of the pattern?"

"Hey! That's not fair." He looked at her, genuinely aggrieved. "I thought you believed me."

"Oh, I do, Harvey, really I do. No one could make up a story like yours. And why on earth would anyone bother? I just think maybe you are part of the picture, the logic of the thing, too, just like Charles and his mother and this mysterious other person if there is one."

"But how could anyone know I'd do what I did? I mean, whoever they were would surely expect me to go to the police, straightaway. Surely no one could guess that I would behave so . . ."

"Stupidly?"

"Er, well, you know . . . well, I guess."

"No, that's true. But you must fit the picture somehow. As you say, there can't be that many coincidences."

———

Harvey didn't get to use Maisie's toothbrush that night. His flesh was quite up for it—although late at night, after drink, had never been his favorite time for sexual endeavors—but his spirit was definitely flagging. She might have said yes. He didn't know her well enough to really tell, and that of course is what made it interesting to ask. But he didn't press the point and when she said maybe it was too soon, he just nodded, pulled what he hoped was a disappointed face, kissed her with everything he had, and then stumbled home to bed and twelve hours' solid sleep.

Maisie left him with a sense of having passed through something unexpected and unprepared-for. What had she intended when she called him and arranged to meet? Thinking, on the last overground train from London Bridge, she looked out at the darkness and surprised an unusual expression on her reflection in the window. There was a contemplative quality to her face, her nose wrinkled in consideration, but her eyes were shockingly alert. Had she really meant to say good-bye to Harvey tonight? Or was that just her fallback position in case he wasn't the same in London, the same now she was single? She looked again at her own face but the expression had gone, replaced by her familiar mirror-look: pretty and prim, or that's how she characterized it tonight. Even that could be reassessed. That was the thing about life changes; even how you looked in the darkened window of a train could be rethought. The orange of her dress was dulled by the darkness and she looked down at it, rather tawdry against the grubby blue of the seat. She had got it on a trip to Morocco with Jeff. That was a lifetime ago, before things went wrong. Had he liked it even then or had he just humored her when he bought it for her? Certainly she had understood, with all the covert knowledge that had become central to their relationship, that she could never wear it when they returned to England. Jeff would have laughed that laugh without a trace of communion in it, and he would have made jokes about joints and communes and all the things he hated. Jeff would have been ashamed of her. And so it had been the right thing to wear to meet another man. Harvey hadn't said a word. No comment at all. For a while she thought about that, and then she thought about the murder. There were things she didn't understand. Quite a few things, actually, that didn't add up. She frowned for a bit and then smiled. It seemed weird to think that she could be happy about murder. But it meant they were going to be together. She could sense that. Harvey had been right, though she didn't know it. We are all the playthings of the god of scale: This was simply too big for either of them to get out of.

CHAPTER NINETEEN

Thursday was delivery day at Inaction Comix, and Josh's favorite day of the week. Throughout the week, new stock would arrive in a variety of vans and private cars from a bewildering array of sources, but Thursday was the day the lorry came from their main supplier; the racks would fill up with back issues of comics they had improbably had a run on. But more excitingly, especially toward the end of the month, all the new issues would start to appear and Harvey and Josh would be the first people, perhaps the first in the whole country, to read them. This job didn't have very many perks, but that sense of being slightly ahead of other comic obsessives was definitely one of them. So in the past, Thursday had been Harvey's favorite day too. But this week he could have done with a day off and some time to think. However, taking a day off would have meant leaving Josh in charge, and they were still trying to clear the shop of the specialist products Josh had decided to try the last time he was alone on a Thursday.

"*When Amazons Rule the Earth* ring a bell, Josh?" Harvey asked as his assistant suggested for the third time that he could manage on his own. "No? What about *Hidden Camera, the European Edition*? Anything happening?"

"Manara's a genius," Josh muttered, "and anyway we sold all that, didn't we?"

"Yes, we did, Josh, and for weeks afterward we had strange old men wandering in to check the graphic novel section. But we are still left with *Silent Flow the Tears: A Pictorial of Pain*. I don't call myself a prudish man, Josh, but you test even my liberality, you really do."

"It's very good. I'd buy it myself if I hadn't read it."

"Excellent. Well, all we need do is find someone exactly like you. That shouldn't take too long, should it? Maybe we'll start with Broadmoor and go on from there." Harvey had been saying things like this since they opened, and Josh was already dispirited.

"You are a miserable bastard," he said, not for the first time. "All you do is criticize. But you buy some weird stuff, too. What about *Whiphand of the Marquis*? You bought that. I feel sorry for bloody Maisie, I can tell you that. A miserable, bad-tempered sadist. She'd be better off with Jeff."

"You know, you are so right, Josh. Oh, and by the way . . ."

"Yes?"

"Fuck off."

Harvey stomped off to the back room and took out the petty-cash box. The *Superman One* was still sitting underneath it, and he wondered vaguely where he had put the envelope that it had come in because it was looking naked and incriminating. Glancing back into the shop to check that he was unwatched, Harvey found a plain A4 envelope, slipped the comic inside, sealed it, and locked the drawer again.

"Harv," Josh called as Harvey was opening the cash box.

"What?" He put some spin on that. When he went to the back room to sulk he expected to be left in peace. That was the law of the shop. He wasn't a terribly demanding or, in truth, very generous employer. But this one rule he expected to be honored.

"Er, it's the cops."

"Right. Don't be a twat, Josh, I'm busy." Harvey got up and stalked through into the shop. "Is it Mary, by any chance?"

"No. It's the cops." Josh said again, this time with a little more emphasis and a slightly stronger American accent.

There were two men in suits standing neatly in front of the counter. They looked about as right and fitting surrounded by the comics and the posters as a social worker at an orgy, and Harvey felt his head lift off from his shoulders, circle the room, and return in time for him to say: "Ahhh. OK. Whatever. Why didn't you say? Problem, Officer? Traffic outside a problem or have we got a shoplifter?" He stopped, ran a hand over the stubble on top of his head, and took two deep breaths. "Please come through to the back." He moved forward himself to lift the flap separating him and Josh from the rest of the world, and it was as if he was inviting wild animals into his house, evil into his home. It reminded him of a horror movie but he couldn't for the life of him remember which one.

"You are Mr. Briscow?" It was the shorter, neater, and more friendly-looking of the two who spoke to Harvey once they were all seated in the back room.

"Yeah, that's me." He wanted to say "I'm Briscow," but it sounded weird in his head, like "I'm Batman." So he nodded and grinned instead.

"My name is Chief Inspector Jarvin and this is Inspector Allen. We are part of the team of officers investigating the death of Mrs. Hilda Odd of St. Ives in Cornwall. I am told that you were in St. Ives at the time of her death and may have known her. Is that correct?"

Well, of course Harvey wasn't expecting a parking ticket or a discussion about a missing dog, but even so it was shocking to hear the words spoken aloud. This was a real policeman, not one of the ghouls that had been haunting his dreams, black and snarly, but a real policeman, a nice one, who was here with the ridiculous excuse that he was investigating a murder case. The police officer's quiet manner made Harvey instantly confidential. If confessing the murder was what it took to allow this decent fellow to go about his important business in the same quiet fashion, then surely it was a small price to pay. Harvey didn't do that. But it was a close thing.

Instead, he said: "Yes. Yes, I was down there when it happened, actually. I just got back the day before yesterday. I hadn't met Hilda for many years, since I was at school really. In fact, until now I never knew her name was Hilda." And in truth it brought him up short. Bleeder Odd's mum had a name. And it was an "H": one of us, in fact.

"Can I ask the purpose of your visit to St. Ives, Mr. Briscow?" So polite, so gentle. Harvey was charmed.

"Yes, of course." He smiled happily and waited for the nice man to ask him another. Then he frowned. "Er, yes. Yes, I went for the reunion, at the school. We've been meeting on and off for twenty years. I go down and see my mum and dad as well, bit of a family do." Policemen liked families, he felt sure of that.

"And did you meet Mrs. Odd's son Charles at the reunion?"

Harvey admitted that he had.

"It is just that we have received some information that we were wondering about. It regards a comic that Mr. Odd is said to have had. A..." Here he consulted his notes. "A *Superman One?*"

"Oh, yes." Harvey looked at the wall, the ceiling, and the door instead of looking at the bottom drawer of his desk. "The *Superman One*. The famous *Superman One*." He felt his smile becoming a rictus and forced himself to stop grinning and do the sigh. "Someone told you about the *Superman One*." Jeff Cooper. Had to be. Bloody snitch.

"Perhaps you could tell us about it, Mr. Briscow." So nice.

"Well, OK. It was just a comic. I swapped it years ago with Charles Odd, when we were twelve. When I had it it wasn't worth much, but it has gained in value and become rather rare. I believe it is quite valuable today."

"How valuable? Do you know?"

"I'm not sure...I suppose it would be worth about two hundred thousand pounds if it was in perfect condition."

Jarvin raised his eyebrows in a rather vague attempt to look impressed. "That much?"

"But only if it was perfect," Harvey stressed.

"And did Mr. Odd know this?"

"I don't know"—God knows he'd wondered—"but I doubt it. I don't think he was very interested in comics."

"Did you talk about comics at the reunion?"

What had Bleeder told them? "Er, yeah. I think it was mentioned. I think I sort of made reference to the swap, reminiscing, yeah? To be honest, I hadn't seen Charles for years and we hardly knew each other at school, so . . . there wasn't much else to talk about."

"One or two of the people we've spoken to mention that he was badly bullied at school. Is that your recollection, too?"

"Er, yeah. Maybe. I don't really know. He was kind of different, I guess, and you know what boys are like?" Inspector Jarvin looked like a man's man to Harvey.

"Some of our informants have suggested that you were one of those who bullied Mr. Odd."

"What?" Now that wasn't fair. If anything Harvey had always thought of himself as kinder to Bleeder than most, one of the ones who gave him a chance. "No way!" He spoke with genuine hurt. "It wasn't me that picked on him, it was other people, especially the rugby crowd; they used to kick him all the time, every day. I was never like that." Did Inspector Jarvin like rugby?

"Mr. Odd himself suggests that you were very cruel to him. That on the day of the comic swap you called him an effing freak. Would that be right?" The chief inspector was watching Harvey closely. Harvey didn't like that so much.

"Bleeder said that?" Then he covered his mouth with his hand. "I mean, Charles said that? I don't think that's fair . . . I mean, everyone called him a freak, all the time . . ." He could feel the beautiful friendship with Chief Inspector Jarvin slipping away. How could you argue that you didn't bully someone twenty years ago when they say that you did? Especially when you called them Bleeder.

"Bleeder." The chief inspector jotted something on his pad and Harvey became aware that the other policeman, Allen, had silently been making notes throughout, recording his words. Shit. "That is what you called him, is it? Was that his nickname?"

"Yeah, Bleeder, Bleeder Odd. But I didn't call him that."

"You did just now."

"No, I mean, I didn't invent the name, it was just what he was called. I was called H, yeah? Everyone has a nickname."

"You were called H?"

"Yes, I was. But not because of drugs! I never took heroin, never have, actually, although I've often thought I should just like to try it once, you know . . . or rather I'm sure you don't and I never have and never will." Jesus.

"Why was he called Bleeder, do you know?"

"Um. No, I don't think I do. Maybe 'cause of the nosebleeds and he had a lot of scabs and stuff. He was always bleeding, you know. So it was kind of descriptive."

"Yes. But not very nice?" It was said to sound like a question but Harvey took it as the statement it actually was.

"Well, no," he said rather desperately, "no, not very nice. But then children aren't nice, are they? Or rather, they can be . . ." Did Inspector Jarvin have children? "But they can not be, if you see what I mean. And we weren't. Or I was but they weren't. The rest of them."

"Yes, I see." Chief Inspector Jarvin sucked the end of his pen for a moment. "So you swapped this comic with him, this *Superman One*? What did he give you in return?"

"Um, God, I don't know. Some length of rope or something, a bit of plastic stuff that he was carrying. I think I felt a bit sorry for him." I'm nice, I'm nice, I'm nice! "So I let him have the comic even though really it was worth a lot more than what he gave me: this piece of plastic. I mean, in truth, I shouldn't have swapped. It was an act of kindness more than anything."

"So, in fact, you might have felt that the comic was really yours more than Charles Odd's, even after the swap?"

Hell, yes. "No, no, not at all; a swap was a swap."

"I mean it must have rankled: that he had this comic, which became more and more valuable?"

"No, not really. I hardly thought about it. I mean, we did the swap, yeah? You don't go back on a swap."

"Not even one that is worth two hundred thousand pounds?"

"No, no." Harvey could feel the hairs on his neck standing up and tickling him, as if trying to comfort him in his moment of crisis. "No, I mean, I never really thought about it. It was so long ago, anyway."

"Yes, although several people we've interviewed have mentioned that you attached a lot of significance to the comic, even though it was a long time ago. And it was not found at the scene. Mr. Odd is vague at the moment about whether it was there or may have been destroyed in the past. But if it was there and was stolen . . . well, you see the connection?"

"Yes, I do." Harvey could feel his face wet with sweat. How clichéd, to sweat under interrogation. "But I don't see any connection to me. I mean, OK, I've mentioned it a few times to people, but that doesn't mean I was going to steal it . . . If that's what you meant . . ."

"No. We are, of course, not accusing you of anything at all. But some people have suggested that you've done more than just mention the comic. That it had become a virtual obsession with you, that you talked of little else."

Who the fuck had said that? Who would squeal on him? The potential list, he realized, was troublingly long.

"I did not. I talked of lots of things, all the time. Of course the comic interested me, as a collector. But there was never any question of me doing anything criminal."

"No. No, I'm sure." The chief inspector's voice was gentle and without any sarcasm. Harvey looked at him hopefully. "And of course you run a comic shop, which is a coincidence, too. I suppose if you did have this *Superman One* you would know what to do, how to sell it and so on?"

"Well, yes, of course. But I haven't got it." Harvey could feel the tip of his nose itching. Was it growing? he wondered. Was he becoming a cartoon himself?

"Ah, right, that was my next question."

"What, whether I'd got the *Superman One?*" Harvey was outraged; were they going to accuse him of murder?

"Yes. Or whether you had heard anything of it. I thought if there was a burglar and if the comic was stolen, then he might have made the same connection and tried to contact you."

"No. Oh, no. I would, of course, have informed the police at once of anything like that. I would never handle stolen goods." Harvey thought uncertainly about the *Batman Returns* complete set he had bought for twelve pounds only two weeks ago . . . but he put that out of his mind. These weren't the comic police.

"So, is there anything else you can tell us about the time you spent in Cornwall that stands out for you, anything out of the ordinary?"

What, apart from scrubbing up blood for an hour or two?

No, not really. "No, I don't think so. Nothing really. Just a typical reunion: see the old crowd. Nothing special."

"I was noticing your eye." Chief Inspector Jarvin put his hand to his own right eye. "You seem to have been hurt."

"Oh, yes, yes indeed."

"What happened?"

"Oh, I fell over." Had they already heard about it? "Bit of horsing around at a party."

"I wondered if it was a punch that gave you that? It looks like a nasty bruise."

"A punch? No, no. Just some messing about. No problem."

"Fine." The chief inspector took a long look at the bruise as he got up. "All right, well, I think that's about it. You won't mind if we get back in touch if we have any more questions, Mr. Briscow?"

"No, no. Call in anytime." Harvey showed them out and then went and sat quietly in his room. Or as quietly as you can with a wide-eyed and hysterical shop assistant bombarding you with questions.

CHAPTER TWENTY

"So, what do we think of Mr. Briscow?" Sigvard Jarvin turned to Inspector Allen as that man pulled their unmarked car out into the lunchtime traffic clustering like a swarm of dragonflies around the swamp of Old Street station.

"Dunno." Allen had a slow lugubriousness that Jarvin always found relaxing. "I thought he was routine till we went there. But now . . ."

"Now . . . ?"

"Dunno."

"You think he's hiding something?"

"He needs to learn how to tell lies if he's going to make it as a villain."

As usual, Jarvin found Allen's viewpoint reflecting his own unknown thought.

"He's done something he doesn't feel happy about," Allen went on. "You can sense that. He's got something going on."

"Murder?"

"Something."

"I wonder what was in those premises. Perhaps he's doing something naughty that's nothing to do with this . . . I don't know. But I agree, there was something there. I wouldn't mind having a longer look around that shop."

"Good place to hide a comic."

"Yes, I thought that, too."

The prostitutes on the Commercial Road were plying their lunchtime trade in a dappled sunlight as the two men drove toward Whitechapel. Jarvin looked upon them with a satisfied expression playing on his gentle features. He had a face that was hard to imagine in displeasure. A slight upturn at the corners of his mouth gave him a dolphinesque appearance, enhanced by his neatly backswept black hair and sea green eyes. Added to that was a genuine pleasure at his current state of mind. He had been put in charge of a case that interested him, and three days in Cornwall had reminded him of why he was a policeman. London sometimes had the effect of making the whole war on crime seem pointless: Everyone seemed so much happier with the lawbreakers than with the enforcers. But St. Ives had returned him to a world where serious crime was taken seriously and the outrage of a small community at this enormity in its midst, even if seasoned with a certain relish, was genuine. There were various people to visit in London. Many of the reunionists came from the city, but none until now had seemed particularly relevant. But again and again as he went round methodically on the neat geographical pattern that Allen had plotted, he heard the name of Harvey Briscow. He was the one who always talked about Charles Odd and his comic. He was the one who had the fight with Mr. Cooper at the party. He was the one that Charles Odd, Bleeder Odd, had spoken to. What a name to call a child, Bleeder Odd.

Jarvin thought of his own son, at school today. Was anyone giving him a name he could never lose, that would haunt him as a shadow of cruelty for the rest of his life? Was he perhaps giving it to some other, sicklier, less confident child? The latter seemed more likely. Jarvin shook his head and watched a drunk stagger into the road and then teeter back to the curb and sit cursing the traffic and the world that contained it. He would have a chat with Jack tonight, just in general, about daring to stand out from the crowd and being kind rather than cruel. He might need to have a word with himself also: to watch out for prejudice against Harvey Briscow, keep an open mind. Just because you bullied someone as a child doesn't mean you killed their mother twenty years later. It would make more sense if they killed you. But then there was this ridiculous comic. Could anyone kill for a comic? Surely only someone who loved comics, who cared about comics...back to Briscow again. He turned to Allen, who was driving with the quiet, undramatic skill that he brought to all his work and letting his boss get on with his thinking.

"When do we go and see Mrs. Cooper, Allen, can you remember?"

"Mrs. Cooper in Croydon, sir? I believe we were leaving her until tomorrow."

"I wonder if you'd mind mixing up our schedule a bit. I think perhaps we should have a talk to her today."

Allen nodded ruminatively. "She was the one the fight was over, wasn't she?"

"Yes. I think I'd like to meet the woman Mr. Briscow was willing to fight for. He doesn't strike me as much of a fighter."

Allen, who was six foot three and had the build of a boxer, shook his head. "No, sir, more of a thinker than a doer, I'd say."

"Precisely. And I'd like to know why he lied about fighting, too. Bit of horseplay indeed."

"Yes, sir, shall we head straight there now? I'm sure we could put off Rob Calderwood. I only mentioned that we might call in to his shop—sporting goods, apparently, rather than comics—I'm sure we could just as easily go tomorrow."

"Good, then let's go and find her, shall we? It's a long drive on the off chance, but I think perhaps I'd like to meet her without warning her in advance."

"Yes, sir." Without rancor Allen performed a neat three-point turn against the traffic and they sped away for at least forty yards before once more becoming embroiled in the unending traffic jam that is the London road system.

———

Croydon is not a pretty place. It has some advantages in terms of connections and rail links to the City, and at night it looks a bit like Manhattan, if Manhattan was rather smaller and full of shaven-headed men with tattoos driving customized Ford Pumas. Its one real advantage is that it has a tram network, which is decorative even though it only connects the town to places no one would ever want to visit. Like Wimbledon. But as a place of escape and safety it has a number of advantages. First among these for Maisie Cooper was anonymity. Nowhere could anyone be quite as anonymous as they could in Croydon. It was a place that seemed almost built to provide faceless, character-less security. And she found it soothing. She liked to walk in the broad, pedestrianized streets filled with the garish familiarity of every town high street. She had fallen in love with the supreme ugliness of the shopping center. She was enchanted by the closed otherness of the faces that passed her own but never met her eye. She saw the ease with which she and anyone could slip into this place, become part of it, and therefore become nothing: an absence of a person, a nonbeing. And while she had nothing to hide from exactly—she was in touch with her husband and indeed had told him where she was going—still this seemed right somehow, to have come to a place where whatever identity she was going to have in the future could wait. She could pause and sit in limbo and for now be without character, blank. She would not stay here, had never intended to. But it was a place to wait and linger, to prepare.

This morning in particular there seemed something right about being there. Waking late, she had breakfast, showered, and then wandered out for a while in all that glorious imper-sonality. She had visited the local shop and failed once again to be greeted by the polite but unattainable Asian gentleman behind the counter; she had bought bread baked on the other side of the city, milk delivered from another county, muffins from another country. And she had wandered through the indiscriminate shallowness of the minicity with a feeling of real contentment, taking her time, using immediate observation to allay any desire to analyze her wider situation.

As she walked back along Cherry Orchard Road there was a fresh wind, but also a hint of the possibility of spring in the way the clouds were carried on it. There were flashes of blue and that yellow-green around the wings of the clouds that spoke of potential and newness. Even the weather was leading her into the uncertainty she needed: opening, clearing her way. Maisie shook her head in the breeze, enjoying the feeling of her hair being whipped against her face. As she fumbled for her keys she might have missed the two men leaning against the dark, unshowy car parked outside Lisa's building. She did notice them when they moved toward her. Though recently fond of Croydon, she was not unaware of its dangers. She stepped back and looked quickly around. Were there any of those faceless nonpeople whom she could call into being for a moment if these men tried to harm her?

"Mrs. Maisie Cooper?" She literally gasped with relief and then felt immediately angry. Rather than speak she pulled a face at the man who spoke, a rather handsome dark-haired man. Her expression said, Don't scare me like that.

"I'm sorry," he responded to it at once, "I didn't mean to startle you. I wasn't sure it was you." He smiled and she found herself smiling back, all fear suddenly gone.

In the kitchen she sorted through her purchases and found fresh coffee and cream. Each day she tried to find something for Lisa, something to welcome her back from her day in the City and to say thank you for letting me stay like this, rent-free and in an open-ended time frame. Yesterday it was a video of *The Pillow Book*, today finest mocha for the dusty *cafetière* she had found under the sink. She opened the packet without remorse. Lisa would understand.

"You are here about the murder?" She found a tray, pink

plastic, but useful in preventing too many trips, avoiding their visit turning into a sort of party, her into a hostess.

"Yes, that's right," the dark-haired one—Jarvin—said. Maisie wondered what his first name was. "You were in St. Ives at the time, I believe?"

She answered honestly and clearly the questions that Jarvin put, his silent companion recording her words, but she added nothing extra. It was not until he asked the purpose of her visit that she reacted.

"I was there with my husband. Keeping him company."

"But you are not with your husband any longer?" Jarvin's soft green eyes did not leave hers and she realized that they must match her own. The dark eyes of Inspector Allen flicked between them and she wondered if he had noticed this rare symmetry, too.

"No. We split up, just the other day. We are living apart now." Again it was a simple answer, so she was astonished to find her eyes filled with tears as she said it. "Shit. Where did these come from?" She said it out loud and actually smiled as she spoke, laughing as she felt her cheeks suddenly sensitive to the morning air from the open window, and getting up she ran for some kitchen roll. "Sorry."

"It's perfectly all right." Jarvin was clearly a man at ease with tears.

Wreathed in floral-patterned towelette, she returned. "I didn't expect that," she said. "I guess I've been saying I'm married for so long, it feels odd to say something else." She dabbed efficiently at her eyes.

"Yes, that must be very hard." She heard in his voice the sound of understanding and smiled at him. He smiled, too. Even Allen was smiling. Suddenly she wanted to laugh out loud. The human species seemed suddenly ridiculous somehow.

"You mentioned parting from your husband. Did that

happen after the party at Steven Weston's house, on Monday of this week?" Jarvin was consulting the notepad that had magically appeared in his hand.

"Yes . . . Well, sort of. I mean, we had a huge row after the party. He attacked another man there . . . But of course we had been on the verge of splitting up for months. I had left him before: last October. I went to my mother's for three weeks, but then we got back together again, mostly because of my mother's plotting. She doesn't believe in divorce." She smiled again, but the tears were still making her eyes shine. "She arranged for Jeff to drop round when she happened to be out and we had another try at things. I think he hoped Cornwall might be some sort of answer. But it was the opposite. A hotel room is a terribly intimate place to be with someone who you know you are going to leave. It is like taking poison; you can feel your insides boiling and your strength just sapping away . . ."

She stopped and looked at the two men in front of her as if they were dressed as rabbits. "Jesus, what am I on about? Sorry. Do all the people you interview start telling you everything like this? You must be very successful if they do."

Jarvin's smile thickened. "It can help to talk things through, I think. And I did ask about your husband. I wonder if you remember the party very well . . . and the breakup."

"You mean the incident?"

"I'm not sure . . ."

"Me and Harvey Briscow out under the willow tree."

"Yes, we have heard something . . ."

"Well, it's not nearly as romantic as I'm sure your other correspondents have made it sound. Harvey was being sweet. He has been sweet every time we've met. I just needed to get out of that dreadful room at that dreadful party so I took him outside for a breath of air. And he, like most men, interpreted this as meaning I wanted to snog him."

"Didn't you?" Jarvin was smiling at her again with what looked suspiciously like a twinkle. Maisie wasn't sure she could handle being twinkled at just yet. She frowned and watched his smile withdraw back into its natural dolphin state.

"No...I don't think so. But Harvey was kind and just wrapped me up in his arms. And then Jeff came out and went berserk..."

"Is he often violent like that?"

"Oh, he can be. He can be very violent..." She caught their looks and shook her head. "Not to me, not really. But when he's drinking— He stopped for a while, a couple of years ago. I think he thought that might sort out the 'marital difficulties.' " She put the inverted commas around the words in the air with her fingers. "But when he found that didn't work he went back to the beer."

"And would you describe Mr. Briscow as a violent man, Mrs. Cooper?"

"Harvey?" She almost laughed but controlled herself. "I can't imagine Harvey doing anything to anybody. I mean, I don't know him very well. He might have all sorts of hidden depths, but my impression is that he's as soft as a lamb."

Jarvin tried and failed to picture Harvey as a lamb.

"And have you seen Mr. Briscow since?"

"Yes, we had a drink last night. Just to talk about things, nothing more..."

"About the murder?"

"Yes..." She looked away for a moment, at the kitchen door, and Jarvin wondered if there was something more. "Yes, about the murder. I mean, we are both in shock about it. Do you have any leads...any ideas who might have done it?"

Jarvin looked at her closely and found himself wishing her eyes were not shining so brightly or her look so eager. She didn't know the victim. She never met the victim, yet her eyes were a little too fixed for a moment on his own.

"No," he said blandly, after a fleeting but heavy pause. "But one question we are asking everyone is where they were at the time of the murder. So I suppose I must ask you..." He looked again into those deep green eyes that so matched his own, bringing back moments from long-forgotten teenage years when he had propped his head against the mirror and looked deeply into what he imagined was his soul. And his soul had been green.

"I don't know. What time was that?"

"We are estimating the time of death at around eleven A.M. on Sunday."

"OK. I don't know. I think we were just out, Jeff and I. We went for a walk, I think, though not together. He went into town for a drink and I went up onto the cliff top and had a look at the sea. I got back about half twelve. We met for lunch in some dingy pub that seemed to carry some memories for Jeff but I didn't ask what they were. We were already at the point where it was better for me not to know. So I suppose I was alone in the morning . . ." She looked for a moment at him with genuine surprise. "Does that mean I'm a suspect?"

"No." This time his smile was reassuring, making her feel like a child. "You are not a suspect. You have no motive and there is nothing to link you to the crime. But . . ." He left it hanging like a peg on a line and she took it down.

"But?"

"But I wonder if you are telling me everything about Mr. Briscow and your conversation. I wish you would, Mrs. Cooper."

This was said so emphatically that for a second Maisie was taken by surprise and he saw it, in the corners of her eyes, like motes of possibility. But she shook her head at once. "I don't know what you mean. But . . ." She tried one on the line also, next to his, but he did not react so she took it down herself. "But I do think you are rather good at what you do."

CHAPTER TWENTY-ONE

"I'm fucking, fucking, fucking, fucking fucked."

"I don't think so, Harvey . . . Look, they're not fools."

"I'm fucked and I might as well face it and just cut my own fucking throat the way they think I cut hers." Harvey dragged deeply on his third cigarette in ten minutes and grappled with his home telephone, which was large and made of bright pink plastic.

"No, I don't think they think that, Harvey. They just have to make inquiries. It's routine—Jesus, I sound like a policeman myself. But it is. They are interviewing everyone."

"Yes, but everyone didn't spend the weekend clogging up their mum's washing machine with blood, did they? Everyone didn't come home in their dad's car covered in old Mrs. Odd's blood. Everyone has a clear conscience. Or almost everyone. I could feel that bastard, that utter bastard, looking into my soul. It was as if he could read my guilt written across my intestines. You know what I mean?"

Is your soul in your intestines? Maisie didn't ask. Instead she said: "No. He was clever, I admit that. But he can't read your thoughts. I found him rather nice." She thought again of the mirror effect of those deep green eyes. "Very fair. And of course if you told him the truth he would know that you were innocent of anything other than breaking a window and being a bloody fool, wouldn't he?"

"Oh, balls." Self-pity had always been one of the more ready options in Harvey's repertoire. He had returned to it now like a migrating bird to the gathering tree. "He'll just see deceit and lies and he'll guess the rest. I should have gone to them straightaway, straight to Truro, straight to the police station, and this would be over now. Jesus fucking wept." He gave a sort of fake sob and Maisie sighed.

"You could still go to them now."

"Oh, yeah, right." For Harvey sarcasm was also a familiar recourse in times of trouble. He often used it on himself and found himself walking home from failed romantic evenings saying, Yeah, right, of course you didn't really fancy her, Harvey, sure thing, inside his head.

"Why not? Nothing has changed. You could tell them everything. I think Chief Inspector Jarvin would appreciate honesty, however belated."

"Don't say that name! I never want to hear that name again. Cunt. Constable Cunt, coming to my shop and fucking asking me questions. I've a good mind to tell him to fuck right off if he comes again. Go and get a fucking warrant, you fucking, fucking, fucking—"

"Yeah, well, if that's all you have to say, Harvey . . ."

"Sorry."

"You need to stop panicking. Chief Inspector Jarvin will do the investigation, and they will find out who did this awful thing, and you will get on with your life. And so will I . . ." It suddenly came to Maisie just how little she knew of what that meant. It also occurred to her that the man at the end of the phone might think that his life and her life were going to get on together. That didn't seem as alien a concept as she had expected.

"Well, I hope you're right. But I could be about to be arrested. I could spend the rest of my life in a prison cell." Harvey wanted to add "and I hope you'll be satisfied" but couldn't really think of any reason to justify it.

"OK, so what are you going to do?"

"What is there to do?" Harvey stubbed out his cigarette on a plastic ashtray in the shape of a woman's breast. It had been a thirtieth birthday present from a very poor friend. He looked at it now with new eyes. "Jesus Christ."

"What?" she asked with what sounded like real tenderness in her voice, and he shook his head foolishly.

"Nothing. Sorry. I just realized I need to sort my life out." He looked round the room: the little flat in Deptford that he had bought when housing prices were low—a good investment, a starter flat, before he moved onward and upward. That was fifteen years ago and Deptford remained defiantly cheap and cheerful and the flat remained his. However, the sense that it was just a temporary dwelling before he moved into the house he was meant to live in—a flat-fronted terrace in Camden, or a glass and steel monstrosity overlooking the river, or perhaps that cottage up in Hampstead; he couldn't make up his mind—had never left him. For this reason he had never really bothered to do anything to it. It remained dimly lit by the bare overhead light, with the sickly yellow Ikea shelves and gray fitted carpeting that it had when he moved in. He had added a veneer of himself to it, most of which originated from smoking: burn marks on the shelves, ash ingrained into the carpet, yellow patches on the ceiling. He looked now at the television set that balanced flatly on top of the video machine on the floor. In front of it was a large, green revolving armchair that he had found in a Dumpster. He sighed and reached for another cigarette.

"You don't need to change your life, Harvey; don't be so melodramatic." He could hear the patient smile in her voice. "You just need to sort this out. Make sure that the police are clear about what happened, where you were on Sunday morning. What did you say when they asked you that?"

"I don't think they did . . ." Harvey was thinking hard. "No, they didn't— Hey, hang on, did they ask you?"

"Yes. They said they were asking everyone."

"But they didn't ask me. Well, fine. Perfect. Dandy-diddly-dee. They didn't ask me because they didn't need to. They already know I was up at Bleeder's house murdering his mother. I'm fucking, fucking, fucking—"

"No, you're not. They must have just forgotten. They'll probably ring you tomorrow and ask. Stop panicking... They'll want to hear your alibi. Do you have one, by the way?"

"One what?" Harvey's voice was still mortified.

"An alibi for Sunday morning?"

"Shit, I don't know. What did I do? I can't remember. I probably fought with my parents and then went out for a walk or something. I don't know. What do you do on Sundays in Smallville? I put on my cape and flew away. I just killed time, I guess..."

"Hmm. Well, I'm not sure I'd give that answer to the police if I was you." Maisie sounded doubtful. "They might think you killed someone else instead."

CHAPTER TWENTY-TWO

When the phones had been put down, with suitable, and in his case at least, heartfelt endearments, Harvey sat in his green revolving armchair. The flat looked different to him tonight. It was the first time he'd been in it and not asleep or drunk since his trip away, and a lot had changed. I'm different, he thought, I am no longer the man I was. He inspected his younger self's living quarters with a certain measured disdain. There really was so little here. Take away the superhero posters and the record and DVD collections and you had anybody's room, anywhere in the western world. A generic, meaningless ragbag of mainstream ugliness. He sighed without rancor. He was saving the big sigh for later. Maybe he wouldn't even do it. Maybe he'd just go to sleep and not worry at all. But that would break the habit of a lifetime. So he sat for a while in the green revolving armchair and thought about what Maisie had said. And then he walked through into the bedroom and sat and looked at the only view from the flat, over the rooftops to St. Alfege church tower in Greenwich. Was this a life change? He seemed to have had so many false starts, so many moments that at the time appeared seminal but which turned out only to be passing possibilities leading nowhere. His view often made him philosophical, and it happened now. Did anything ever lead anywhere really? In the end, whatever you did you ended up dead. Like Mrs. Odd, that twisted gray face, that terrible stillness. That's where you end up, and all the pretend revelations of life can't spare you. He did the sigh after all. It felt good to do it about something as ordinary as death; it pulled him back into the majority for a second.

The bedclothes were all on the floor where he had flung them that morning. So he picked them up and for the first time in a while, he made his bed properly. Then, to his own surprise, he did not light a cigarette, or go to the off-license. He had a shower—washing off a grime that seemed ingrained—and went to bed. There, he lay naked in the dark, awake for a while, something rendered rare by alcohol, and he thought about Maisie, and, across all the multiplicity of roads and rooftops and people's lives that lay between Deptford and Croydon, he wondered if she was thinking about him and whether her thoughts were as warm and wistful as his own.

In the morning the rare pleasure of sober rest had done its job, as if the sleeping Harvey had been waiting a long time for a chance to speak and had a lot to say. Alongside the images of randy horses chasing young maidens up trees, which Harvey found filling his dream recollection over breakfast, was the knowledge that he could not just sit and do nothing. His restful self had made a call to arms. Up, up, it said, and be doing. Which, Harvey reflected, was easy for him to say. It had been a while since Harvey had felt driven. He had wanted an iPod quite a lot when they first came out, and had queued up for the premiere of *A Scanner Darkly*, but that was about it in the last few years. So this felt different, new and yet familiar. It was, he realized, the call of a younger and more physically fit Harvey. Jesus, if one night of sobriety did this to him what would a week or a month be like? He pictured a slimmer, gym-toned figure running to work, eating a salad, and getting a decent haircut. Worried at the turn of his thoughts he sat and smoked the second cigarette of the day: always his favorite, the after-breakfast one, slower, more sensual, less desperate than the wake-up choker. And then he went to work.

Was it all about this? Once Harvey had passed the shocked Josh, who had been appalled by this new, clean-shaven, polished, on-time man in his life, Harvey had repaired once more to the back room and slipped the comic from the bottom drawer. Then he had looked at it for a long time.

Was this really enough for an old woman to die for? Harvey's was not a sentimental soul. He could understand killing someone for a comic; the problem was how anyone could ever reap the profits. It would be big news on the Internet already. The comic world would share his lack of sentiment. A missing, mint-condition *Superman One*, that was the story. One dead old woman more or less would not excite the Internet obsessives. Gingerly and with great caution he opened the plastic sheath in which the comic was wrapped. He recognized the seal on the package that was stuck as he had stuck it in 1982. It had never been broken. Bleeder had never read it. The comic was old then, of course, not as valuable as it was now, but old. Forty years old. He remembered the job lot he'd bought from the Conservative Club Christmas Bazaar: toys, various. Twelve action figures, including a Spider-Man with racer, a whole lot of worthless plastic bits and pieces, and the pile of comics, all untouched, stored at the bottom of an old crate in someone's loft. He hadn't liked comics. He'd wanted the figures and the lumps of plastic: Lego bits and other rubbish. He almost threw the comics away. Random *Fantastic Fours* and *Silver Surfers*. But instead he read them. Lying around in his room with nothing else to do, he read them one after another and got lost there somewhere, in that world of strength and goodness, of grace and beauty and perfectly turned humor. *Silver Surfer* was his first love: so beautiful, so tragic. He, too, yearned across the wastes of infinity for the woman he once loved and could never know again as a mortal man. He, too, looked cool on a surfboard, although in fact it was bloody cold surfing in Cornwall and he'd tended to prefer sitting on the sand watching the girls walk past.

From there he discovered *Spider-Man* and found his true alter ego. Silver Surfer was too damaged, too unreachable in the end. Spidey was human: secretive, wistful, passionate, and sarcastic. As human as any adolescent might hope for, more really than anyone he had known. Spider-Man had so much power, and yet he could never use it in any way to help himself. All that potential and he ended up alone. He was also in love with Mary Jane. And Harvey was just discovering Penny Trayland who wore skintight jeans with a flower stenciled on the left buttock. Flowers played a big part in Harvey's dreams at that time. So he discovered comics from that first encounter. And those early purchases formed the beginnings of the collection that would one day be the basis for this shop and in many ways for the whole life that he had constructed on those rather flimsy foundations. The only one of that first historic haul that didn't interest him was the *Superman One*. It was for kids; you could see that. "The daring exploits of the one and only Superman": It sounded ridiculous. The artwork was tired. The story was petty: nothing like the complex, angst-ridden, existential explorations of the *Silver Surfer*, or even the homey but tragic sufferings of the *Fantastic Four*. So he'd given it away, swapped it for a bit of nothing, as an act of kindness to a bullied child. Saint Briscow, Saint Harvey of fucking St. Ives.

He flicked through the pages disconsolately, although he did so with instinctive care not to damage the paper. This was worthless now, completely valueless. He knew that. He could never sell it without being accused of murder, and even if the murder was solved it wasn't his to sell. It belonged to Bleeder. He should destroy it, chuck it in a Dumpster or something on the way home. All this promise, all this power that he held in his hands, and all it could possibly represent was trouble, tragedy, and ruin.

Just like Spider-Man, in fact.

———

"And back again and back, ever decreasing circles of likelihood." Sigvard Jarvin was in a poetic frame of mind and Allen allowed his own mental inclinations to follow his leader.

"We are getting rather stuck with Mr. Briscow, aren't we, sir?"

"Yes, we are, and I don't like it. I can't see him as a murderer somehow, and nor could Ms. Cooper."

"Yes, sir. And are we attaching a lot of significance to Ms. Cooper's opinion?"

Jarvin gave him a look. "No more than to anyone else's, Allen. But I always find intuitions like that interesting."

"Yes, sir. A very attractive woman, Ms. Cooper." Allen took a swig of tea and waited to be put in his place.

"You can drop that tone of voice right now, Allen," Jarvin duly obliged. "I take every view as it comes. Ms. Cooper's is just as valid as anyone else's." He nodded emphatically once with a sharp jolt of the head, a characteristic and bullish motion. Allen nodded, too, but more slowly and gently.

"So back to Briscow," he said.

"I suppose . . ." Jarvin looked round the café in which they were taking lunch. It was a favorite of Allen's, which Jarvin had long given up complaining about. Red Formica tables along each wall with halfhearted booth effects around them; black-and-white pictures of boxers, one per booth; and, unaccountably, red flock wallpaper. The day's specials were written in flamboyant if inaccurate hand on a large sandwich board placed in the middle of the aisle. Jarvin did not need to look to know what his order would be. Or his colleague's. Lamb chops and mash for Allen, spaghetti carbonara for him. Some people said a partnership was like a marriage, but he disagreed. He would long since have tired of any romantic relationship as predictable as theirs. He was, he felt, in many ways an adventurous man; he had even been called brave at times over the course of an eventful career in the army and now in the force. But he did not require surprises from Allen. Nor did he find it sad to provide so few himself.

"Fancy a chop?" he said and his colleague nodded ruminatively without comment. "Yes, back to Briscow. Literally I think. We'll go and pay him another visit. I want to know how he fitted together with Charles Odd. I wish we could interview him again, too."

"Mr. Odd is planning to stay in Cornwall?"

"Well, yes, apparently, for the time being. Now the inquest is over there'll be the funeral on Wednesday. Inspector Roberts down there seems happy enough with him. What Mr. Odd told us the other day still holds: He was at church first thing Sunday, plenty of witnesses to that, and then he walked down into the town to get the Sunday papers and read them in a coffee shop. Nobody remembers that bit so far, but why should they really? Then he took the long way home, having a look round the town. He stopped off for a drink in the pub at lunchtime where he was seen by most of the reunionists, bar Harvey Briscow, who wasn't with them. He then returned home and assumed that his mother had gone out. He came in by the front door and so didn't notice the broken window in the kitchen until later on. So he sat in the sitting room and read the paper, then went for a bit of wander round the old neighborhood, exploring his roots . . . up onto the headland for a breath of air . . . Lot of walking these people do. Half of them seem to have been out on hikes that Sunday. It's very inconvenient."

"Yes, Ms. Cooper was walking, too, wasn't she?"

"Yes, she was. She was on the cliffs, too. I suppose it's what you do at the seaside in the winter, but I do wish they'd all stayed put where people could see them." He shook his head and smiled. "Nobody considers us policemen."

"No." Allen smiled, too. "And where was Mr. Briscow, I wonder?"

"Yes, that is a good question, Allen. Where was Mr. Briscow?"

"I notice you didn't ask when we visited him."

"No, I didn't." Jarvin shook his head thoughtfully. "But perhaps I will, eh? Perhaps Mr. Briscow was surrounded by twenty people at eleven that morning. Perhaps we can cross him off our list and forget all about him. What do you think?"

"I think he was probably out for a walk," said Allen mournfully and then brightened visibly. "Chops," he said and fair beamed at the arriving waitress.

Once their orders were placed, the two men sat in silence until the waitress returned with their meals. Jarvin was grimacing at the familiar flavor of a sauce he had long since had to accept as the best available, when Allen unexpectedly asked: "What about this comic business? I've been thinking about that a bit and I can't say as I've ever heard of anyone being killed for a comic before. It might be a whole new motive for murder. What do you think, is there anything in it?"

"I don't know." Jarvin enjoyed the excuse momentarily to spare his taste buds another mouthful. "It is certainly worth a lot of money. I had a look on the Internet last night and the collectors are willing to pay four hundred thousand dollars for a 1939 first edition of a *Superman* comic. It seems an incredible amount of money but it's still a bit behind an *Action Comics* Number One, which is worth nearly a million dollars. A million dollars for a comic, Allen, doesn't that make you shudder? *Action Comics* is where Superman started, of course."

"Yes, indeed." Allen nodded as if this was the most obvious piece of information. "It's not what I'd spend two hundred grand on."

"No." Jarvin didn't ask what Allen would spend it on. Visions of extended decking areas and enlarged sheds swam briefly through his mind—he did know his subordinate's tastes rather well. "But I don't think it could really be called a new motive. Greed is, after all, as old as history, isn't it?"

"True, sir. That is true." Allen filled his face with a laden fork, which bore all the food groups at once, and then champed happily for a moment or two. "But it's the only motive that could make any sense for Mr. Briscow, isn't it, sir?" he went on after a noisy moment. "I mean, why else would a man go and kill an old lady? He doesn't seem like a pervert or a weirdo or anything. So..." He left it open and refilled his mouth. The chops came with almost liquid spinach as well as the mash and he had made a nice green goo by mixing the two together. Jarvin looked elsewhere.

"I don't know," he said. "But killing her seems excessive anyway, don't you think, even if the comic is relevant? I mean, if the mother of an old school acquaintance discovered you in her house one day, would you cut her throat with a knife? Or would you blush and say something about dropping in to see Charles and apologize for accidentally breaking a window... something like that? I mean, it might be a bit embarrassing... I don't know."

Allen could, on occasion, become biblical and he did so now. "But what if the lust was upon him, sir? What if he had just found the comic and she tried to take it from him..."

"The comic lust?" Jarvin tried not to laugh and stirred his carbonara with a fork. "Well, maybe, but it's a bit hard to imagine, isn't it? 'I was so overcome with passion for *Superman* that I lost all sense of proportion, m'lord.' It might work as a plea, but I can't really see it myself. I tend to think there may be more to this bullying matter. That seems to be the only relationship between them, other than the comic, and even that is mixed up in that early stuff. Yes, if Harvey Briscow bullied Charles Odd, and Mrs. Odd found out... I wonder if there is anything there. Well..." He returned to his pasta with resolution. "We'll get after Mr. Briscow again and perhaps we'll find out." He closed his eyes and began, stoically, to eat.

What to do, what to do? Harvey had put the comic away and taken it out again three times before Saturday had really started. It was weird how few hiding places a room held when you really looked at it. Maybe Edgar Allan Poe just couldn't think of anywhere else to stick it. God knows, it wasn't as if they were tidy, it was just that there was almost nowhere that Josh might not go at some point. For a time he toyed with the idea of murdering Josh. Hiding Josh certainly seemed a lot easier than hiding a *Superman One*. Saturday was their one busy day in the shop, when the customers actually came in enough numbers to require two members of staff. But even as he haggled over a *Darkman* series, and watched Josh try to press obscure manga on unenthusiastic collectors, he was thinking about the drawer and how easy it would be simply to go back there with a lighter and solve the problem in one short burst, which, for all his hopes of a new sense of purpose, he had so far not dared to do. And as soon as the frankly meager morning rush had begun to ebb, he went to the office, took it out again, and then stood, irresolute, like Hamlet—in *Classic Comics* form.

"Harv, can I go and get some bananas?" Josh wandered into the back room now, causing Harvey to double up and twist around in a sort of contortion of concealment.

"I told you I wanted peace." Standing up he pushed the *Superman One* into the back of his trousers. "What that means, Josh, is that you leave me alone. You don't come barging in asking me about bananas. What the fuck do you want bananas for?"

"I could make banana custard." Josh was unmoved by Harvey's annoyance. Josh was always either deeply offended or unmoved. Harvey had long wished for an assistant with something in between. "We've got a tin of custard powder in the cupboard, I found it yesterday when I was tidying up, and I was thinking I could make banana custard, bit of a change from the norm. Something different." He eyed Harvey keenly through his spectacles, which shone with an eager light. Harvey shut his eyes for a moment and took a deep breath.

"Yes, Josh," he said, "banana custard would be lovely. If you think you can make the gas ring work and if you think you can find a saucepan that isn't contaminated and if there are two bowls from which we could eat it, then I believe you should spend our busiest day of the week making banana custard."

"Nice one." Josh headed for the petty-cash drawer and then stopped and looked hard at Harvey. "You're not going to assault me again, are you?"

"No, why?"

"I need some money to buy the bananas. No tackling, yeah?"

"No, no. No tackling." Harvey watched patiently as Josh extracted two pound coins from the metal tin and wrote it carefully on the reckoner they kept inside.

"Right." He beamed. "Banana custards are go."

When he'd gone, Harvey took the *Superman One* out of his trousers, put it on his desk, and then sat in his chair and looked at it once more. Suddenly and unexpectedly he wanted to cry. He could feel a great sob forming at the bottom of his windpipe and beginning to rise like a bubble in the bath. He recognized this feeling. It was the feeling of being punished for something he hadn't done. When did he last have this sensation, that seemed to go into his system, as if the tears were mixing with his blood, making him go floppy and frantic? It was at school, the day he was accused of stealing from the charity fund. Somebody nicked the money raised from the charity bed-push, and he was suspected. He could remember now that mingled feeling of impotence, righteousness, and desperation. He almost got expelled for that and he was entirely innocent.

Whoever had done it had never been fully explained but he had his suspicions: That bloody rugby lot had laughed their socks off. Carl Butcher and his friends, Jeff bloody Cooper among them. Harvey felt back there now, back waiting outside the head's office on that awful green sofa, knowing that his mum and dad were on the way, and knowing, with a terrible certainty in one so young, that they would side with the headmaster and would indeed argue for whatever sentence was passed to be increased. It was a feeling of isolation and of being involved in something far too big and serious for anyone so small. How old was he then? Eleven? Maybe twelve . . . He was a grown man now, of course, but still that same feeling welled up from wherever it was kept, tidily tucked away for when it was needed. He put his head in his hands and felt the tears begin to well against his palms.

He sat and shook, rocking himself back and forth and muttering against an unyielding adversity.

"Oh shit, oh shit, oh shit, oh shit," he said slowly and in a sort of terrible whisper. "What the fuck am I going to do?"

"Hello?" Josh had left the office door open and someone was leaning over the counter and looking through the open gap.

"Oh, hello, Chief Inspector." Harvey jumped up and moved to the door. "All right?"

CHAPTER TWENTY-THREE

"Are you all right, Mr. Briscow?" Jarvin and Allen both looked at him with concern. Harvey wiped his nose on the long-sleeve Sepultura shirt he was wearing.

"Er, yeah, yeah. Touch of the flu." He stood in the doorway and felt his eyes beginning to brim over with tears. He also felt the *Superman One* on the desk behind him burning a hole in the back of his trousers.

"We wondered if we might have another few words with you. But if this is a bad time . . ." Jarvin's sympathy made Harvey close his eyes for a moment to block out the desire to tell him everything. This caused the tears to well up and begin to trickle gently down both cheeks. He opened them again and shook his head.

"No, no problem," he sniffed. "Let me just clear up a bit. We're in a mess. Ah, is that Josh?" He looked over Jarvin's shoulder and then as both men turned he stepped swiftly backward and slammed the door. "Right," he muttered, "get it together, Briscow." He rushed to the desk, grabbed the comic, thrust it into the drawer, slammed it shut, and locked it.

"Mr. Briscow?" Jarvin's voice from the shop was surprisingly clear.

"Yeehes?" Harvey sang his reply as he finished locking up, trying desperately not to jingle the keys; then, grabbing the dirty towel from the bathroom, which was draped over the back of the sofa, he rubbed it all over his face. At a run he got back to the door and opened it. "There we are." He beamed at them, his face a mess of mingled tears, snot, and gray matter from the towel. "Thought it was Josh coming back but it wasn't. Come in, come in."

"Well, only if you're sure . . ." Jarvin stepped forward slowly, "and if you wanted to clean up . . ."

"All done." Harvey beamed the more. "All done, just then, I cleaned up. No problem. Come in, come in." Once more he lifted the flap of the counter so that they could walk through into the back, and once more he felt as if he was inviting something rather large and unlikely into his space, like bringing a walrus into a Ford Cortina. But this time he felt more in control.

"You forgot to ask me the other day, didn't you?" He was still smiling, with glistening eyes, when they were all sitting back in their places, him at the desk but facing away from it into the room, Jarvin on the sofa, Allen in the frankly unsafe wooden chair behind the door.

"Forgot to ask you?"

"My whereabouts. You've been asking everyone their whereabouts on the day of the murder, Sunday morning, I mean, about eleven A.M.," Harvey prompted, "but you forgot to ask me."

"Did we? Perhaps we did. Would you like us to ask you?" Jarvin was smiling too.

"If you want you can. Or I'll tell you anyway." Harvey suddenly had a desire to tell them, or rather for them to have asked. "I was out for a walk," he said and Jarvin managed not to look at Allen. "I have tried to reconstruct that morning for you." ("Thank you," said Jarvin politely.) "And I have come up with the following." Harvey paused importantly and then sniffed, aware that the tears, so ruthlessly blocked, were now trying to make their way down his nose. "I arose at approximately eight-thirty, which is earlier than usual but my dad woke me up. I got out of bed and had a shower. I then went downstairs and ate breakfast. I then went out for a walk at about nine-thirty. I then walked into town and looked at the shops and then I went onto the beach and walked along the shore. I then went back home and got there about twelve-fifteen. We had lunch at one." He smiled at both of them expectantly. Jarvin nodded and made two observations. The first, to himself, was that the study of comic books did absolutely nothing for your narrative style. The second was aloud: "And what did you do after that, Mr. Briscow?"

"After that?" Harvey stared at him. "She died at eleven A.M. What does it matter what I did after that?"

"I just wondered." Jarvin watched Harvey carefully. "I wondered what you did in the afternoon."

"God, Jesus, I don't know." Surprise and terror combined in Harvey with irritation. What business of Jarvin's was it where he was in the afternoon? He had just told him the absolute and unalloyed truth, for Christ's sake. He really would have liked a little bit of credit for that.

"I was at home," he said uncertainly, "I think. Or did I go out? I'll need to work it out. But I think I was at home for a bit and perhaps I took my dad's car out for a bit. I don't know."

"You were at home with your mother and father?"

"Yes. No. I can't remember. They were probably about, but I'm not aware whether I was with them. I may have stayed in my room."

"For how long?"

"I'm not sure. Most of the afternoon, I guess."

"That would be a long time to just stay in a room on your own. You would probably have wanted to spend time with your family . . ." Jarvin tried to help.

"You haven't met them," Harvey muttered. "But no, perhaps I did, I just can't really . . ."

"And then you went out in your father's car?"

"Maybe. I can't really . . . was that Sunday? Or another day? You see, it's all rather vague . . ."

"Perhaps we could ask your parents? If you give me their number I might give them a call, just to clarify . . ."

It isn't easy to make an internal volcanic eruption appear in the form of a scratching of the head and a grimace of uncertainty, but Harvey attempted it. The fact that he turned from bright pink to very white in around twenty seconds was the only obvious signifier of the turmoil within.

"No, I'd rather you didn't do that," he said slowly. "They are easily upset. I could check with them, but really I just need time to think. I'm sure it will come back to me." Where the fuck could he have been that afternoon? All he could see was blood-soaked washing-up gloves and bottles of bleach. He also heard a renewed echo of his mother's words about washing his clothes and trainers. She would definitely remember.

Never had he had a stronger desire to encourage people to leave. He needed this conversation to be over and he needed to ring his mum. Jesus, what could he say to her? Remember those things under my bed? Well, they didn't exist, OK? It never happened, got that? Gangster movies were always about families. That was probably why the gangsters always got caught. Never let your family get involved in your affairs; that was the simple rule of life. Harvey had done his best to apply it for many years, yet here he was at his moment of crisis having to ring his mum. Once he got rid of the police, of course.

"It is just that we would need to corroborate what you say about the morning also." Jarvin was continuing with the conversation just as if all this wasn't going on inside Harvey's head. "We are checking on everybody who is involved in any way. But we can come back to that. I also wanted to ask you about Mrs. Odd. I am trying to get a picture of her and while there are people who knew her in Cornwall, of course, I was wondering what Charles's friends remember of her."

"Friends? I wasn't his friend really . . ."

"I was thinking of the swap?"

"Yeah, well, that was a one-off. I hardly knew him, to be honest. And I certainly hardly knew his mother. As I told you last time, I didn't even know her name. I did tell you that . . ."

He petered out and looked at Jarvin with something close to pleading in his eyes. Why didn't he go?

"So you were never in the house?"

This took Harvey by surprise. "What house? The Odds' house? No, of course I wasn't, or actually I was, but ages ago. Of course, a long time ago, not recently. Years and years ago."

"You visited as a friend?"

"Yes. No, not a friend, as an acquaintance, once. Only the once."

"Why was that, Mr. Briscow?"

"Why was what?" Harvey wanted to ring his mother. He could tell her they were stolen goods or something. He had been arrested once before, for shoplifting when he was fifteen. It was still mentioned regularly by his father whenever the subject of criminality of any kind came up. All it needed was some gruesome murder or armed heist to come on the news and Harvey's crime would be aired once more: a point of comparison, a reminder that evil wasn't only on the television. It was another reason why he so rarely went home. Perhaps now he could say they were stolen goods. They would certainly believe it. But would his mother cover for him? His dad wouldn't. Indeed, he wasn't sure his dad wouldn't report him immediately. He sighed and shook his head and then looked back to Jarvin, who was waiting politely. "Pardon?"

"I was wondering why you went to Mrs. Odd's house just the one time, all those years ago."

"Oh, God, I don't know. Does it matter? It was just a visit." Why had he gone? It was a good question. It wasn't as if he had any desire to know Bleeder then or now.

"You don't think it might be significant?" Jarvin's eyes had gone gentle and they seemed to slip off his own rather than fully meeting them.

"No, of course not; it was years ago."

"So you had no real impression of Mrs. Odd?"

"Impression? Well, she was mad, wasn't she?"

"Mad?"

"Well, not mad. Just a bit . . . odd. You know, she was Mrs. Odd and Mrs. odd. Capital letter and lowercase . . . That's what people seemed to think of her anyway. I never knew her, of course."

"No. But that is how you thought of her . . . as odd?"

"Yes. She had a reputation, you know."

"A reputation?"

"Yes. She was a bit . . . well, odd. She let men sleep with her, or so they said. I wouldn't know, of course; too young. But she didn't wash very much. She shouted at people in the street . . . ranted." Harvey tried to put into words what Mrs. Odd had been. She was just a part of local life really, to the point that he'd never really analyzed what she represented. In a small town there were always people like that, weren't there? Strange, local legends really. "I suppose she would have been a witch," he said after a pause, "in another time, I mean. Sort of crazy and very there, you know, always around, wandering about, wearing weird clothes, muttering. I can imagine her cursing wells or whatever in, like, medieval times, yeah? But in the 1980s she was just a bit . . . well, odd. A bit eerie. You didn't want to get too close to her in case she sort of infected you." That didn't sound very good. "I mean, now I'd be sympathetic, right? But then you just wanted to keep clear of her really. And you kind of laughed at her." And you would have done, too, Mr. High-and-Mighty Policeman.

"Yes." Jarvin nodded thoughtfully and Harvey felt the eyes change so that when he met them it was he who looked away. "A very difficult sort of person to have for a mother."

"Yeah, yeah, I guess." Harvey had always thought of his own mother as the most difficult sort to have, but he had to admit that maybe Bleeder's had the edge. "I suppose that now, Blee . . . Charles would have gone into care or something. But then, he just sort of had to cope, kind of thing."

"And of course what friends he did have would be very important to him. I doubt he would have invited many to his house." The look continued and Harvey smiled vaguely into the middle distance. "So if you do remember anything about your visit to the house, it might be useful, Mr. Briscow...Perhaps you could ring me if anything does come to mind..." He turned slightly to Allen, who silently fished in his pocket and wrote a number on a card. The two men rose and moved to the door. Never had Harvey been happier to say good-bye.

"Oh, and perhaps you could just let me have your parents' telephone number so I can tick them off my list."

"What? No!"

"You'd rather I didn't call them?"

"No, I said so. They'll be upset. I'll call them..."

"Why would they be upset, Mr. Briscow?"

"Because they're not at ease with the police." Harvey got creative. "They are easily frightened, especially my father. You must let me ring them and explain. They're old; they are easily scared..." Where was all this coming from? Anything less like his parents and the unbridled joy they would feel at being involved in a murder inquiry was hard to imagine. He had a vision of his new parents, old and broken, cowering in their home, starting at sudden noises. If only life was really like that. "I will ring them and check about what happened. Honestly." If you will just fuck off I'll do it now.

"All right, and perhaps you'd ask them to ring me on that same number." The piece of white card with the number had been placed in Harvey's hand and he was holding it up in front of him as if it was attached to the string of a kite.

"Ring you. Well, I don't know. All right." He could think of no reason to deny Jarvin this. As he had with Josh earlier, he now toyed with the idea of killing Jarvin and his assistant. It would certainly make things easier for a few minutes. But he looked at Allen and put the idea away: He was bloody enormous. The two men made their way out of the shop calling their valedictions. Harvey waved a vague hand, with a white card in it, and then ran back into the office and grabbed the phone.

CHAPTER TWENTY-FOUR

Two customers shambled into the shop as Harvey began to dial and he frowned at them suspiciously. One thing he didn't need right now was trade. They were both familiar patrons, who he knew would spend a lot of time and very little money in his shop. He considered throwing them out but then decided it was easier simply to shut the door and leave them to it. Criminality was uncommon among comic book fans: They all wanted to be on the side of righteousness.

The number was engaged. Which was, when he thought about it, inevitable. What was it about parents that meant they could annoy you even when you were miles away, even without knowing they were doing it, unconsciously, without any premeditation? Normally, when he rang, he prayed that the number would be engaged, and it never was. There was always that long set of rings, just so long that he began to believe that they might be out or away or dead or something, and then always, just as he was about to put the handset down and beam with relief, his mother would come on the line and in her little tiny voice, the one he didn't recognize, the one she saved for other people, would say "Hello," as if she had never spoken on the telephone before and she might be punished for it. And he would grunt "Hi, Mum" and she would alter into someone quite different from that all-right-sounding little person. "Harvey, darling!" and they would be off on the first game, which was her trying to find out about his life and him trying to prevent her, which segued swiftly into the second game, which was her trying to keep things going even without any information to work with and him trying to bring things to a close without actually being rude. But now, of course, when he needed to speak to her she was busy with someone else. And, of course, she continued to be for some time. (It did not occur to him that his father might be using the telephone; his father was not good with telephones.) Josh would be returning with his bananas very soon, and this was a call that demanded privacy. The way Jarvin's voice had carried from the shop made Harvey wonder if he really was alone in the back room, especially if he started shouting, which in any call to his parents was a strong possibility. And also, was Jarvin telling the truth? What if he already had his parents' number? It was in the book, for Christ's sake. What if he was just playing with Harvey, testing him out? What if he was the person engaging his mother? He redialed with renewed vigor, but the most irritating woman in the world continued to say, "The number you are calling is engaged, please hang up and try again." He had been aware of a desire to kill this woman for some time, ever since she had first appeared unannounced on the normal *beep-beep* noise that signaled an unattainable number. He hit redial every twenty seconds or so and got her each time, then about the third minute it struck him that he might have misdialed the first time and might even now be ringing a wrong number while his mother talked things over with Jarvin, so he dialed from scratch again. He was just beginning to wonder if his memory was playing tricks with him—was this really his parents' number at all? Perhaps he had just made it up from thin air—when it rang.

"Hello?" Harvey's joy at finally getting through was instantly removed by the sound of his father's voice.

"Dad, hi." Where was his mother?

"Harvey, don't ring us during the daytime, it costs a fortune. Ring after six o'clock."

"Yeah, OK, Dad, but—look, is Mum there?"

"Why do you want her? Has there been a tragedy? Because

if there hasn't I'm putting the phone down; it's sinful to waste money like this."

"Dad, shut up and get Mum, I need to ask her something."

"What?"

Jesus Christ. "I need to know her plans for your funeral. Just get her, will you?"

"All right, but keep it short, boy. You can't be making that much money from that shop of yours . . ."

Harvey listened to the sound of his own breathing, heavy and ragged in the handset, then heard distantly: "It's your son. He's presumably won the pools and rung us to celebrate . . ." and his mother's chirrup of delight—"Is it Harvey? Oh, Donald, how lovely . . ."—and then at last her voice on the line, "Hello?" all questioning and full of expectation. Harvey briefly wondered what her mind had formed for itself in the time it took her to get to the phone. He so rarely rang during the day that presumably she was optimistic: He was getting married, that was the most likely. He'd got a job in a bank maybe second.

"All right, Mum?" The impatience of ringing meant that he hadn't thought to plan the conversation. He'd just have to wing it.

"How are you, darling? Are you all right?" He could feel the worry and longing mingling in her voice. He shook his head and heard his voice take on its usual guarded tone.

"Yeah, not bad. Just wondered if you were OK."

"I'm fine, we're both fine. It's lovely to hear from you . . ." How could that be a question? But it seemed that it was.

"Yeah, just thought I'd give a ring to let you know I got home safe the other day, yeah?"

"Yes, dear, that's kind of you." Harvey could hear his mother's effort not to say, "But you've not bothered before in the last twenty years."

"And, er . . . I had the police round. Thought you'd want to know about that . . . Have you spoken to them at all?" He couldn't think of any subtle way of introducing it.

"The police! Donald, Harvey's had the police round."

"Well, there you are. Drugs, I suppose." His father's voice came to Harvey as a distant presence, but approaching, and he pictured him moving through from the sitting room into the hall to listen in.

"Actually, I was hoping for a quiet chat with you, Mum," he said rather desperately.

"Oh, yes, dear . . . he wants a quiet chat, Donald. You'd better stay in case he needs your advice. Now, darling, what did they want? Was it about drugs? Because if it was, frankly I'm not surprised. I remember when you bought that T-shirt with a cannabis leaf on it from the beach shop. Your father took it back but we were both so worried and now, well—"

"I was eleven, Mother, for Christ's sake. I thought it was a peace symbol, and anyway it was a T-shirt, not a crack pipe. Besides, it's not about drugs."

"It's not about drugs, Donald," his mother translated.

"Tell him it's better to tell the truth and get it over with. No point in lying."

Harvey literally wiggled with irritation. "Fucking hell, Mum, how have you stood him all these years? What kind of mad world does he inhabit? Why would I ring up to lie? Why would I ring up at all? Why did I ring up at all? Jesus fucking wept."

"Language, Harvey. He says it's not about drugs, Donald."

"I know he does, but what is it about, then? Has he been arrested for murdering Mrs. Odd when he was down here? 'Cause if so he'll get no help from me."

Mrs. Briscow was giggling, "Your father says have you been arrested for murdering Mrs. Odd, Harvey? Remember the old lady who was killed when you were here. You knew her son—now what was his name? What was his name, Donald? Charles, that's it. You knew him, Harvey, you must remember . . ."

Harvey wondered if it was possible to commit suicide with a telephone handset. He attempted it by bashing it against the side of his temple several times.

"Harvey? Harvey, what's that noise?"

"Nothing, Mother, just the sound of a final nail entering a coffin . . ."

"What, dear?"

"Never mind. Look, it is sort of about the murder, yes." He hurried on over the gasp and the sound of his mother passing on this information to his father. "Because I knew Charles, the police wanted to know about what happened that day. It was Sunday and I remember what I did: I went for a walk in the morning and in the afternoon I was out again walking. I took the car for a bit, and then I was up in my room and then I went out for a drink, you remember?" Harvey was quite glad that he had never pursued the life of crime that he had sometimes fantasized for himself; he could sense a lack of aptitude, a certain amateurishness in his work.

"Oh, but you didn't get back until quite late, darling, and we hoped you might stay in but you went out very late with your friends." His mother clearly remembered very well.

"OK, fine, but you remember I went for a walk that afternoon, yeah?"

"Well, I remember you went for one in the morning, dear. And you came back for lunch and then you borrowed your father's car, didn't you, in the afternoon and I remember you came back very dirty and I had to wash your clothes for you; they were under your bed where they didn't belong. But I don't remember you ever saying where you'd been . . . Donald, Harvey wants to know if we remember where he went on Sunday; the police need to know."

"Why?" Harvey heard his father's voice close to the handset and suspected that he had been listening for himself.

"Yes, why, Harvey? Why do they want to know?"

Why do you bloody think, you stupid woman? "It's just routine. They're checking on everyone who was at the reunion."

"They're checking on everyone at the reunion, Donald."

"Well, we can't give him an alibi if that's what he wants. He went out and he came back. That's all we can say. What he was doing I don't know. It seems a very long time to be out for a walk; anyone would think he didn't want to come home."

"Yes, Harvey, you were out a long time for just a walk. I wonder what you were doing all that time." His mother was clearly trying to guess, really just as if he hadn't told her, as if he wasn't there at the end of the phone line to ask. He shook his head more quickly and did the wiggle again.

"Look, there's no need to wonder. I've just told you: I was walking. I just need you to tell the police that."

"You want us to tell the police? Oh, Harvey, what have you done? Why on earth would the police want to ask us?"

Oh, Christ. "I haven't done anything. That's the point, Mother. If I had done anything I wouldn't be ringing you—"

"Oh, but the police don't need alibis for no reason, Harvey. You must have done something, mustn't you? He does need an alibi, Donald; the police are going to ring us."

"Well, he'll get no alibi from me. I'll not tell a lie to a policeman, nor to anyone else. He must take his medicine if he's done wrong, simple as that."

"Yes, your father's right, Harvey. If you've done wrong you must say so and tell the truth."

Harvey closed his eyes very tight and put his fist holding the telephone against his face for a moment. He could die here. He could die right here and then it would all go away.

"I haven't done wrong, Mum. That's the whole point. I haven't done anything. I just need you to tell the police what I'm telling you, that I went out in the car and went walking in the afternoon. It's as simple as that."

"But why would they need to ask us unless you'd done something you shouldn't, Harvey? It doesn't make sense." Harvey had pictured his parents in Nazi Germany more than once. He often felt that they had missed their calling.

"Just tell them that, all right? I have to give you their number." He still held the piece of white card in his hand and he looked at it now and found that it had been twisted and bent until it had torn. He read the number into the telephone while his mother flapped about and tried to find the pen that was beside the phone in plain view, so plain, in fact, that Harvey could see it in his mind's eye and direct her to it; and then dropped it on the floor and had to put the phone down while she got it and then his father got to it first and insisted she recite the number to him rather than writing it herself, and she said it wrong and then his father got it wrong so that by the end he was bellowing the number at the top of his voice, each digit separated by either a blasphemy or an obscenity, or in many cases, both. Finally she read it back in her "I'm rather useless, aren't I?" voice, brought on by his own and his father's critical remarks about her note taking, and, by unexpected intervention of grace, got it right.

"Brilliant." Harvey was literally sweating with effort. "So ring him, his name is Chief Inspector Jarvin, J-A-R-V-I-N. No, I don't know what time he'll be there, just give him a bell and . . ." He paused for a moment. "Look, just between us, Mum, I wouldn't mention that evening, after I got back, you know—me lying in my room and you washing my clothes and stuff, I wouldn't mention all that if I was you. Just tell him I went for a walk and went up to my room and then went out for a drink. Stick to the facts, yeah?"

"Yes, all right, Harvey, don't worry, we can manage."

His mother was speaking with the forced competence she sometimes took on when she was offended at being treated like a fool. Harvey took note of this tone. "I should ring him right away, Mother, OK? And try and get it right."

"Yes, dear, I'm quite sure I can handle that without any problem, thank you."

Harvey put the phone down and reopened the door to the shop. The two customers were still there, just as he had left them, and he drummed his fingers loudly on the counter until they were encouraged to go. The call hadn't gone as badly as he'd thought it would, actually.

CHAPTER TWENTY-FIVE

Sunday was the day of rest for Harvey, although in truth most days were fairly restful, so Sunday was really the day of more rest than usual. It meant he had the chance to lie around his flat thinking and listening to the washing machine going round and round cleaning his one set of bedclothes in preparation for another trying week for them. It also meant he could catch up with his telephoning and stay in touch with his friends. So on this particular Sunday he rang various people, including several of the old crowd, of whom he asked tentative and subtle questions about the reunion and was met with ribaldry regarding Maisie and hilarious reminiscences about the fight at Steve's house. After several of these he stopped shouting, had a shower, and spent some time examining his stomach in the bathroom mirror. Because the mirror was at head height this involved standing on the toilet and leaning backward. It was, he decided, after several moments' consideration, definitely larger than the last time he did this: about three Sundays ago. A resolution to lay off beer and to eat better in future was only slightly weakened by the memory that he had made exactly the same vow the last time.

Sunday was also the day he sometimes rang his mother and the thought that he had already done it on Saturday and therefore didn't need to do it again was a warming and harmonizing one. The fact that he wouldn't see Josh today was equally satisfying. Josh had returned with a large bunch of unhealthy-looking bananas and had proceeded to make custard on the gas ring; this had boiled over because the gas was set too high, and the custard had spilled onto the floor. Josh had collected it carefully with a spoon and a piece of paper, returned it to the pan, and allowed the same thing to happen again. Harvey had taken the spoon from him and attempted to knock him on the head with it. Scalding custard had sprayed off the spoon and he had got some in his eye. He could still feel a slight pain in his right eye—the same one that he had been punched in—as he wandered around his flat. So not seeing Josh was all to the good.

However, Sunday did always present the challenge of how to spend his time. It seemed to reinforce and exaggerate the sense of purposelessness in the rest of his existence. Surely a man of his age and lifestyle should have a variety of things to do between lunch and dinner on his only free day of the week, but he never seemed to. There always seemed this need to do his washing or go and buy a paper because if he didn't he would just have to sit and stare out of the window. And this week the uncertainty seemed more pressing than usual. Not that he wouldn't welcome a certain amount of boredom: Ennui suddenly seemed a rather desirable commodity. It was just that there seemed so many things that he should be doing, like . . . well, something surely. If you are a suspect in a murder inquiry you should be doing something. But he couldn't really think of anything. Or at least there was one thing he could do: go to the shop, get the *Superman One*, and destroy it. It might stop him dreaming about drawers and red fingerprints every night. Several times he almost made it to the door to set off, but each time he sat down again. What if it was important that the comic did exist? That was the question troubling him. It was the only proof he had that someone was trying to set him up. Someone who had perhaps waited a long time for this. Harvey thought back over the reunion; someone must have been waiting for Bleeder's return, just as he had been. Who else was there? Who else knew Bleeder? And into his mind came the image of Bleeder talking to someone at the reunion; that old maths teacher, what was his name? Harvey thought about him for a while. Had he, too, been waiting for Bleeder? Waiting for one of his star pupils to return? Was there something else there? Was there something that didn't involve the comic? But then who sent the comic to him? How was he being set up? And why? He was sitting on the bed, looking out over London, when the telephone rang.

It was his mother, which caused Harvey a certain degree of outrage: He had rung her yesterday, done his duty for the week, maybe for the month. This was against all the rules. But it turned out she had a reason for ringing, which was that she had spoken to Jarvin. He lit a cigarette while she talked about what a nice man the chief inspector seemed and he waited for her to get to the part that he needed to worry about. It didn't take all that long.

"We talked about last weekend," she told him, "and what a bad temper you were in most of the time, rolling home drunk and sleeping in with a hangover. And I told him how you came home filthy that Sunday. He was quite interested in that."

Harvey was suddenly standing up and breathing hard. "You told him that?"

"Of course I did. And Donald said that you had left a stain on the driver's seat of the car, which I didn't know about and I'm really very cross with you, Harvey, we only got that car last year. So Donald suggested that the police might like to have a look at the stain. And Mr. Jarvin said one of his men would come round today if they could. Isn't that efficient? I do think the police are very efficient, don't you, Harvey? All that nonsense in the papers about them I think is just rubbish."

"When are they coming round?"

"I don't know, sometime today, which means we have to wait in, and I must say we don't appreciate that, Harvey, we are busy people..."

She would probably have said more, indeed perhaps she did, but Harvey put the phone down at this point and sat quietly taking a long, penetrating look at his view. Then he rang Maisie and demanded that she come out for Sunday lunch. As it was two o'clock by this time—Harvey having followed his usual practice of rising late on the sabbath—she suggested that dinner might be a better idea and they arranged to meet at seven in Islington. This left Harvey a fair amount of time to think. He paced the floor in bare feet, leaving faint footprints in the grime of the carpet, and it was this that made him consider cleaning up. The majority of his brain was fixed on the fact that he was clearly about to be arrested—the stain had to be Mrs. Odd's blood; he didn't leave stains on seats as a rule—but one small part of his thoughts did return to the subject of sex. You can't seduce with a messy flat: simple fact of life. So he fetched the ageing and underemployed Hoover from the cupboard in the hall and dug out a duster and spray polish from under the sink. With a horrible feeling of familiarity he began to clean. There was no blood here, but still the motions of cleaning were remembered by his body, and remembered too was the revulsion of that day, one week ago, almost to the minute. In his muscles he could still feel slight twinges of familiarity, tiny points of pain from his previous exertions. As he knelt to pick up some errant fag ends his knees recalled the movement and protested. He had cleaned away a murder and he had left a mark of it on his father's car. In his mind he pictured a huge stain across the Fling's cheap gray seats. He saw it like a map of Africa, or like Gorbachev's birthmark, some symbol of vast and various meaning. And the primary meaning was guilt. Jesus, he had taken on this murder like growing a boil; it had become attached to him. As he worked he gritted his teeth and sobbed between them. And the sobs this time were uncontained, forcing their way out of the knotted coils that had formed inside him, coils of horror and guilt and anger and fear, until he had to stop and just kneel in the dust, with all his cleaning materials around him, a pot of Mr. Muscle still clutched in his hand, and watch his tears form black splashes in the gray dust of the floor.

How long he sat like that Harvey wasn't sure. It was a significant moment, definitely; he had had few enough of them to recognize one when he saw it. He didn't exactly kneel down a boy and stand up a man, although that thought did drift through his mind. But he felt sort of different afterward, stronger and a bit less weak and hopeless. When he tried to characterize it to himself his thoughts came back to his stomach. It was as if his stomach had been making all the decisions so far, and they were therefore flabby, excessive, and self-pitying. From now on, whatever else happened, he was going to think with some other part of his body. Maybe his heart could have a say; maybe his brain could work things through rationally. It was with a firm nod that he grasped this slightly obscure metaphor. But of course it wasn't really his heart or his brain that was doing the thinking. The cleaning was for Maisie and her seduction, so it was his genitals that really had the floor. But at least they were making decisions that the rest of him was happy with. And as he set off for Islington, although his fingers were shaking as he locked his flat, there was a trace of a bulge in his trousers and some difficulty in his gait as he strode down the stairs.

Chief Inspector Jarvin's smile was biologically determined and therefore unreliable as a guide to the inner world. His son, Jack, who had inherited the green eyes but not as yet the dolphin jawline, was examining his father's face for more than a genetic appearance of goodwill.

"I am absolutely serious, Jack. I want you to pal up with Oliver a little bit. Make him feel like he has some protection at least, if not a real friend." Oliver was the victim of bullying in Jack's class, and Jarvin had developed a protective feeling for him.

Jack shook his head in anger. "You are interfering in the

dynamics of my relationships, Dad"—Jack was studying psychology—"and you are letting your job influence your family life. Who I am friends with is up to me."

"Yes, it is. But who you bully isn't." Jarvin was able to admire his son's intelligence at the same time as objecting to backchat. This was in part a product of his own background: his English mother, so gentle and liberal in his youth, opening his mind to so many possibilities, and his more traditional Finnish father imposing a variable and unpredictable restraint. How he wanted to be the best of both of them in his relations with his son, and how often he felt that he was the worst.

"I'm not a bully! Other people pick on Dawson, not me."

"Dawson? You don't call your friends by their surnames, why do you call Oliver that?"

"Because everyone does; he's Dickie Dawson...He's Dawson's Freak. That's what they call him."

" 'They, they, they'...? When did you ever learn to make choices based on what 'they' think?"

"When you sent me to comprehensive school, Dad, remember? I have to take care of myself. I can't be nursemaiding anyone else." Jack got up and made for the door, thereby declaring this father-son chat concluded. Jarvin sighed and for a moment looked almost like Harvey Briscow. He shook his head, too.

"Just do your best, Jack, that's all I ask."

"Yeah, sure. But I've got to live my own life." And his son was gone on what was, Jarvin had to admit, a pretty unanswerable exit line. He got up and did what he rarely did, which was to look in the glass cabinet in the corner of his sitting room. The room was light, with a bay window opening onto a tulip tree, just beginning to bud, and the sunlight was calling him into the garden. Instead, he looked for a moment into his past. Susan, his wife, had arranged his memories for him in the cabinet. Army photos: him in desert gear and camouflage; his two medals, displayed so nicely in a frame; his trophy for winning the marksmanship contest for his year; passing out from Sandhurst; his first commission; Hendon, class of '84. What was this all about? He looked at these memories for a while with real uncertainty. What had he intended when he chose this course, this institutional, controlled, frankly authoritarian path in his life: his father's path, not his mother's? If even his own son was potentially delinquent, potentially making another human being's life hell, and if he, Jarvin, didn't really care, so long as Jack was OK, so long as he survived it and made it through to the unpredictable delights of adulthood, why do this? Why not get some desk job, or go back to college and study engineering as he'd sometimes dreamed? His thoughts turned now, as perhaps he knew they would, to the case in hand. Mrs. Odd and her poor bullied son, and his strange City financier existence; Harvey Briscow and his comic shop and his unexpectedly guilty demeanor; Maisie Cooper and her deep sea-green eyes, and her distant, bitter husband. Jarvin had been to see Jeff Cooper the day before and had come away troubled. What had Allen's words been? "Pretty near the boil, Mr. Cooper." And Jarvin had known exactly what he meant. Something was bubbling in Mr. Cooper. Was it just the loss of his wife? Jarvin thought again of Maisie and had to acknowledge that the loss of her would certainly be a blow. But he thought most of Charles Odd, Bleeder Odd. Where was he today? He would like to meet him again. Being so far from Cornwall was a problem. To prevent things like Mrs. Odd's murder: Was that why he did it? As he straightened up from bending to peer at a picture of a younger, smiling, seemingly carefree Jarvin at the back of the cabinet, he allowed himself this one generous thought. But as he made his way outside for half an hour's weeding before lunch, he was unsure that it was anything but a palliative, unsure that there was really any reason at all.

CHAPTER TWENTY-SIX

They met in a Pizza Express. This wouldn't have been Harvey's first choice for what his genitals were characterizing as one of the more important evenings of his life. He was not without romantic common sense and had some insight into how women thought. He would have preferred somewhere intimate and personal; somewhere that they could perhaps call their special place; somewhere that they would always go back to on their anniversary and point out fondly to their grandchildren. Unfortunately, he hadn't been able to think of anywhere. So they met in the weirdly unreal, postmodern splendor of the Islington Pizza Express. The way Harvey was feeling perhaps it wasn't such an inappropriate choice.

"You look terrible." Maisie had taken his hand as he stood up for an awkward peck on the cheek. The kiss had been mistimed and he had bashed the side of her head with his chin.

"Oh, thanks." They both sat down, with Harvey attempting to retain her hand as they did so, almost knocking over the rare and unlikely foreign flower with which the table was inevitably adorned. He let go and sat heavily.

"I mean, you look worried. Are you worried?"

"Oh no, I'm fine. Not a care in the world." Harvey shook his head and closed his eyes. Then, remembering he wasn't speaking to Josh, but to the woman that parts of his anatomy had been dreaming about almost unceasingly, he opened them again and sighed. "Sorry. I don't mean to be mean, yeah? But I'm having a bad day."

"Another one?" Her smile reached across the table and her hand came with it to reclaim his. "Tell me," she said. So he did.

"Shit, OK, so now we know where we are." They had ordered pizzas and were sharing a mixed salad and garlic bread in preparation for their arrival. And Harvey, while telling her about the stain in the car, had revisited a little of his earlier sorrow. He pronged a moody cherry tomato and shook his head.

"I know where I am: in bloody Reading Gaol, that's where. Bang to rights and doing stir. Bastards."

Maisie was not sure who this last expletive was directed at but decided that it was probably better not to ask. "No, now you will have to tell the truth, and that is a good thing, Harvey. If I was you I would go to Jarvin first thing tomorrow. How long does it take for them to analyze a stain? Probably a day or two, so you'll have plenty of time to go and sort everything out." She saw the look on Harvey's face. "I'll come with you if you like," she said gently. "It really is for the best."

"They'll arrest me." Harvey could feel the tears from the cleaning session still hanging in his vocal cords. "They'll put me in a cell and hold me. They won't let me go once I tell them. Jesus, I'm so stupid."

"Well, perhaps..."

"I don't mean that. I mean with Bleeder. Why didn't I talk to him when I had the chance? I keep thinking of that. When I saw him at Steve's party he wanted to tell me something, I know he did. Stuff that I don't know about his mother and about the past. Jarvin thinks the murder is linked to the past and to Bleeder. He obviously hasn't told the police very much." He stopped and bit his lip. "I just wish I could talk to him, just get everything straight in my head. Because they will lock me up, Maisie, you must see that. If I go in there and tell Jarvin that I was at Mrs. Odd's house, and that I broke the back window, and that I saw the body and that I wiped up all the fingerprints, and then add, 'Oh, but by the way, I'm not the murderer,' he is never in a million years going to just say, 'Oh, fine, well, thanks for popping in.' He is going to chuck me in a cell and give me a small bucket to piss in and a bar of soap to protect my honor in the showers. Shit. I need to talk to Bleeder."

"All right." She spoke with sudden authority and took him by surprise. "We'll go down there tomorrow. I'd been thinking about it anyway, actually. You should speak to Charles; he obviously wanted to talk to you. And I'd like to set eyes on him myself. If this is the center of our lives and he is the pivotal figure, I'd at least like to know what he looks like. We'll get this straightened out." She said it with such certainty that Harvey was moved.

"That's really kind," he said softly and she smiled at him. "But I'm not seeing my mum and dad!" he added suddenly with real vehemence. "And I'm not fucking staying at their house."

"No, OK, we'll find a B and B." She smiled. Harvey grinned back and his genitals gave a little shimmy of delight.

After the pizza there was wine. There had been some during the pizza, of course, but not enough for Harvey to attempt romance. But once the eating was over and the decision was made, he was able to let his genitals really take over the planning of the rest of the evening. He ordered a bottle of red and drank it quickly and efficiently and ordered another, so that within a fairly short space of time he was able to worry about the garlic bread he'd eaten earlier and just hope that she had had her share, because he was kissing her over the table. She tasted as clean as a broad bean; how did women do that? He wasn't sure what he tasted like, but when he went to the bathroom, he found that his teeth had turned a nasty sort of glistening purple color. They were making good progress on the second bottle by that time and Harvey had been doing more than his fair share to keep up the pace. He wasn't really a wine drinker, except at parties, where he would drink anything. But these days he went to fewer parties than in his youth and beer had rather taken over. It is, of course, possible for a man in his midthirties to go up to the bar in a straight pub and order a glass of red wine for himself but Harvey had never actually seen it done. When examining his teeth in the bathroom, he noticed that he was also rather red in the face. Kissing did make him red; he knew that of old. Kissing and tennis. When he returned she was still there, which while hardly unexpected was not necessarily a sure thing in his experience.

They kissed some more and then came his least favorite bit of any romantic evening, when they got their coats and paid the bill and didn't look at each other's face in case they caught the wrong sort of expression there.

"Er, shall we get a cab, or are you heading straight off?" Harvey had used this question before. It wasn't perfect but it did allow some suggestiveness without crudity and some freedom without rejection. It prevented, in fact, the worst scenario, where he said "please" and she said "no" and then they had to make conversation for half an hour while they waited for two separate taxis to arrive.

"I'd like to see where you live."

He wondered if she'd used that before, too, because as far as he was concerned it was just about perfect.

"Cool. We'll do the taxi thing, yeah?" And they got one almost at once, which was in itself pretty miraculous, and the driver was only mildly sarcastic and bitter when Harvey mentioned their destination. And they kissed some more in the back with the driver talking about West Ham, and apart from one moment when Harvey had to pause to correct him about Bobby Zamora, the journey was unusually trouble-free. And when he surfaced occasionally for air Harvey saw that the Old Kent Road had never looked so beautiful, nor so exotic and strange, as if he had left his usual bubble existence and was experiencing how someone else might see southeast London: the eyes of someone from another dimension perhaps, who had seen it before but never quite like this. This idea so caught his imagination, and he became so involved in the visualization of how it might work as a comic, that he almost forgot to kiss her.

Deptford isn't lovely, but Harvey reminded himself that she had been living in Croydon and relaxed. He opened his flat door with something of a flourish: No point in doing all that cleaning if you didn't show off a bit. The kitchen he'd spent extra time on, even going so far as to throw out the milk cartons and beer cans that he usually stored on the window ledge for decorative purposes, so he led her there.

"Er, you know, there's not much to it." He saw a certain something in her face. Was that disappointment? "You were expecting something a little bigger, yeah? Well, I kind of live at work mostly. I just need a place to crash really so this is like my crash pad, and . . ." She laid a hand on his arm and he stopped. For some reason he had started trying to talk like a Miami drugs baron. He was even beginning to work in a little of the accent.

"I like it, Harvey." She said his name to bring him back to earth, or at least to the right side of the Atlantic. He nodded and felt the red wine swoosh from the back of his head to the front.

"Er . . ."

"But I just don't see anything of you."

"Oh, right, yeah, it's just a place to crash." He stopped again. "I guess I haven't really done much with it." He tried his own voice instead. "I'm not here that much."

"How long have you lived here?"

"Um, well," shit, "about fifteen years."

"Fifteen years? Harvey!" She walked through into the pine-fresh lounge, and once he'd put the kettle on he followed.

"I know, I haven't really been here that much." He said it again but even to him it sounded hollow.

"What can I learn about you from this flat?" She looked around interested, as if playing a favorite game.

"Er, well, not much probably." Jesus, what did she expect, cushions and cut flowers?

"The posters of course are distinctive." She examined a *Tomb Raider*—with Lara swinging from a rope—as if looking at some rare collector's item. It was a generic poster, really common-place now since Lara had got so popular. He should have taken it down and gone for one of the Japanese ones: same graphic but with Japanese writing . . . bit less common . . . his brain sort of came to a standstill. He hadn't got what she wanted. Perhaps she hoped for Impressionist prints or something, but he'd never really got on with art. "I know a lot about art, but I don't know what I like." That was his favorite line when asked, which wasn't very often, and this was fortunate because it was entirely untrue. He had done Art History for A level, but that had mostly been eighteenth-century English art, and all he could remember was a lot of horses and really weird trees. If he hadn't fancied the girl who sat next to him he might have swapped to cookery. What was her name? And why didn't she ever come to the reunion? Women like men who like art; that was a truth that he had learned down the years. It had almost got him laid when he was seventeen, but it seemed to be coming back to haunt him. Maisie shook her head, as if slightly disillusioned, and moved on to his records and CDs. Harvey felt a welling of relief: This was an area he was more at home with. But of course women don't care what music you like. That was an-other truth, even harder to bear than the art one. And it wasn't that he wanted her to take in all that he'd got in one glance. What mattered was what he didn't have: Elton John and U2 and George Michael and all that other shite that people who don't like music always owned. This was where he was revealing his character: in what he hadn't got in his record collection. But she didn't stop to consider. She just smiled at the amount and moved on to the DVDs. Here Harvey had rather let himself go. Deptford Market had a healthy trade in slightly suspicious DVDs and he had begun collecting several years ago. From a first, primal choice: *Blade Runner Director's Cut*, through the *Die Hard* box set and right up to the *Matrix* interactive edition, he had, he felt, found a cross section of modern cinema to rival . . . well, anyone else he knew.

So it was with a certain sinking of the heart that he heard her words: "Wow, you sure like action films, Harvey, and what is it with you and science fiction? You're not an alien, are you?"

This last comment was especially dispiriting to Harvey as it wasn't actually the first time that he'd heard it. Indeed, for a time in his twenties when the shop was getting started he had moved in a circle of friends, mostly from Camden, who were, frankly, too cool for him, and the suggestion that he was an alien who had recently landed had become something of an in-joke. On his birthday one year they had all arrived wearing deely-boppers and had given him presents themed around space, including a silver hat to protect him from rays from other galaxies. They had not remained his friends for long, and the last he heard the coolest of them all, a terribly witty gay man with impeccable taste, named Peter, was working as a supply teacher at a comprehensive in Stafford. But it was as close as he had ever been to feeling like Bleeder Odd, and that realization made him close his eyes for a moment and wince.

"Hey, are you OK?" She came over and put the back of her hand to his forehead. "Did I say the wrong thing?"

"Yeah, no, no problem. Just, you know. I don't like being called an alien."

"OK."

He could sense that she was trying not to giggle and he frowned the more. "It's kind of a sore spot."

"I see. Does it happen a lot?" The giggle made its way out

and he felt his shoulders go up, and despite himself he gave a little snort of amusement.

"Yes, actually." They both snorted in sync and then she moved into his arms in such a slinky, sensual sort of way that she was almost being satirical, but not quite. He kissed her and she let him and then smiled and said "Mmm, hello" in a way that made his genitals awaken and begin to plan ahead.

"Let's, er . . ." He tried to explain what his groin was saying but it was a hard language to translate.

"Do you have a bath?"

The question was so unexpected that Harvey was jolted into articulacy: "Er, yeah, in the bathroom." He pointed to make the position clear.

"Come on then, show me."

So he showed her his spotless bathroom, and she ran the taps and found some bath foam to pour under the hot water, just like in a proper person's house. Admittedly it was Thomas the Tank Engine bath foam, which came with a free game where you pressed buttons to make Thomas go round a track . . . but it was a genuine bathroom product. The fact that the bathroom now smelled heavily of strawberry bubble gum seemed all to the good. She then exclaimed aloud and ran off to the sitting room, returning with three fat little candles from her bag, which she claimed were meant to be a present for Lisa. But she sat them on the corners of the bath and he lit them with his fag matches, and then she turned off the light and made him a stranger in his own bathroom. How did women do that: transform somewhere into somewhere else in a minute? The water pressure in South London is quite low so it took some time for the bath to fill, but he made up for that by kissing her. And at the end of one kiss, she grabbed the back of his T-shirt and peeled it up over his head. Harvey felt a powerful desire to fight her off and drag it back down. His stomach hadn't looked too good in the clear light of a Sunday afternoon, but the candlelight and the steam, he realized, would give many things a genuinely sexy glow. Would it work for his stomach? He wasn't entirely convinced, but vague memories of other romantic evenings from the past brought the thought that if he allowed her to remove one item of his, then he could do one in return. He stepped back and sucked in his breath as hard as he could—first impressions last—and then reached out for her. She was wearing a tassely, beaded sort of shirt with buttons that came down to her cleavage and he fiddled with the buttons, and then, fearing that he might wait too long, just sort of grabbed the bottom and heaved. It came up and he could hear her giggling, and she seemed to be about to ask him to stop so he pulled harder and she emerged, rather red in the face, but with a pretty smile, from underneath.

"You animal!" she said sweetly and then turned to test the water in the bath. She was, Harvey realized, far more at ease with this than he was. Which was unfair as he was the one who had been single and out there for the last . . . well . . . forever really, and she was the one from the loveless marriage. He was meant slowly but firmly to show her what love could really be like now that she had left her evil husband. Instead, here she was unhooking her bra and letting it swing playfully from side to side, while he stood with his arms squarely folded over his belly, trying not to panic. He wasn't complaining, mind, it was just an observation.

In the end, she did lose her nerve and made him turn around while she stripped, and when he looked again she was lying back under the foam with her hair up in a disheveled bun, looking like one of those adverts for bathroom products at the back of the Sunday supplements, which Harvey always found it very hard to flick past.

"Shit, you're beautiful." He reached for his belt and then paused to consider: which side to give her? Full frontal or his arse while he took his pants off? Tricky. But of course she was better at this: Perhaps some people are just born good at sex, like with chess. She just put her head back against his pale green bath and closed her eyes with a long slow "mmmm" of plea-sure. She was a cat, he thought...only one that liked water... not a great image, but enough to calm him a little as he whipped his trousers off with panicked efficiency, tore off his pants, re-membered at the last moment that he still had his socks on—that would have been an error—and tried desperately to decide how to get in. He went for the tap end. Not as romantic as snug-gling in next to her but, frankly, he wasn't sure he'd fit. It's a fine line between eroticism and ludicrousness for most people and Harvey had found himself way too close to that line on a num-ber of occasions. Once he was in she opened her eyes and looked at him with great sweetness. "Look at us two," she said softly, lifting a dappled foot and running it up Harvey's chest. He was glad of the bubbles because without them his penis would have appeared above the water, *Jaws*-like, rather earlier than was appropriate.

"Yeah, amazing." Perhaps he'd leave the dialogue to her. He took the foot in his hands and kissed it; she squealed as he ran his tongue along the sole and a wave washed along from her end to his.

"I'm very ticklish, Harvey."

"Are you?" He tested this claim by moving his hand from her foot up her leg, like silk in the soapy water. The back of her knee felt so soft and interesting to his fingers that he stopped there for a while and just stroked it gently, causing her to wrig-gle but not to squeal. He'd always liked legs; long or short, there were very few female legs that didn't stimulate his curiosity. He liked the funny knobbly bits of them, the ankle bones and the knees, the way they widened as you moved up them, the muscle lines that seemed to lead you, as if you were following some sort of map. If you looked closely at a woman's leg he believed it was possible to suggest that it was designed to lead you where you wanted to go. He explored her knee and then his hand fol-lowed the map of her body up the inside of her thigh and she closed her eyes and made a low, very satisfactory sound.

CHAPTER TWENTY-SEVEN

There are some experiences in life that seem sent to haunt us and render us unhappy. Some because they are so terrible that they cannot be fully forgotten or left behind, others for the more bittersweet reason that they are so perfect we can never fully experience anything similar without drawing critical comparison. When Harvey awoke on Monday morning he knew that the previous night would, for him, forever be something he would strive to repeat, without any real likelihood of success. He woke early, needing to pee and with his mouth feeling as if it had been chemically corroded. In the bathroom, after the simple joy of a relieved bladder, he examined his mouth and found that his tongue was still purpled by the wine. Who drank this stuff, for Christ's sake? He fetched his toothbrush and scrubbed his tongue with it. But he did have to admit that the wine had been a help, in ways that beer might not have been. His penis, for all its cavalier behavior earlier in the evening, had behaved itself when it mattered. They had stayed in the bath for a while, and he had had a bit of an explore. She was so soft. As he scrubbed now and spat purple liquid into the sink he thought about that: It had been like sliding his finger into warm butter. He snorted noisily at the crudity of this image and then stifled it, lest she hear him sniggering in the bathroom. Then they had both sat up and kissed and looked into each other's eyes for a while with their hands underwater touching and exploring. It was very possibly the most erotic experience of his life. Was it better than the time he saw Jenny

Ainsworth's knickers as she climbed over the stile when they were sixteen? Hard to judge really: It certainly went on a lot longer. Her hand discovered his penis, standing patiently to attention with a smile on its face. Returning the smile, she ran her fingers down it as if they'd been meeting like this for ages. Harvey, to his embarrassment, made a sort of whinnying noise as she did it. It wasn't a noise he had made before, and it sounded almost pathetic with desire. It had been such a long time since he'd had any sort of sex, and almost beyond memory since anyone had touched him with such tenderness. With a broadening smile she had slid forward a little so that their bodies could entwine, her face right against his, and he could bring his hands up and run them foaming over her breasts. As he turned the toothbrush over and began to descale the roof of his mouth, he thought again of the sheer availability of her. He had wanted her since he first set eyes on her as she walked into the reunion, and while this wasn't in truth a very long time, an awful lot had happened since. Perhaps he had always wanted her. Perhaps she was meant to be his, destined. He spat again and imagined himself, not for the first time, on a silver surfboard crossing the infinite wastes of space. After a bit of fiddling about she had put one hand on his shoulder and, with her eyes never leaving his, had lifted herself up and forward and then slid downward so that her knees were tucked outside his legs, and his penis, directed by her other hand, slid neatly and perfectly inside her. He hadn't expected her to do this and it was so totally, electrically erotic that for a moment his penis considered simply exploding with emotion. Which is where the wine made up for its many disadvantages. With a final grimace at the mirror he made his way out and back to bed. But the thoughts in the bathroom had warmed him and stopped him feeling tired. So he woke her up.

———

"So, are we going to go?" They were sitting at his breakfast table and Harvey was wearing the slightly smug look of a fully satisfied man. He wouldn't previously have said that he owned a breakfast table, because he always ate muffins and coffee on the train to work or sent Josh to McDonald's when he got there, except on Sundays when he allowed himself a fry-up at the local café, Sid's—not wanting to become too much of a health freak. And so breakfast had not entered his flat for many years. But it did so now, and he was surprised by how easily such a major invasion could be carried out. It seemed a change into some past life, as if Maise's presence had carried him back to another more innocent age before choc-chip muffins and lattes. There was bread and milk and tea and Marmite, and they laid all the elements out on the table exactly as if they were going to sit around and eat like grown-ups. They might even have had boiled eggs, but didn't fancy it. But they could have done; that was the point. He had performed for her, he had satisfied her, he had fed her, and he had entertained her in a tidy flat. As he sipped his tea, he did so with an air of almost complete complacency.

"Go?" he said.

"To Cornwall. Remember we spoke about it last night?" She had been sitting on his lap for a bit while the bread was toasting under the grill and he had wondered, as many men wonder, how women manage to smell so good first thing in the morning. But now she was sitting across from him and looking at him with eyes that seemed filled with a green warmth, as if she was radiating care and concern and support across the table.

"Oh, yeah." Of course, he was a murder suspect; he'd rather forgotten. "Um, OK, but I think we should maybe plan it a bit, yeah? I mean, we can't go this morning—I've got a small delivery at the shop first thing. But we could go after lunch. Maybe stay the night and see Bleeder tomorrow. Why don't you come down to the shop about twelve and we'll go from there? What do you think?"

"You've got a delivery first thing this morning?"

"Yeah, so what?"

"Well, it's twenty past nine."

So it was that Harvey arrived disheveled and sweating at Inaction Comix. If he had had a car that worked at least there might have been some drama attached to a life-or-death race through the heaving streets; but by public transport he just got the same trains as usual only he swore and smoked more while he was waiting for them. But even all his efforts, including a heroic final run down Old Street from the tube to the shop, were not enough and he arrived panting at ten-thirty to find the deliverymen gone and Josh standing looking very pleased with himself beside a large cardboard box. At least it wasn't Thursday. That was the only positive thought that Harvey could muster as he ignored his assistant's cheery greeting and stood, breathing hard and eyeing the box with a cold distaste.

"What have you bought?"

"All right, Harv? Good weekend?"

"What have you bought, Josh?"

"No problem opening up for you this morning, don't mention it." The sarcasm was accompanied by an ingratiating smile, which rather spoiled its impact. Harvey was troubled by the smile. For, while most of the shop's merchandise arrived on a Thursday, the Monday van delivery was also important. Particularly significant was the fact that you could buy anything loose directly from the driver. This was how the shop got many of its more idiosyncratic items. The South Park key rings that said "You killed Kenny" in Spanish, for instance. Or the photo book of stills from the making of Deep Throat. These were items that Harvey liked to think gave the shop its specialness, its originality, that separated it from other comic shops. But there was one simple rule for these sorts of identity items: Josh was not allowed to buy them.

"I've told you, if I'm not here, either ask them to wait or tell them to come back next week. Haven't I told you that, Josh?"

"You have." Josh was beaming like a lighthouse.

"So what is in the box?"

"Bargain."

"A bargain?"

"Yeah, you are going to flip." Josh made no move to open the box and indeed was slowly backing behind the nearest comic rack.

"OK." Harvey put his hands to his face for a moment and closed his eyes. "Show me." He slid the hands away.

Josh reached round the rack for the lid of the box with the air of a conjuror about to perform his greatest trick. Indeed, when he flung back the lid he even said: *"Voilà!"*

Inside were two thousand packs of *Pokémon* game cards.

"You won't believe what I paid for these, Harvey." He chuckled with delight and then slipped quickly round the rack and ran for the door. "*Pokémon*'s coming back, Harv, we'll clean up."

He just made it out and away down the street before Harvey could reach him. "Bastard, bastard, bastard, bastard!" Harvey stalked back to the box, grabbed a handful of cards, and hurled them into the air. Fucking *Pokémon*. All these years of resistance, of battle, of denial. And all that time like an insidious voice of temptation had been Josh: "We need to move with the times, Harv"; "We need to know what the kids want, Harv"; "It's Japanese modern art, Harv." And now he'd done it. One Monday morning and all Harvey's principles were shot to shit. And it was almost certainly a fait accompli. Josh would have paid cash for these. They always paid cash to the travelers who came on days other than Thursday. He'd have paid cash. Harvey leaned against the *Ninja Turtle* section and lit a cigarette. Then he walked through into the back room and unlocked the bottom drawer of the desk. The petty-cash box was at the bottom with the envelope containing the *Superman One* lying neatly on top of it. Had Josh opened it? It was hard to imagine Josh not opening a private letter. But Josh would also have been desperate to do the deal and get the salesman away before Harvey arrived. Harvey swore and smoked for a few moments. Surely even Josh would have mentioned it if he'd found a stolen copy of one of the rarest comics in the world in the bottom drawer? Relocking the drawer, Harvey sat for a while in his office, glad of the peace. Perhaps he should allow Josh to buy ludicrous things at great expense more often, then he might have some time to rest and to think. He had a cup of tea and thought about Maisie and wondered if she had got back to Croydon all right and whether she was now on her way to meet him. It was some time before he ambled rather aimlessly back into the shop again and he was startled to find he had a customer.

"Oh, hello," he said. He hadn't heard the door and he spoke more in surprise than in any desire to engage in conversation. The man, who had been leafing through the *Incredible Hulks*, turned and grinned.

"Hello, Harvey."

"Oh. All right?" Harvey said.

It was Jeff Cooper.

There was a long silence broken, for Harvey at least, only by the sound of a small, low fart of fear that escaped him as he stood rooted behind the counter. The last time he had seen this man was from a prone position as Jeff's trainered foot connected with his stomach. Was this to be a repeat performance? Had Jeff returned to finish the murderous work that he had begun only one week ago? To Harvey's mind came the nightmare thought that things were moving in weekly cycles—Sundays: clean up; Mondays: get shitkicked. Fuck, what happened on Tuesdays? Before he could really work this new theory through,

Jeff, who had been contemplating him as a cannibal might consider a missionary, now approached the counter and put both hands down flat on its grubby surface.

"Harvey Briscow," he said, and he smiled again. Harvey nodded nervously and attempted a grimace in return.

"Er, yeah," he said, "that's me." Where was Josh? That was the question. Not that Josh would be any use in a fight but at least he might be a distraction, or at worst a witness. Would Jeff assault him in front of Josh? What if Harvey threatened to sue if he did? Jeff had done it in front of a whole party full of people in Cornwall . . . why hadn't Harvey sued him already? How did you sue people when they beat you up? He was sure he'd heard about it on television. His thoughts began to wander to afternoon advertisements for compensation lawyers, and to *Ally McBeal*, but Jeff's voice dragged him back to the moment.

"And here I am. You and me, Harvey. Old friends reunited, and with no need for a special Web site. You and me back together again."

"Yeah, lovely." Harvey was unsure that there was much to celebrate. He peered hopefully past Jeff's visibly muscular shoulder in the unlikely fantasy that a customer might come in.

"Old friends, Harvey," Jeff went on. "Old friends who grew up together, went to school together. Old friends who meet for a reunion. Old friends who steal each other's wives, Harvey. Old friends, that's what we are." Jeff was pausing between each line in frankly Pinteresque fashion.

Troubled by this rhetorical style, Harvey put his hand to his mouth for a moment. "Look, Jeff . . ." His middle finger was under his nose and he noticed a pleasant aroma; he sniffed more closely and realized it was Jeff's wife. "Look . . ." He whipped the hand away. "I think we need to discuss this. I mean, I haven't stolen anyone. I hardly know Mais—your wife. Yes, we were under a tree at the party but she was upset, I don't know what about, but I expect you do, and I put my arm round her. I shouldn't have but I did. The next thing I know you are going after me like Mike Tyson after a lamb kebab and I'm still bearing the scars." He risked putting his hand up again—reasoning that Jeff was unlikely to vault the counter and sniff his finger—and indicated the still purpled patch round his right eye. He looked closely at Jeff and considered his options: run into the back room and lock the door was probably his best move, the counter being too high for him to jump and get out the front. But the office door was troublingly thin, even if he could lock it in time. Would Jeff break down a door? He looked again at the shoulder muscles and tried another smile. "We are old friends, Jeff. You're right. And as such we shouldn't be fighting. We should talk. Look, would you like a cup of tea?" Once he was in the back room he could phone the police. How long would they take? Knowing this area, it would be quicker to ring the undertaker direct. Jeff didn't move. He remained with his hands planted on the counter, spread unnaturally wide, neck forward. He resembled a bird of some kind and Harvey filled the pause by speculating as to which breed. He had settled on an African vulture when Jeff spoke again.

"Who said anything about fighting, Harvey? Did you think I had come here to fight?" Some people can do melodrama and some can't. Harvey had never been much good at it and tended to mumble his lines, but Jeff was obviously a professional. He spoke with a clear and ringing menace that reminded Harvey of James Mason. There was just enough of the psychotic in the tone to make him return his hand to his face and bite at the skin around his thumbnail.

"I'm not here to fight. If I wanted to hurt you I would have done so at the party. I would have given you a few more playful slaps . . . but I thought you might die of it. You should at least have put up some sort of fight. I mean, I don't mind losing Maisie to another man, but to you . . . It's amazing—women are unknown quantities, aren't they, Harvey? So what do you think of her?"

Harvey had been considering Jeff's suggestion that he should have hit him back, which hadn't actually occurred to him before. It had about it something of the idea of punching a force of nature, smacking a landslide, kicking a flood. "Er, well, like I said . . ."

"She's good in the sack, I will say that. Like a little animal she is, or rather was, with me. Is she like that with you, Harvey? I must say it's hard to imagine it. Perhaps she takes pity on you, does she? Pretends? Makes you feel good? Maisie would probably do that for a poor lost soul, eh?" Harvey frowned in thought for a moment; had Maisie been faking last night and again this morning? Hard to tell. He was slightly shocked that he didn't really mind if she was: Sex had never seemed to him a suitable arena for competitive sport and if she was faking, then frankly he appreciated the kindness. He gazed at the ceiling for a while thoughtfully, and then glancing back at Jeff realized that his cold gray eyes were watching him like a vulture watching a tortoise on its back.

"Er, I wouldn't know, Jeff. Like I said, we only really met in Cornwall. I haven't seen Maisie since then. I assumed you were still together, actually, but I suppose she's left you, yeah?" He tried not to give a little grin as he said this but failed and saw the eyes narrow.

"So we are not enemies then, Harvey? That's a relief. I would hate to have a man of such substance for an enemy." The bird eyes circled round the shop and Harvey remembered vaguely the claims to grandeur that he had made at the reunion. Then the eyes returned to hold his. "We can talk as friends, eh? Not enemies, but allies?" Jeff turned suddenly and began to pace down the central aisle, both hands held out at the sides, riffling his fingers over the soft plastic of the comic sleeves. "We can talk about it all. What happened, the past, we can talk about it

all, Harvey, get it out in the open, eh? Get everything out in the
open?"

"Oh, yeah. Absolutely." Harvey moved back toward the
door to his office. "We can talk about everything."

"Everything?" Jeff swung round and looked piercingly in
his direction. "We can talk about everything now? Yes, I suppose we can. Now she's gone we may as well. It's all over now
anyway. I guess you sort of hold it together . . . But when it falls
apart it all comes back . . . I knew when we went down to the
reunion. I knew then that it had all fallen apart—it was like
everything that had been holding it up just collapsed. We sat
around in that bloody hotel room like two strangers, two people who had never known each other, but she was mine,
Harvey, she's been mine for twelve years, you have to understand that. It's hard to give that up. To let it all slip. When it's
meant so much . . ."

"Of course it is, of course it is." Harvey was still inching
backward, his mind filled with a new thought: He shouldn't
call the police, he should call the vet: Jeff was barking.

"We can talk about the past, about Bleeder, about the murder, about everything. I guess I didn't think you had it in you,
Harvey: I guess I doubted that I did. But now it's done I don't
know what to think, don't know what I think of you. I guess
that's why I had to hit you, you took something away as well as
giving something. You know what I mean?"

"Er, yeah. Sure thing, Jeff, but like I say I didn't shag . . . I
mean, I haven't seen your wife since Cornwall, so, you know,
this is a bit pointless . . ."

"I'm not talking about Maisie, Harvey." Jeff had returned to
the counter now and his face was changed. There was a wistful-
ness, an eerie gentleness that Harvey had not seen before. It
made him even more nervous than the menace. "I'm talking
about Hilda Odd."

"Right, yeah. What?"

"Hilda Odd, Harvey. I'm talking about Hilda Odd and I'm

talking about the murder and I'm talking about you. We said we could talk about everything, didn't we? Well, I want to talk about that."

He was going to confess to murder. Jeff was going to confess to him and then he was going to kill him. Harvey had backed as far as he could go and was standing now in the doorway, his fingers on the handle. "Um, look, Jeff, we don't need to do this, yeah? Whatever you've done, whatever's happened, it's in the past, OK, I don't hold anything against you."

"No!" Jeff had straightened up and was back in the vulture position. "And I don't hold anything against you, Harvey. What she did, what she did . . . it's funny, the past, isn't it? You think it will fade but it never really leaves you; you still carry it, you just shore things up, use other things, marriage, sex, houses, cars, all that stuff, all that stuff . . . and then one day it all falls away and there you are. Back there in that room, that basement in that fucking house, that terrible, terrible house, with that woman standing over you . . ."

Harvey glanced quickly behind him; where were his keys?

"Standing over you with that length of plastic wire in her hand. And you are being held down and she's laughing, she's laughing . . ."

"Eh?" The keys were on the desk, and Harvey had measured the leap and planned the run back to slam the door, ram the key home, turn it . . . but he paused. "You what?"

"You know, Harvey. You know as much as I know. You've been there, too. We've always carried that knowledge with us. We carry it but we can't leave it and in the end we face it . . . we face it."

"What do you mean, I know? What do I know? I don't know anything." He was still considering the leap, he could still make it. It was simply a matter of timing.

"Jeff?" He had been so startled by what Jeff was saying that Harvey hadn't registered the sound of the shop door opening, and now Maisie was standing directly behind Jeff, gazing at the scene as if she had entered the stage set of a Russian play. Harvey could see her hair, lit by the weak sunlight from the open doorway like a messy halo, as if she had floated in from some safer, better, holier place, rather than from Croydon. "Jeff," she said again, "what are you doing here? What is this, Harvey?" Why did everyone ask him?

Jeff turned round slowly, his eyes half closed as if he had taken a blow to the face. He turned and faced his wife and she caught for a moment a look she had never seen in his eyes before. But his eyes closed and then reopened and there was Jeff, just as she had left him.

"Ah. So you haven't seen her since Cornwall, Harvey? Interesting." Jeff's back was to the counter and he did not appear to be about to spring but Harvey jumped and grabbed the keys anyway, then shot backward and slammed the door, dropped the keys, swore, fumbled, tried the wrong key in the lock, swore again, found the right one, forced it in, turned it, and then stood panting with his back against the door. It was only after he had stood there for several moments that he became aware of two things: One was that he was not pursued, indeed he could hear the mumbled trace of what sounded like a rather civilized conversation proceeding in the shop; the second was that this was perhaps the most cowardly thing he had done in his life. This did not prevent him feeling deeply relieved to have done it. Jeff wouldn't kill Maisie; they would talk through their differences and then Jeff would go and he and Maisie could go to Cornwall and solve the murder, although really there seemed very little to solve. Jeff was clearly raving bonkers. It occurred to Harvey how very close this was coming to his fantasy: Jeff in prison, and Maisie in his bed. Cool. Maybe all the pain and suffering he had been through was in a good cause. For a moment he was almost religious in his thinking: Maybe it was all for a purpose, to finally bring him some semblance of meaning and reward in his otherwise inexplicable existence. He was very happy now that he hadn't thrown out the

Superman One. Who knows, maybe he could sell it and they'd live happily ever after on the proceeds, sharing some of it with Bleeder, of course. Perhaps they could open a superhero-themed coffee shop together in New York . . . He shook himself physically to pull back into reality. Then he moved to the phone but couldn't think of anyone to ring. So he sat down beside it at his desk and tried to hear what was going on in the shop.

They seemed to be speaking with great solemnity. That was the word that came to his mind. A feeling of solemnity and even of serenity, almost as if they were conducting some sort of religious ritual, a rite. The voices rose and fell, without seeming to falter, as if a script was being followed. This sense was added to by the fact that they rarely seemed to overlap each other, as if politely waiting for each other to finish before speaking. It was rather restful and Harvey, though more than usually happy about it, had had an abbreviated sleep. He settled back in his chair and was just beginning to eye the couch, when the telephone rang. It was Jarvin.

"Mr. Briscow? After much work, our forensic team in St. Ives believes that it has found some DNA evidence that might be relevant to the case. And I wondered if you might come down to the station for a chat this afternoon? We would also need to take a blood sample from you, as from everyone involved."

"This afternoon?" Harvey felt his stomach tighten—something it rarely did. "I'm not sure this afternoon is possible, I . . . I have a lot to do this afternoon."

"Well, it is fairly important, but perhaps we could come to you . . ."

"Of course, of course . . . Let me think. What if I came to you this afternoon? That would probably be the best—yes, give me the address where you want me to come. I could come at about four, would that be all right?" Harvey carefully wrote down the address of a police surgeon in Kensington on the back of an envelope and hung up the phone. Then he carefully tore the

envelope into twenty-six pieces and threw them up in the air.
For a long time he sat in silence. It was only after the long time
had become almost unbearable that it struck him the silence
was significant. Why had they stopped talking? Perhaps Jeff had
murdered her while he was on the phone. With the air of a
mouse in a cattery, Harvey gently re-turned the key in the lock
and pulled the door an inch toward him. The silence continued
and he dared a fraction more. Maisie was sitting on the counter
facing him, with her legs swinging in front of her and a look of
thoughtful sorrow on her face. She had been crying. Stepping
carefully in case of hidden rugby players, Harvey ventured out.

"Hello, Harvey."

"Um, hello. You OK?"

"Mmm. Jeff's gone."

"Oh, right."

"Yes. Thanks for leaving us alone like that just now, it was
very discreet."

"Er . . ."

"In fact, it was the fastest bit of discretion I think I've ever
seen." She smiled a bit crookedly and brought the tissue in her
hand to her face.

"Yeah, sorry, but I thought, well, you know, you'd maybe be
better just sort of thrashing it out, yeah?"

"Yeah. And we did sort of thrash it out. We are going to get
divorced. Jeff's going back to Cornwall. I think he might even
move back there to live. I think he should. We both grew up in
small towns, but where I stayed and dreamed of escaping, Jeff
moved away without ever really leaving. It was one of our many
incompatibilities." She shook her head, no longer framed in
light, but still, to Harvey's eye, angelic.

"Cool. I mean, difficult, but cool, you know? It may be hard
but when it's over you'll be yourself again, yeah? I mean, you'll
be sad and stuff but it'll be you being sad and that's got to be
worth it, because you are really worth it." It didn't sound very
much to Harvey, indeed it had the deathly ring of a shampoo

advertisement, but it had the effect he'd intended. She beckoned him toward her and then climbed off the counter into his arms. And when she wept now it was into the thick roll-neck of his red fisherman's sweater with the holes in the sleeves.

She stayed like that for some time and Harvey let her, wanting to smell the groove of her neck, wanting for a little while to see the world through the tangled sanctuary of her hair. Unfortunately, as he tried this latter pleasure what he saw was Josh, standing pop-eyed about three feet away. Harvey did the sigh. He wouldn't have thought he could do it in her arms, but he did. She tried to give him a squeeze, but he politely disengaged himself.

"Er, Mais, this is Josh."

"Oh, hang on." Maisie did some dabbing with her tissue and turned round. "How do you do?"

"Er, yeah cool. All right, Harvey?"

Harvey was inwardly thrilled. Surely no woman could look at him and Josh and come to any conclusion but that she had made a sound choice in selecting him from the gene pool.

CHAPTER TWENTY-EIGHT

The English countryside somehow looks better when you see it from opposite your new girlfriend. The rolling fields full of factories and pretty industrial estates that separate London from the feral south are given added appeal when there is a genuinely beautiful bit of English nature resting her head against the window and sighing. Harvey, who didn't like to face backward on trains, could see what lay before them down the line. And not just literally, either. He had already planned a whole future for them, perhaps a cottage in the country, to supplement the flat in Chelsea. Was she rich? He didn't know or care really. But even if the *Superman One* angle didn't work out they were going to have a future with money in it. He felt sure of that. He couldn't imagine starving with Maisie beside him. She would inspire him to expansion, to invest in a whole new way of living in the world. He was just concluding his vision with a pony for their first child, and seeing himself suddenly cast rather unexpectedly as Rhett Butler in *Gone With the Wind*, when she turned her eyes to him. She had been lost in reverie for a while, letting the view carry her along like a nanny holding her hand. Apart from the offer of a tin of Watneys, Harvey had respected her need for peace. Now she shook herself like an animal recovering from a shock and smiled. Should he tell her about the phone call from Jarvin? There hadn't really been time at the shop and she had been keen to get away, due no doubt to the emotionally tumultuous experience she had just passed through, but also to the presence of

Josh. Josh had responded to her with a mixture of brooding jealousy and unbridled curiosity. After being thwarted in his attempt to persuade Harvey to join him in the back room alone for a "conflab," he had made some muttered remark about married women, which, when asked to explain, he had denied making. After several less audible mutterings, he had then begun the questioning that had finally driven them out, the words "Well, I'm only asking, I mean she is your bird now, Harvey" still ringing unhappily in their ears. Perhaps Josh didn't reflect so well on him, when Harvey had time to think about it; after all, he had chosen him as his assistant.

"I wonder what would have happened if I hadn't come to the shop when I did." Her head now was tilted down a little as she considered him, and he admired the small freckled-ness of her nose.

"Dunno. Probably have kicked my head in." Harvey sipped delicately from the one can he had allowed himself.

"Yes, perhaps. But I wonder . . . what were you talking about before I came in? I looked through the window, through a tiny gap between all your posters, and I couldn't believe my eyes. I was going to run in and save you, but then I realized he wasn't attacking you, you weren't even shouting. What were you doing, Harvey?"

That was another thing there hadn't been time to tell her about.

"Um, well, we were talking. About you. At least I thought we were. In fact, I'm sure we were at first. But then I think I went on talking about you, but Jeff started to talk about something else."

"What did you say about me?"

"I can't remember."

"Yes, you can. What did you say? What did Jeff say?"

"He said he missed you." Harvey drank more deeply. He might need another, he reflected.

"Did he indeed? What else did he say? The truth, Harvey, please."

He met her eye. Shit.

"He said you were good in bed."

"What?"

"And that you were probably faking any orgasms you might have with me. Which I must admit I don't mind at all. If you are, I mean. Or actually, I'd rather you weren't, if you get me. But if you are, or rather if you did, last night, I mean, and in fact this morning, then, well, thanks very much." He paused, feeling that really that had come out better than he might have expected.

Maisie was shaking her head and Harvey knew what was coming. He did the sigh internally. She might be the most extraordinary woman he could remember meeting, but she was a woman for all that.

"You really mean that after all those years together all Jeff can think of to talk about is sex?"

Harvey sipped his beer and let his mind wander a little; he had enough experience of women to know exactly what was coming.

"And you, when confronted with the ex-husband of the woman you say you like, a man you have known since you were a small boy, a friend you have lost, all you are worried about is whether I fake my orgasms?"

Harvey was aware that while the carriage was fairly empty— the trains usually were quiet after lunch, in his experience— still they had passed one or two people as they made their way to their seats. He didn't worry too much about the noise Maisie was making: This would liven up what was, frankly, a fairly dull journey until they reached the Tamar. He sipped again and then realized she had paused.

"Oh, er, yeah. Well, no. I'm not saying that's all I was concerned about. I'm just giving you the gist of bits of it. He said you would have to fake it with me because I am a wimp or something like that, and I just wondered whether you did or not. It was no big deal. We just talked about lots of things really."

"I see." There was a dangerous note in her voice and he kept his eyes on the landscape. "Well, for the record I have been faking it, as you so elegantly put it, for months. The first time I haven't for a long time was last night. Does that make you feel better?"

Harvey sipped his beer again to disguise the fact that yes, it did. Once again, Rhett Butler came into his mind, "Frankly, my dear..." No, perhaps that wasn't the line, but even so, Clark Gable, Clark bloody Gable, no problem.

"I can't believe how shallow he could be. I must admit it only makes me feel better about being out of there. We'd never talked properly about divorce until this morning, and it had a horrible sound to it when he said it. But now...I guess he's just a waste of time really...a complete waste of time..."

"Well, I don't know..." Harvey had said the words before considering them, and was now struck by the strangeness of standing up for the man who beat him up and from whom he was stealing this woman. "I mean, he might not be perfect but...I doubt he was just a waste of time."

"Are you defending him, Harvey? Is this some manifestation of male solidarity that even I never imagined? Do you think I should give him another chance?"

"No, no," Harvey said hurriedly, and then paused. What was it he was trying to say? "I don't know, it's just—I think there was something going on that you didn't see, in the shop I mean. Jeff was...there was something about you that kept him like he was, if you see what I mean. And now you've gone...I dunno, it's as if he's gone back to where he was. And he's a bit lost and maybe he did something because of that...Oh, shit, I don't know what I'm talking about."

"Hang on, what *are* you talking about? What else did Jeff say?"

"Well, I don't know really." Harvey tried to remember. "I just got the impression . . ."—it sounded silly now to put it into words—"well, the murder and all that. Jeff seemed to be thinking about Mrs. Odd, something like that. I don't know . . ."

"The murder? Jeff didn't know anything about the murder. He can't be involved with that. Why would he be?"

"Well, I don't know, but then why would I be? Except that I went to the house and cleaned up the blood and that—well, OK, maybe I am, but that doesn't mean Jeff isn't. Jarvin seems to think this is all about the past, and remember Jeff was one of the ones who bullied Bleeder the worst. What if there was some memory that he'd forgotten about because he was with you and because it was a long time ago, and then you left him and everything fell down . . . that was what he said: It all fell down, something like that. So he remembered, yeah? And he went back to St. Ives and killed Mrs. Odd."

"Jeff killed Mrs. Odd? Harvey, that's ridiculous." She was looking at him with openmouthed disbelief. "Why Jeff?"

"Because he's a violent bastard, that's why. And he was upset about you 'cause he knew it was over when you went down there, and he was one of the ones who bullied Bleeder. That's why." It did sound a bit thin now that Harvey put it into words. "Well, I don't know. I don't claim to know, but he was certainly a bit psycho in the shop. I thought he was going to batter me, and then he went all sort of mellow and faraway and then he looked like a vulture, although not in that order."

"What are you talking about?"

"I don't know. But there was something weird about him, and then you came in and he went back to being how he always is. Or at least I think he did, but I was in the back room for most of the time, of course."

"Yes, you were, and he certainly seemed just like he always is to me, sadly. I always thought he might change, you know, open up to me. I tried so hard to get inside Jeff, but he never let me in. After twelve years together it still feels like I've been with a stranger. And now this whole breakup has happened and still he just stands there and grins like it's all kind of a joke and as if it all just meant nothing. Maybe it did just all mean nothing, Harvey, maybe it was all just a waste..." She buried her head in her hands and wept.

Harvey had to admit that the fellow travelers who had chosen the 2:27 from Paddington this afternoon were getting their money's worth. From sexual jealousy to murder to marital breakdown. They could have stayed at home watching daytime TV and got no more. He reached across the table and awkwardly rubbed her arm, which was the only bit he could really reach. He considered getting up and going round but that would have meant a struggle past his duffel bag, which was on the seat next to him, and it would have meant sitting down with his back to the engine, which always made him feel sick. So he rubbed her arm and used his free hand to pick up his can and pour some of the Watneys into his mouth and some down his jumper.

When he had cleaned up a bit she had stopped crying and was looking better.

"I'm wondering about his maths teacher," Harvey said brightly when he was sure she was ready.

"Pardon?"

"Bleeder Odd's maths teacher. He met him at the reunion; I saw them together and I was wondering what they talked about."

"Mmm. OK, so it wasn't Jeff, it was the maths teacher?"

"No, I'm not saying that." Harvey wiped his mouth delicately with his sleeve. "I just wonder what they talked about. I bet Jarvin doesn't know about him and I think we should interview him. What if Bleeder told him something important?"

"Like what?"

"I don't know."

"But I thought we were going down to see Blee—I'm not calling him that—to see Charles. We can ask him directly, can't we?"

"Well, yes, we can." To Harvey this seemed somehow rather too easy, like watching *Star Wars* the week after it opened rather than queuing overnight. Surely they should creep up on Bleeder, surprise him with his maths teacher's new evidence, shock him into a full confession . . . that it was Jeff. He said something along these lines to Maisie and she laughed at him and then she got up and came round to remove his duffel bag and settle down cozily in the seat beside him and slid her hand up his leg. Harvey rather lost interest in the countryside for a while and his only thought was that their fellow passengers were perhaps going to get a finale that even daytime TV rarely delivered.

CHAPTER TWENTY-NINE

A town can look very different when you are not staying with your parents in it. It can look even more different, and indeed better, when you are sitting in front of a full English breakfast. Even when you are preparing to meet someone you don't know who may well be going to cause you a certain amount of unhappiness or confusion, it can still look pretty good. Harvey gazed out across the wisps of mist that lay beneath them toward the wild white horses of the sea beyond. They were sitting in the conservatory-style restaurant of the hotel to which they had awarded their business the night before. Harvey had decided that a B and B just wasn't what a youngish couple in something very close to love really needed, and anyway he had long wanted to visit this hotel again. The Atlantic Rollers was set, in an act of glorious Edwardian vandalism, actually on St. Ives's principal outreach from the shoreline, Porthminster Point itself, as if all the people who traveled so far to look at this chunk of wild nature would be delighted to find that their hotel was its principal feature. And indeed it seemed they were, because in the foyer every postcard on sale featured the hotel prominently. The boy-Harvey had looked up at this hotel and one or two others of the same vintage that were dotted along St. Ives's bayfront and wondered at their sense of belonging to another world: like bubbles in which a different air was breathed, city air, with a taste of cigarette smoke and engines and danger in it. And the teenaged-Harvey had, with Steve and Rob in particular, sometimes broken into these vast hotels—forced a fire door or found a broken window, and run down their dark, looming passageways, daring his friends to turn corners, to go further into their vast emptinesses, and then fleeing with smothered shrieks. What he remembered most was the fire escapes that he and the boys would scale to run free on the rooftops, like football fields of white. And always he had wondered what it would be like to come not as a starstruck local boy, nor as an adolescent intruder, but as an adult, as a guest, received and welcomed at the daunting, if faded, splendor of the front door. Having failed so signally to provide Maisie with a memorable location for their first meal, Harvey had sensed that this might be the opportunity to provide their relationship with the sort of romantic mise-en-scène that he was sure all women required.

"Pretty, isn't it?" He sipped his coffee complacently and indicated the view.

"Yes, it is." Maisie spoke across the devastation of a hearty man's breakfast table. She had had toast and coffee; Harvey had had tinned grapefruit segments, porridge, kippers, sausage, eggs, fried slice, beans, and tomatoes. And toast and coffee. "Do you feel like a good long walk before we meet Mr. Simes?"

Harvey had placed both his hands on his stomach to better enjoy the feeling of being absolutely drum-tight, but now he raised them in an attitude of defense.

"You are joking?"

"Perhaps walk off our breakfasts?" She twinkled sweetly and he found that he could deny her nothing.

"Um, OK." He had thought of a little lie-down, possibly followed by a bit of unscheduled sex to fill in the time before eleven-thirty A.M., when Simes had agreed to meet them in the hotel bar. They had got his name and telephone number from Steve. Maisie had suggested that Harvey's parents might remember him, but Harvey had said Steve would be a better bet. Steve had been excited to hear that Harvey was back and had demanded that they meet that evening "for many beers." This nuisance apart, Harvey was satisfied with his progress. Indeed, he was satisfied at this moment with just about everything. Had he not been a fugitive from justice, he might even have whistled as they made their way out into the bracing air. The sea looked even better with the wind whipping their faces from the west. Maisie allowed him to put his arm around her shoulders and cunningly shield himself from it with her body. They walked down the path from the hotel to a gate that led out onto the headland itself. And there the grass was springy and the scent of gorse mingled with the smell of the sea.

"Oh, it's fantastic," Maisie shouted into the wind, and freeing herself from his grasp she ran down the track—distinguished only by a narrow line of more beaten grass—and on between the gorse bushes into the banks of heather beyond. The gorse was not in full flower but the odd yellow head showed itself as an irrational flash of brightness against the massing logic of deep greens and purples. While all for playfulness in its right place, Harvey was unenthusiastic about physical exercise this early in the day. He lumbered after her for a moment or two, but feeling the breakfast shudder dangerously within him he slowed almost at once to a walk. There was a hint of a stitch in his side and he put his hand there and puffed. Then, realizing that she had turned and was watching him approach, he stopped doing both and attempted the confident, outdoorsman's stride. She came to meet him and put her arms round his neck. "God, this place is alive! It makes me feel alive!" This last word was shouted out into the spinning air and she turned and ran again, leading him on down the path where the grass turned to shale and then up onto the rocks beyond. The rocks, black from the mist, lay like great whales beached on a foreign shore, in a reassuringly wall-like formation. Once over the whales' backs, though, they stepped onto a great disc boulder that marked the edge of the cliff and from which they could look down the spinning drop to the sea below.

"Shit." Harvey stepped back and put his hand to the great

blue-whale rock that reared up beside him. "I haven't been up here for ages. I'd forgotten how high it was." Dreams of falling, of rolling down the sides of cliffs, clutching on to tufts of grass that slipped from between his fingers, returned to him. That was the advantage of London, of course: You only had muggers and skinheads infesting your sleeping hours, and the likelihood of being blown into the sea was virtually nil. Maisie did not share his concern and, stepping right to the edge of the great disc, looked down for a long time at the waves boiling against the base of the cliff below. She breathed deeply the stinging salt water in the air and it scoured her lungs, cleaning away the residue of the last few days in London. Harvey stayed back on the whale's flank, patting its smooth, cold, damp sides for reassurance with one hand and feeling for his cigarettes with the other. Before he could locate them, she turned back to him, her hair flying in the wind, a blizzard of curls. Striding forward she looked at him as she had looked at the sea and he felt it carried in her eyes; the green of the deep water washed over him and made him gasp. She pulled up his jumper and ran her hands, icy soft from the wind, over his chest.

"Fuck me, Harvey," she said in a voice he had not heard before. "I need you, right now." And Harvey, wide-eyed with fear at what sex on the edge of a cliff might entail, but also suddenly consumed by the desire to be desired in this all-consuming sort of way, turned her and pushed her back against the whale's side. Then, with a passion that he would later characterize as "a bit D. H. Lawrence," he scrabbled the buttons of her jeans undone, tore them down, and, kneeling on the wet rock, buried his face in her crotch before standing and having what he would also later refer to as "an old-fashioned knee-trembler." The wind beat their bodies but they felt no chill; indeed Harvey was sweating like a racehorse by the time they finished. As they ended she gave a great howl into the wind and listened to it as it was whipped away from her, over the whale's soaring flanks and off inland. Harvey too cried out, though with a more grunting intonation that wasn't carried at all but seemed to stay for ages as a sort of echoed, animal noise under the rocks. She clung to him for a bit, and then with a little laugh found her knickers round her left ankle and restored them and her jeans. Harvey turned from her and, putting his back against the whale, dragged in great gouts of air. He really wouldn't have eaten that breakfast if he'd had any idea . . . He groped in the pocket of his unbuttoned denim jacket, found his cigarettes, somewhat crushed, and then spent several cursing moments attempting to light one in the swirling eddies of the wind.

"That was amazing, Harvey." They had returned to the hotel and were now, red-faced from the sting of salt in the air and from their exertions, sitting in the bar drinking hot chocolates. Still breathing rather heavily, Harvey nodded his agreement. He was already busy writing up the memory in his mind for future repetition to several of his friends. Much of his teenage years had been spent attempting to orchestrate knee-tremblers on headlands, and mostly it had been a history of terrible failure and shame. But now when his mates played that "strangest place" game and someone came up with "in a hammock on a catamaran" or whatever, at least Harvey could provide a half-decent riposte. He grinned at the warm place that he had prepared to keep the memory; it was already part of the new bit of himself that he was calling the Maisie'd bit. It was a part of himself that he wanted to see a lot of.

"You seem to bring something out in me," she went on, making it better and better. "I'm not usually like this, I assure you. I was never like this with Jeff. In fact, he always did all the work, if you know what I mean. But with you . . . I can't keep my hands off you!" She laughed out loud, perhaps slightly longer and louder than Harvey would have chosen, but at least she was smiling—not always a certainty after sex, in his experience. He sipped meditatively of his chocolate and considered whether he should have a doughnut to go with it, but realized that a woman who has only recently watched a man eat a breakfast of frankly heroic proportions might balk at elevenses. So with a little sigh, no more than a breath really, he did his best to take sustenance from the warm thick drink while he watched for Simes. They had never met, and when the old teacher came nodding, birdlike and punctual, into his sight, Harvey considered him with a cool eye. He must be seventy, he thought, and was showing signs of the development of a naturally fit man who has spent too many years sitting down. He stooped and bobbed round the tables, his eyes seeking an ex-pupil that he had never taught, an irritability and potential excitability combined in his darting glance. With the air of one putting another out of their misery, Harvey stood up, startling Maisie slightly as she was telling him about Bristol, and waved his hand.

"Mr. Simes?"

"Yes. Mr. Briscow?"

Harvey got him settled in one of the low green armchairs with battered gold arms and then fetched him a hot chocolate from the bar. When he returned, the old man was telling Maisie about the headland outside and how in past times a hewer would sit in a little hut among the rocks and watch out for the schools of pilchards as they swam into the bay.

"He would have a huge horn," said Simes, "and he would blow the horn when he saw the fish."

Harvey, who was behind Simes at this moment as he returned to sit down, caught Maisie's eye.

"So, he had the horn at the end of the headland?" she said with great interest and Harvey returned to the bar. Once in control he sat and smiled at the testy but eager expression on Simes's face.

"So, thanks for coming," he said politely and Simes nodded. Harvey explained the purpose of their visit. When he had done so Simes regarded him with his head on one side, like a bird considering a Brazil nut.

"You want to know about Charles Odd. Well, that was a long time ago, of course. Although I do remember him well. And I saw him recently at the reunion. He was in the maths club that I used to run, and that was what he spoke to me about. He was very animated, telling me about how much the club had meant to him, as if he felt it necessary to thank me. But it was strange, like he was talking about something else altogether, in a way." He paused and looked thoughtful at that.

Harvey was thoughtful, too. He couldn't remember ever being invited to join the maths club, or in fact any club at all. Where was his club? He ignored the impulse to ask and instead said vaguely: "Right, so a good student, yeah? But a bit knocked about, no? I mean, Bleeder Odd and all that."

Simes considered this illiterate response with a little grimace of distaste. "If you mean Charles was badly bullied at school, then yes, I am inclined to agree with you. But I'm still not clear what your interest is. And"—he turned his attention suddenly to Maisie—"I'm afraid I don't even know your name."

"Oh, sorry. I thought you might have introduced yourselves. Maisie, this is Mr. Simes, Mr. Simes, Maisie Cooper."

"Cooper?" Simes jumped a little at the name and narrowed his eyes. "You are Jeffrey Cooper's wife?"

"Yes, I am." It was Maisie's turn to be surprised. "Do you know Jeff?"

It was a simple enough question but it seemed to stir Simes up to a great extent. He made as if to stand up and then stopped and perched himself on the edge of his chair, glaring at them both. "I feel that I am here under false pretenses, Briscow. You did not tell me that Jeffrey Cooper's wife would be here. I do not understand what you have come here to ask me, nor do I understand what interest you have in this murder." White patches formed in his reddening cheeks, giving him a look, to Harvey's eye, something of the rosetted guinea pig. Maisie glanced, for a moment uncertain, at Harvey, and then she, too, sat forward so that her face was quite close to Simes's.

"What do you know about Jeff?" she asked softly.

The rosettes began to fade a little as Simes sat back and regarded her, then he said: "It is history, of course. Old history. Hardly the need to dredge it all up now." He looked at her for a while and Maisie had the good sense to sit quietly and let him think.

Harvey sighed. If only he had ignored his probably imaginary concerns about Maisie's attitude and got a doughnut earlier it might be easier to concentrate. There was a bowl of them on the bar, fresh-baked and smothered in icing sugar. Shame to waste them. But as he was about to get up Simes spoke again.

"But perhaps it is right that this story should be told. Perhaps to the police . . . well, I will tell you." So Harvey sat back again and bit his fingernails instead.

CHAPTER THIRTY

"It was in 1982," said Simes, "the year Trehendricks won the junior rugby cup, and your husband was one of the best young players we had, Mrs. Cooper." Maisie nodded with, Harvey was pleased to note, a long-suffering air. "He was a bit of a rogue, I think, and he was a bit of a bully. All the rugby lads tended to be high-spirited. They played tricks and could be cruel, but he was the worst by some distance. He had, as I remember, a very domineering father . . ." He glanced at Maisie again and she did the nod with the same air and Simes copied it. "Yes, very domineering, and Jeffrey brought the home into the school. He was unkind to a lot of the smaller, weaker boys, and I was aware of that. For some reason mathematics seems to attract a disproportionate amount of such boys." His eyes gleamed and Harvey and Maisie smiled on cue. "Perhaps it is nature's way of compensating . . . Anyway, several of my boys were treated unkindly by Mr. Cooper, but none as unkindly as Charles Odd. It was as if he had done something personally to enrage Cooper, and he was brutally treated."

"Yes, I can believe that," Maisie said quietly.

"Well, one did what one could," Simes went on. "Although, looking back, I think we might have done more to protect poor Charles, because Jeff Cooper seemed intent on bringing him misery. He would follow him home, ride up and down outside his house on his bicycle shouting out obscenities, singing cruel songs . . ." Harvey felt his bladder tighten and he gulped audibly. "And then Mrs. Odd would come out and chase him away down the road, no mean employer of obscenity herself, by all accounts. We knew of all this because there were complaints to the school, lots of them. From Mrs. Odd herself, although these were somewhat confused and difficult to grasp, but also from other residents in the area. The pursuit of Charles Odd was known about and abhorred by many local people. But still it continued for some time until Cooper was caught." Simes looked round impressively and Harvey realized just how much the old man enjoyed telling stories. He was aware also of the fact, felt instinctively, that he had not told this one before, that this was its maiden voyage.

"He was caught?" Maisie spoke as if she was grasping something that she had missed and was needing to ensure that she heard correctly this time. "Caught by the school, you mean?"

"Oh, no. We'd caught him lots of times, but a bit of bullying in those days, especially by the star of the rugby team, was not a very serious offense. No, this time he was caught by Mrs. Odd."

"Oh, right." Harvey, who had had his head down, looked up sharply at him and then his eyes went very far away. "Caught by Mrs. Odd?"

"Yes. Mrs. Odd got hold of him. Perhaps she was lying in wait. She could be a rather frightening woman, I found. Anyway, she got him—knocked him off his bicycle. The bicycle was badly damaged. I remember that because it seemed to be the only thing his father was really concerned about. But she got him and took him inside her house. Charles was there, too, of course. And she beat them. Both of them. Took them into a basement of the house, stripped them, and beat them with a length of plastic tubing."

"She beat them?" Maisie's voice was clear and sharp now. "These were children, twelve-year-olds?"

"Yes, just children, and she whipped them." Simes nodded, more birdlike than ever. "When he got home, Jeffrey Cooper's back was ripped to shreds. He had to go to the doctor, I believe. The school was appalled: It was about this same time of the year, early spring perhaps, and the rugby season was up and running. But of course the school did everything it could to help cover things up. That was what schools did in those days. Still do, perhaps . . . Certainly, the Coopers were only too keen to participate in smoothing everything over. They didn't want any scandal in their family, though as I say Cooper senior was concerned about the bicycle." He stopped and smiled without pleasure. "Why some people have children I don't understand. But there we are. Jeffrey went into hospital but Charles was at school the very next day, business as usual for him. I only discovered the details of his beating because I found him crying outside the maths club. I made him lift up his shirt at the back. I'd never seen anything like it in all the time I was a teacher. I wanted to call the police, call social services, call someone. But the headmaster opposed it. Bad for the school. Not the done thing. So we did nothing and Jeffrey came back to school and nobody said a word. Even when it happened again a few weeks later, when someone else was caught by her and Charles was beaten again. Still, we didn't speak. All these years we didn't speak . . . And Jeffrey came back and the school won the Junior Cup. Glory days indeed. But the bullying stopped from that quarter at least. I don't think Charles Odd ever had to worry about Jeffrey Cooper again . . ."

Simes turned again to Maisie. "You didn't know of this, Mrs. Cooper?"

"No." Maisie was seeing into another picture than the hunting scene on the hotel wall. "No, I knew nothing about this. Jeff never told me. I wish he had."

"Well, of course, it is not an easy thing to speak of. For a proud, rather arrogant boy like that, and with those parents of his . . . very difficult."

"Yes, yes, it would be." Maisie nodded, as though solving a crossword puzzle clue.

"Well, now, was that what you expected to hear, Mr. Briscow?" Mr. Simes, kindly now, and touched by his own narrative, turned his eyes across the table to where Harvey was slumped. There was a silence for a moment and then Harvey roused himself as if slapped.

"Er, yeah," he said, "good one. Thanks. Fast times at Trehendricks High really. I don't remember that about Jeff; don't think I ever knew. I guess it makes sense of what he was saying in the shop, eh? And of course it gives him a great motive for murder." He laughed loudly and then realized that he was doing it solo.

"You know, really I think that is a dangerous thing to say." Simes shook his head and Maisie joined him.

"Yes, Harvey, please don't say that. This makes everything different somehow. Poor Jeff. And his god-awful father . . ."

Simes's kindliness got even kindlier and while he was patting Maisie's hand Harvey snuck swiftly to the bar. He returned with a large white plate with two doughnuts on it and placed it with a little ceremony in the middle of the table. "Anyone?" he said.

Maisie gazed at him. "I don't believe you're eating again, Harvey, and now of all times . . ."

"Er, no, no, I'm not." Harvey sought to clarify this point. "I just thought Mr. Simes might be hungry. He is our guest."

"Yes. Yes, of course he is. Please do have some, Mr. Simes."

"Oh, thank you kindly. Very nice."

So Harvey had to watch Mr. Simes eat the two doughnuts.

CHAPTER THIRTY-ONE

"You do realize that they are probably looking for me. When I didn't show up for the meeting with him Jarvin probably put out an APB on me across London." Did they have APB's in England? Harvey wasn't sure, but for once the issue didn't seem that significant. He was dissatisfied, and he feared that Maisie was sharing the emotion. "I am on the run and you are my accomplice. Bonny and fucking Clyde."

Maisie took a chip from his plate and licked the salt from it with a certain disdain. "I am not your accomplice. I am your girlfriend and I am helping you to sort out your life, not to flee justice. Anything you may or may not have done in the past I cannot be held responsible for."

Harvey did the sigh. From sex on the cliffs to the sigh in three and a half hours: not bad. "I mean, I am in trouble and all you can seem to focus on is Jeff and his teenage angst. That was twenty-odd years ago, Maisie. I mean, I need help right now."

"OK." She smiled, but registered, in a slight lift and drop of the shoulders, the hard work involved in doing so. Harvey was good at body language. On a clear day he could take offense at up to a hundred yards. He bridled at once.

"Fucking hell, Maisie, we're meant to be saving me. Jeff is history, yeah? He's the past, your past. The future is me and you. Jeff, he could be in jail soon—the sooner the better really."

"He won't be in jail, Harvey. Or if he is, I will be with him . . ."

They were sitting in the Greedy Mackerel on the high street

and Harvey was eating his way methodically through the tastes of his past. On his plate were the remains of a large Cornish pasty, a pile of chips, half a gherkin, some tomato ketchup, and an unused wooden forking device. Beside his plate was a large Coke with lots of ice. Maisie had refused any sustenance, suggesting, again purely through body language, that she was too emotionally involved in what had recently passed to eat. This did not stop her nicking his chips, Harvey noticed. He would have liked to express with his own body language the fact that when emotional he preferred to eat. It didn't mean that he was insensitive; it was just his way, his form of compassion. This was a difficult concept to communicate nonverbally and he wasn't sure it had got across. He lifted the remains of the pasty to his mouth and forced most of it inside.

"I wish I could just talk to Jeff. Maybe I should ring him. But I'm not sure where he is." Maisie had produced a mobile phone on the walk from the hotel into town and she had been fiddling with it ever since. "He said he might come to Cornwall but he didn't say when. He might even be in town right now. Perhaps I should just try our old number . . ." She looked for assistance across the blue plastic table with a picture of a large, grinning dolphin on it. But Harvey had overused the rhetorical potential of the pasty and was now struggling with the implications. She sighed. "I don't know what to do; this has completely thrown me. Why didn't he tell me?"

Giving up the contest, Harvey simply swallowed a large chunk of crust whole and then sat with his eyes screwed up tight as it went down. "That's the fifteenth time you've said that, Maisie, and I wish you'd, like, rest it, yeah? He didn't tell you because he's a closed-up English guy who keeps the family secrets rammed up his arse. Secrets are the currency, you know? You don't give them away; you store them up for the future."

"But I've left him, Harvey." She looked at him with real sadness. "What possible future could there be for us? What could he have been waiting for?"

Well, Harvey could answer those: "No future whatsoever," and "Until after he had killed old Mrs. Odd." Easy. But women, of course, can never see these things and when he tried to explain it she returned to dissatisfied, if she had ever left it.

"No, Harvey. Jeff can't be the killer. You must forget that. It's your fantasy."

Shocked by how true this actually was, Harvey shook his head vigorously. "Why can't he be the killer? You've said yourself he could be violent. He's got a brilliant motive: Anyone who got beaten like that would want to kill Mrs. Odd. He hasn't got an alibi for that morning. He's got standard serial-killer's parents. He's the perfect murderer. Don't protect him; face the facts." He took up three chips and ate them with relish.

His satisfaction was so complete that Maisie found herself laughing despite her better feelings. "No, Harvey," she said, "he has no more motive than you. You wanted the comic," she went on as he tried to protest. "That's the perfect motive, much better than some grudge from the past; you have no alibi; I'm sure you can be very violent when you want to be. In fact, I know you are quite the animal." The fact that her toe suddenly appeared on his inner thigh when she said this had two effects. One was that Harvey did not feel so like protesting at her outrageous reasoning, and the other was that he almost choked on the chips and had to cough pronouncedly and with accusatory glances in her amused direction for several minutes. The pasty and chips were Harvey's suggestion as a way to kill time in St. Ives before Bleeder arrived. They had rung him on Maisie's mobile after getting his mum's number from Directory Inquiries. This had taken rather longer than he had expected: There were a lot of Odds in Cornwall and a fair few in St. Ives. When Bleeder had answered the phone it had been in a strange voice that Harvey had assumed was someone else, but when Harvey announced himself it turned into Charles Odd, successful financier. Bleeder had been unexpectedly amenable to the meeting, and if Harvey had been in an imaginative frame of mind he might almost have said he was expecting his call. But Harvey wasn't, so that possible thought, like so many others he might have focused on at this time, drifted away while Harvey thought about lunch instead.

The toe on his thigh had disappeared while he had his coughing fit, but it returned once more and ran up and down his upper leg while Maisie gazed out at a light drizzle on St. Ives's high street. Harvey had been to this café and others very like it along this road many times in his life. But he had never had an erection in one, not one that he could remember anyway, not a proper grown-up erection. Was she a nymphomaniac? That was a question that popped into his mind. Shagging on the cliffs and then only a few hours later giving him a hard-on in a chip shop. Was this a sign of pathological sexual tendencies? Harvey could only hope so. He glanced at his watch and reached for a napkin. Exploring her psychosis would have to wait, because it was time to go to the pub.

CHAPTER THIRTY-TWO

Bleeder was late. The rain had stopped, so they sat out in the long garden that ran down from the main road and gave the pub its character. Inside, the Golden Lion was fugged with the smoke of too many cigarettes and the unhappy sound of a darts team practicing. So Harvey and Maisie sat at a damp wooden bench in the garden and Harvey felt his incipient piles give a nervous twitch. He had fetched a pint and a half of lager and they waited in silence. Was it the pleasant, restful silence of two people who are at ease in each other's company? Harvey wondered. He had heard tell of such a thing, but had no actual experience to go on. Perhaps it was a pregnant silence. He glanced uncertainly at Maisie, but she was deep in thought and gave him only a vague, not-now sort of smile. Perhaps it was pregnant with all sorts of significances that he was missing. Harvey had always considered himself a sensitive person, but had realized somewhere in his early thirties that he only had one sort of sensitivity: the one that meant he was easy to upset; he did not have that other sort that meant he knew what was going on. Mostly he had seen this as a positive thing. Who wanted to know the insides of other people's minds, for heaven's sake? It was bad enough knowing his own. But it was, he had become certain, a factor in his relative lack of romantic success. Relative, that is, to actual human beings. Compared to Josh he was Warren Beatty, but this fact was bringing him less and less satisfaction. He looked again at Maisie, but she was gazing past him down the crazy-paving pathway that led from the road and Harvey heard a footfall behind him. Turning, he found that it was Bleeder Odd.

"Um, all right, mate?" Now that Bleeder was here, Harvey suddenly had the irrational wish that he wasn't. He often did that: spent weeks arranging something and then at the last minute wished it wasn't happening.

"Good afternoon, Harvey. Good afternoon..." He smiled vaguely at Harvey but his eyes were on Maisie. "Mrs. Cooper, perhaps?"

"Yes. You must be Mr. Odd." Harvey wanted to laugh but didn't. Was there a Mr. Odd in the Mr. Men? He couldn't remember. He made a mental note to check when he had a moment. There certainly should be. "Mr. Odd liked to hang round school playgrounds waiting for little Miss Dainty..." He shook his head hard to break the spell and watched Bleeder climb awkwardly onto the wooden bench beside Maisie.

"Drink, Charles?"

"A drink? Yes, all right. I'll have a peppermint cordial." Harvey looked at him for a long moment. Was he being made a fool of? Neither Bleeder nor Maisie was smiling. He got up heavily, keeping his eyes on Bleeder's face, and made for the bar and the inevitable comments of the darts team with measured tread.

Bleeder had turned to Maisie and she to him. Because they were sitting side by side, they found that they were now rather close together and they peered uncomfortably into each other's eyes.

"I suppose I am wondering why you have come, Mrs. Cooper," Bleeder said, turning his gaze to a pink cement toadstool that enhanced the herbaceous border running down the garden beside the path. "I thought perhaps I would see your husband at some point. I did wonder if I would hear from him..."

"Yes, of course, you knew him, didn't you? You knew Jeff?"

"Oh, indeed. We were in the same year at Trehendricks."

He radiated such easy assurance that Maisie felt she could ask him. She turned for a moment to check that Harvey had gone and then said: "I am glad actually of a moment alone with you, Mr. Odd, or Charles, is that all right?" Bleeder smiled his agreement. "And I'm Maisie, by the way. I don't want to rush into things but we may not be able to speak alone like this very much, and I have heard a rumor about my husband, about when you were boys together here in St. Ives, and I was wondering if I could ask you about it."

"A rumor? Oh, yes." Bleeder nodded thoughtfully. "I suspect I can guess what that rumor was, but I'll let you tell me."

"Well, 'rumor' is an unpleasant word, actually. I don't mean that anyone has been gossiping about you or my husband. It's nothing like that. But I did hear a story from the past. It concerned Jeff and it concerned your mother, Mrs. Odd. The story I heard involved her punishing Jeff, beating him, beating you both, if the story is true. A very cruel punishment . . ." She was watching Bleeder's face, but his eyes remained on the toadstool. "It is just that Jeff never told me this story. I heard it from another source altogether. The story also suggested that he had been very cruel to you, that he was a bully and that in many ways he probably deserved what he got. But he has never spoken of it, you see. And I just wondered if it was true. Somehow it would kind of explain some things about our relationship, our marriage. It would sort of add up to something different than it did before, if you see what I mean . . ."

"Yes. It would add up differently." There was a slight change to Bleeder's voice and again she tried to pull his eyes round to meet her own, but they remained fixed, very still in his very still face. She noticed that the ginger hair was thinning at the back and that he had carefully combed the strands across the gap. She wondered if that was for her.

"Did she punish him, Charles? It would really help me to know. The story said that she grabbed him as he was cycling around shouting abusive comments. I assure you that I wouldn't pass any judgment on her at all; it sounds as if Jeff behaved terribly badly, wickedly really. I just really need to know . . ."

Bleeder's head did turn but it did so rather too slowly, so that even though she had called them to her, by the time his eyes met hers she was wishing they wouldn't. Finally, he looked straight at her for a moment in absolute silence and she held the eyes for a second and then turned to the toadstool herself.

"Yes, my mother did catch people who rode their bicycles outside our house," he said slowly. "But it wasn't the shouting, it was the singing. She didn't like the singing." And to Maisie's horror a high falsetto voice emerged from the face so close to her cheek that she could feel his breath hot and sour against it.

" 'Bleeder Odd he's a runt, he looks like a spastic and his mum's a cunt.' That's what they sang, Maisie, outside my house. My mother hated the singing. So she would hide sometimes by the wall with a stick, and when they came she would jump and throw it into the spokes of their wheels. She caught one or two that way. She caught Jeff, that's for sure. And she caught Harvey Briscow. Oh, yes." He reacted to her face, which swung much faster than his, to reconnect with his eyes. "Oh, yes, Harvey sang that song, too, or some variation on it. They were quite creative. There were lots of different versions."

"Oh, Charles." Maisie reached out and instinctively took his hand for a moment. "I'm so sorry."

"Bastards." Harvey gracelessly plonked down a wineglass with a pale liquid in it on the table. He had also bought himself another pint, which he put down with more care.

"Who?" Maisie jumped and gazed up at him with an expression both of annoyance and of doubt. As she did so she felt Bleeder's hand slip from her own.

"Those bloody darts players. They thought it was hilarious that I wanted a peppermint cordial. I had to order a pint as well just to stop them saying it was for me. Do you really drink that stuff, Charles? Or are you just having a laugh?"

"I rather like it." Bleeder picked up the glass and sipped it delicately. "I got the taste out in Saudi Arabia, where I worked for a time. One learns to live without alcohol and this is a popular substitute."

"Right, well, OK. But we're not in bloody Arabia now, are we? When at home, beer is the correct drink." Harvey finished off the remains of his first pint in a single gulp and carefully substituted the full glass for the empty. "Now, what have you two been chatting about?"

"Nothing that you need to hear." Maisie glanced at Bleeder, wanting to welcome him into a confidence, but his eyes had left hers and were riveted on Harvey.

"OK, fair enough. But I do need to ask you some things, Charles, OK?" Harvey was very aware of Bleeder's gaze. It seemed to root him to the spot; even moving his head from side to side felt strangely performed in the face of this piercing witness. He took a long pull on his drink and then added: "So let's chat."

"All right." Bleeder spoke with the same eerie slowness that had unnerved Maisie. "You can ask me anything you want to know. But I think perhaps it might be better if we spoke alone, H. There are things that you might want to hear alone."

"What? No, no, that's all right." Harvey was suddenly panicked. "Anything you say to me you can say to her, to Maisie, I mean, no problem." But Maisie was already getting up.

"I think Charles is probably right, Harvey. He does need to speak to you. There are things that you need to hear, things that come out of your past. And I need to think about this. I need some space, actually." Suddenly she was up and ready to go, needing to be away from these people, needing for a moment to be just herself and to make some kind of sense of all the new information that this day had brought her. "I'll take myself for a walk, get some air in my lungs. I'll see you later, Harvey, OK?" She stopped for a second and put her hand on his arm. "It'll be all right, just let it happen, OK? Let it be."

And with that she strode away down the path. Harvey watched her rear view appreciatively. That's got a wiggle in it, he thought with a hint of proprietorial pride, and then turned his attention back to Bleeder. "So," he said, and grabbed his glass as a prop, "we need to talk, yeah? I mean, I think we were going to at Steve's but I kind of had to go and stuff. But you know, I guess it's about the past and your mum and so on, really. If you want to talk, I mean, you know, no problem." He was drinking fast; this really wasn't his territory. Was this how policemen did it? He felt more like some sort of amateur psychologist. Bleeder was sipping his peppermint cordial with every appearance of pleasure and made no immediate response. But then suddenly he stood up. Harvey, though unnerved, was also thrilled; he was leaving, thank Christ for that.

Bleeder looked down at him for a long moment and then said: "I think we should walk, too, don't you, H? I feel like I need to move; this is hard to talk about over a pub table." He set off down the path and Harvey watched his arse with less enthusiasm. Bony butt, he thought. It was also Bleeder's round, of course. Harvey shook his head at this display of bad manners, threw his head back, poured the rest of his drink down his throat, and got up. For a second his own arse entered his mind and he wondered how it would appear as he followed the path to the gate. He attempted a sexy wiggle, stumbled, and almost fell over the pink toadstool. "Ridiculous bloody thing," he muttered and then sped up to catch Bleeder as he walked away down St. Ives's high street.

CHAPTER THIRTY-THREE

They walked for a while back the way Harvey and Maisie had come that morning. Bleeder set a faster pace than Maisie and also he didn't hold his hand, so Harvey enjoyed it less and wished they could stop. However, he could see that discussing murder in the high street with numerous Cornish people—a type renowned for their inquisitiveness—milling about was not really such a wise idea, so he followed meekly as Bleeder led them back toward the headland. Perhaps they could go in the hotel bar or something, find a quiet corner, get it over with. In truth, he'd have been happy to stay in the pub garden, have another beer, watch Bleeder go and order a peppermint cordial in front of a room full of drunken comedians; that would have been fine. But he followed Bleeder's narrow arse and watched it make its slightly mincing journey through the busy streets and out onto the quieter, open road that led to the headland. There Bleeder paused and waited for Harvey to join him, then side by side they walked down through the gorse toward the waiting whale rocks.

"So the time has come for us to speak, H. I guess I always knew it would." Bleeder had slowed now and Harvey, relieved, came to a full stop.

"Er, yeah, OK. It's good to talk." Harvey put on an attempt at a cockney accent when he said this last sentence, remembering Bob Hoskins. He glanced ahead at the rocks and felt a warm glow of memory. He'd shagged up there.

"To speak about the past, both distant and recent. To talk it all through . . ." Bleeder's voice was fading in the breeze. "To finally let it all out. It is something I have been doing in different ways for many years. I have had psychoanalysis, H. I have been through that process, and I have trusted it to bring me here, to this point where I can stand with someone I once knew, in a place where we grew up, and feel not anger, nor bitterness, but hope. Dare I say it, I can almost feel pity." He looked at Harvey with an expression that did seem pitying and Harvey reached for his cigarettes. He hardly knew what to say. Psychoanalysis? Jesus, he knew Bleeder was mad. There followed a similar performance around lighting the cigarette, although it didn't last as long as it had earlier because the wind had dropped and Harvey had got slightly better at it. Once he had taken a long drag to chase any hint of fresh country air from his lungs, he said: "Er, yeah, OK, Charles, we can talk, but I wouldn't get too many hopes up, yeah? I mean, I don't do that much of this, you know?" He gave a sort of laugh at the end in the hope that Bleeder would smile and they could maybe just have a bit of a joke instead, but Bleeder did not. He nodded in a way that Harvey found rather patronizing and then turned to gaze into the distance.

"I suppose I should say that for a long time I hated you the most, H. More than Jeff Cooper or Carl Butcher or Rob Calderwood or any of those other sports boys, 'the jocks,' as the Americans would call them. They were cruel to me, of course, but your cruelty was greater."

"Um. OK." Harvey stepped back and prickled himself on a gorse bush. "Fuck, ow. OK." Did Rob pick on Bleeder, too? He couldn't really remember but he assumed Bleeder must know. He really had managed to unite the school, quite an achievement. Harvey began to grin and then turned it into what he hoped was a sensitive grimace.

"You probably want to know what I mean," Bleeder went on without turning back, thus wasting Harvey's expression, "because, of course, you didn't pick on me the way those others did."

That was right. Harvey nodded vigorously; he didn't bully Bleeder, whoever told Jarvin that he did was wrong, he was one of the good guys, on the side of righteousness and justice. He pictured Spider-Man for a moment, how he looked after Aunt May died and Mary Jane left him. So unjustly dealt with. He took a long sad pull on his cigarette. He knew that feeling.

"And what I mean is that I looked to you for help. You were one of the people I really thought might stop what was happening. You could have done. You had the status in our year to stop it. You could have made friends with me. I just needed one friend, H, and then I might have been OK. If you had done that I might have survived what happened, might even have had a youth I could remember without a professional there to help me. For so long I hoped that you would be my salvation. That's what my analyst said: You were my fantasy, the one I dreamed would save me. And then I heard the singing outside my house. I heard Rob Calderwood's voice, and next to it I heard yours. Do you remember that day, H? Do you? Do you know what it felt like to have been through that with Jeff only a few weeks before? And to be back there, locked in that house with my mother, hearing those voices again, singing that same song, hearing Mother going out to hide by the wall to try to grab another of them, and then to realize that one of the voices was yours? Can you imagine that, H? Is it in your range of possibilities? I think that was the greatest betrayal of them all. I think it was the moment when I realized it wasn't ever going to be all right. Do you remember, Harvey, the day my mother caught you?"

"Eh?" Harvey's mind had begun to wander slightly at the point when Bleeder said he had status in the school. He did really. He'd been popular and influential. Where had that status gone? Why didn't he have any status now? If the boy is the father of the man, where was his position and influence in his current life? Bossing Josh around, that was about it, and Josh bought *Pokémon* cards. He wanted to do the sigh, but realized that it might really be Bleeder's prerogative. As for the rest, that was bollocks and Bleeder should know it, especially if he'd had therapy. Nobody could save anyone else. Harvey had known that as long as he could remember. But this last remark caught him by surprise and he choked a little on smoke.

"When she caught me?" he said, spluttering.

"The day you were singing outside my house, not the first time probably, but the first that I realized it was you, recognized your voice alongside the others. And she came out and grabbed you, don't you remember that?"

Harvey thought for a long moment, then slowly nodded.

"Er, yeah, kind of. She sort of told me off and stuff, and you said I was your mate and that I didn't do it before, so let me off. So she did, sort of thing." Harvey shrugged. He did remember, of course, bloody scary it had been, but what did Bleeder want, a letter of thanks? Madwoman grabbed him and shouted at him. He should have had her arrested. He took a last drag and flicked the butt, with insolent skill, into a rabbit hole.

"Yes, I saved you. You see? You would have been beaten, like Jeff, but I stopped that. And then I was beaten instead." He had turned to look at Harvey now and reacted to his expression. "Oh, yes, I got my licks for being friends with someone who would sing like that. My analyst made a lot of it. I wanted so much to be saved but instead I saved you. You see?"

"Er, yeah, yeah. Nice one. Clever. I mean cheers, thanks for that, saving me and so on. I didn't know you got whacked."

"Oh, yes. I got 'whacked' when I saved you, but I couldn't save Jeff. Or at least I didn't. I let him be beaten, with the plastic tube. I let him see just what could happen. And I think he saw what life might be like. I mean, after that he pretty much left me alone. But I saved you and took the beating on my own.

And I stole the strip of plastic, to bring to you. Do you remember, H? That day we did the swap? The length of plastic that I brought to school. I wanted you to see it. It still had my blood on it, you know? I was waiting for you, and you didn't even notice the blood; you wanted it to play at snapping off the nettle heads with. So you swapped it with me, for a comic, a *Superman One*. The *Superman One* that I kept for so long. That was in the box at my house. You do remember, H; I know you do, because you were the one who reminded me."

Bleeder's voice had been rising and he had begun twisting his head from side to side as if shaking away the memory, as if keeping it at bay as a horse does with a swarm of flies. But now he was slowing and speaking with more precision. "And I had forgotten that. Blanked it out. Forgotten that day so deeply that even in analysis I didn't speak of it. Even when I thought I was cured it was out there in history, in this place, this cruel and vicious place." He turned right around, spreading out his arms to encompass the great sweep of Porthminster Point, with St. Ives Bay away behind it and the sea on either side. Two passing hikers gave him a funny look and stepped round his arms. "Afternoon," one said, and Harvey, who had been watching their approach over Bleeder's shoulder, nodded politely. Bleeder paused until they had passed away down the path and disappeared where it snaked around the rocks. "I had forgotten." He spoke more quietly and with a limpness in his shoulders, as if the spell holding him together had been broken. "I had forgotten until you spoke to me in the car at the reunion, asked me if I still had that comic. And it all came flooding back. I remembered that I didn't even tell you what you'd done. That was what I think was buried deepest. That I let you have the strip of plastic as if I was giving away a toy. I remember looking at your fingers as you took it to see if the blood made them red. It's funny how vividly I can remember what was so recently buried away. And I did it for a comic. Is there a more ridiculous story than that? I gave away everything for a comic..." He had turned and was looking away, back toward the hotel, the roofs of which could still be seen above the rise of the land. But as he spoke again he swung back, as if unable to be still. "And that's why I killed her, I suppose. Because that memory was just one too many, and too suddenly recalled. I still needed to make some kind of reparation, you see. To put right what had been done so wrong. So that morning, on the Sunday, when I woke up I knew what I had to do. It was as if my dreams had told me—and they can; my therapist explained that to me. My dreams had brought it to a point, the necessary point where I could finally end it and stop it all. It was easy really. Killing is really very easy."

"Er, what?" Aware of the gorse bush, Harvey didn't step backward again. But he wanted to. Bleeder's eyes were riveted on his own. This would have been so much better in the pub garden, he felt. He glanced round, looking for the hikers, but they were long gone into the rocks. Were they having it off? he wondered vaguely, and the picture of the two midseventies male hikers pressed up against the whale rock was so startling that it snapped his attention back to Bleeder.

"I killed her, Harvey."

"Um, right you are." Harvey could feel that he was so far out of his depth now that he might as well have been swimming across the bay. What on earth did he say now? "So you, er, you did the deed, yeah?"

"Yes, I did the deed." Bleeder's voice was calm and clear now. "I don't know why I haven't been arrested for it. In some ways it would be easier if I was." Harvey nodded vigorously. "But apparently the police have found other evidence of someone breaking in. I don't know what that is about..." He tailed off and shut his eyes for a moment. "I had thought it would be the solution, that everything would be different afterward, and for those first few days it was, I think. But you know, I'm not sure it works like that for long. I'm not sure it isn't still all there

really. It may even be that in the end this will only be one moment, another stage in all the stages I have been through..."

"Yeah, right, well, hey, maybe you should, like, tell the police, you know?" Despite the gorse, Harvey had moved away a
little and could feel it clawing at the back of his trousers. "I
mean, it wouldn't be fair if anyone else gets kind of implicated
and stuff, yeah? And also maybe that is what you need to do,
maybe if you confess, it will be a release and you will experience closure." Even as he spoke Harvey was rather proud of his
words. Even under pressure like this he could bullshit with the
best of them. And he'd always known it was Bleeder: That was
the thing. If he ever got off this headland and out from the laser
beam of Bleeder's attention he would tell the world, or Maisie
at least—and bloody Jarvin—that he'd known it all along:
Bleeder, obvious.

"In many ways I suppose I have fulfilled my destiny,"
Bleeder continued. "My analyst was rather a Freudian, rather a
traditionalist; I suppose for him I am something of a success
story." And Harvey was horrified to hear a sort of cackle at the
end of Bleeder's words. As he finished speaking them, Bleeder
moved off down the path. "Come on, Harvey. I want to show
you something." And he set off toward the rocks.

Harvey was rooted momentarily to the spot, uncaring of
the sharp points in his lower buttocks. His mind worked fast.
He was on a headland with a self-confessed murderer; he had
been accused of being that murderer's worst enemy in childhood; the murderer was leading him toward the cliff edge. He
stood for a long moment, uncertain, then shrugged his shoulders and followed Bleeder down the path to the whale rocks.
Mad or not, it was still Bleeder; he could take him out, no problem.

CHAPTER THIRTY-FOUR

What Bleeder wanted to show him, Harvey had already seen. The disc of rock where you could stand and look down to the angry entrapment of the waves below looked no better with Bleeder on it. Harvey put his back to the blue whale where he'd so recently stood with Maisie and indulged in a happy memory. This time he lit his cigarette with no trouble at all; he was getting used to outdoor smoking, something he was very good at in his youth. After he had lit it and put the pack away he remembered his manners and offered one to his new confidant, but got no coherent response as Bleeder stood peering over the edge. Harvey had never stood on a cliff top with a murderer before, but was pleased to find that he quickly adapted to the experience.

"Um." He cleared his throat and then broached a subject that was close to his heart. "About that comic, the *Superman One*, Charles, did you, I mean, was it found at the scene sort of thing?"

"The comic?" Responding this time, Bleeder stood up straight and turned back from the edge. "Yes, oh, yes, it was in the box in the cellar. That's why she died. I started going through my things and there it was, clean as a whistle, just as I left it all those years ago. But you must know that already, H. I sent it to you at your shop."

"You sent it to me?" Harvey was astounded. Bleeder sent him the comic; after all these years of dreaming exactly that, it had come true. Was this perhaps the time in his life when everything he had ever hoped for just happened? Why hadn't he hoped for Britney Spears? He put that thought away where it belonged and gazed at Bleeder, who nodded.

"Of course, where did you think it came from? It just seemed right to return it to you. It was yours, after all. And now you run a comic shop. You had nothing to run away from, you see; in your past there was nothing to hide from so you stayed where you were: reading comics and doing swaps and listening to pop music, all that. That's what I meant about feeling pity. I have come so far from here, but you have stayed right where you were, right here in St. Ives."

This was so catastrophically unfair that for the first time since they met at the pub, Harvey became genuinely animated.

"You fucking what? I moved to London, mate. I live a life as far away from this as it's possible to bloody get. I mean, OK, your mother was straight out of the Bates Motel, but that doesn't mean nobody else had problems. I had problems."

"Like what?" Bleeder was doing that piercing thing with his eyes again and Harvey withered beneath it.

"I don't know, stuff, problems, my parents didn't under-stand me kind of stuff, you know. I mean, OK, I wasn't getting the lash every twenty minutes but that doesn't mean everything was easy. You should meet my dad, he's fucking weird."

"Yes, yes, I'm sure." Bleeder nodded and spoke without sar-casm but Harvey was aware that the words weren't really adding up.

He sighed a sort of medium strength and said: "OK, look, I mean, thanks for the comic, yeah? I didn't expect it, and I have to say it kind of freaked me. I thought someone was setting me up for murder sort of thing. But I should say that actually it is worth a bit of money, you know, not loads, but, well, quite a load really. So I don't know if maybe you should have it back, or we could share it or something . . . Whatever you think, yeah? Charles?"

But Bleeder was moving away from the edge, past where

Harvey stood and back along the path. Harvey, with another expert flick of his cigarette over the parapet, followed. Did Bleeder not realize what he'd just said? It was as if he hadn't heard. And Harvey had just made the most generous offer of his life. All he'd dreamed of—the coffee shop with the superhero pictures, the wealthy married life with Maisie, all of it—he'd just offered to give it up, to give it back to Bleeder. And why? Shit, why? Oh, because Bleeder saved him and Bleeder needed a friend back then, but didn't get one, so he would be a friend now. All this was moving through his mind and melding together to form a large black blob of hurt feelings. This was as moral as he got. This was all he could do; there really wasn't any more. He almost ran after Bleeder, who was now pacing the path with swift foot. It had begun to drizzle again and Bleeder's hair was shining in the gathering light of the afternoon.

"I mean it, Charles. You can have it back." But Bleeder didn't respond in words; he simply stepped off the path and stalked away between two gorse bushes across the high back of the headland. "Charles?" Really quite plaintive this time, and then Bleeder turned.

"I think I need some time on my own, H. I've said more than I'd planned and I need to take stock. Let's ... let's talk again . . ." He was moving away, the second person that afternoon to need time apart from him to think, and the hurt feelings grew and solidified.

"Well, that's charming," said Harvey. "Thanks a bundle."

"I'm—what do you mean?" Bleeder paused, astonished.

"The comic. I offer it back to you and you don't even respond. It's worth money, Charles, for Christ's sake. I could have sold it if I'd wanted to, you know. I could be well off now. But I didn't, I kept it for you, and all you do when I offer it to you, for nothing, is ignore me." There were reasons why this wasn't a terribly good speech and Harvey could kind of see them, but really everyone seemed to be just saying what they were thinking today, so it just boiled out. And if it wasn't really true as such, it did at least reflect honestly how he was feeling. Sort of. Bleeder gazed at him with a kind of faraway amazement on his face and then closed his eyes for a long moment.

"I think you should keep the comic, Harvey. I think that is probably what you should do, all right? I think perhaps the comic is what this is about for you and I'm glad we could discuss it. But now I must go for a while." And he turned again to the narrow space between the bushes that formed a little pathway across the headland and he followed it until it turned and bore him out of sight.

Harvey stood for a while where he was. I am experiencing conflicting emotions, he told himself. But it wasn't really true. Jesus Christ, it's mine! And he set off, suddenly pumped up with emotion, until he broke into a run and gamboled like a flat-footed lamb along the path, back toward the hotel. The murder was solved, he was rich, and he'd got Maisie, and everything was going to be just totally, totally perfect.

CHAPTER THIRTY-FIVE

Maisie wasn't there, which was the only setback of the
day really. There was no one guarding reception so Harvey simply leaned over the counter and stole the key. Once in his room
he paced the floor for a while and then had a shower, being still
slightly sticky from the first encounter on the cliffs and sweaty
from the second. But when she didn't return after about an
hour, he went out again. He couldn't be still. Feeling sure that
he would meet her on the return journey, he left the hotel, untended as far as he could tell, and walked back into town. He
needed a drink, and someone to drink with, preferably female
and gorgeous. He made for the Lifeboat, still waiting to meet
her eye in the faces that he passed, still expecting her voice to
call to him in a way that meant she had been looking for him.
But she didn't come. The Lifeboat was the pub they always
drank in on Friday nights when he was seventeen, good for
pulling and good for scrumpy that made you sick after only
three pints. He had entered and ordered lager when he heard a
voice in his ear.

"Hello, H, you're early, I thought we weren't meeting till
seven." It was Steve.

"Er, yeah, all right, mate?" Harvey allowed the situation to
occur without any comment on his part.

"It's only half six. Is this the new Harvey Briscow? Weren't
you always fashionably late for everything?"

"Er, yeah, but I've not much to do today." No point in not
lying.

"No? Try having a baby, there's never not much to do. That's why I had to get out: bit of peace and quiet. I'm not allowed out that often, but for the great H. Briscow, Jean makes an exception. What am I having, by the way? Oh, pint of Tribute, please, thanks, Harv."

So Harvey ordered Steve a drink and relaxed onto his bar stool.

It was a longer night than he had planned, but he wanted to be with someone. Harvey rarely shared confidences, and certainly told Steve nothing of the day's unfolding, but he did like someone there to exchange pointless platitudes with, someone whose shoulder he could look over in the hope of spotting someone better to talk to. Irrationally, he kept thinking she would walk in and their eyes would meet and he'd blow off Steve and she would sit on the bar stool next to him and she wouldn't tell tedious stories about child care and childhood; rather, she would listen, rapt, as he recounted the Bleeder experience. Because he was suddenly desperate to tell someone what Bleeder had said. He was off the hook; the nightmare was over. No more tears, as both Johnson's Baby Shampoo and Ozzy Osbourne had put it in their time. No more tears. He did the sigh a few times during the evening. He was off the murder rap and he was rich. But still he had to listen to Steve retell how he deflowered Melanie Simpson in the back of a Ford Capri. It lacked that feeling of momentousness really.

When at last they left the pub he found it was nearly midnight and the stars of his youth, mysteriously absent in London, had returned to the night sky. They steered each other in somewhat haphazard style along the seafront, where the roar of the surf seemed so like the call of home that for a second Harvey almost thought of relocating the superhero café and going back to his roots. This brought to mind a song and he sang it with Steve in enthusiastic if misguided harmony. They carolled American-style harmonies together and then stepped down from the roadway onto the sand and Steve fell over and Harvey fell over Steve and then they lay and smoked on the sand for a bit until Harvey realized that it was bloody freezing.

"Come on." He roused his friend who was in danger of sleep and, cursing now and stumbling, they made their way along the road and up the hill toward his hotel.

"Igothisway." Steve said it as one word and, slapping Harvey brutally across the shoulder blades, moved away into the deep darkness of a small country town in winter.

"Yeah, and I go that." Harvey nodded, confident on that point, and set off toward the deeper black of Porthminster Point for a third time.

Whatever magic carries drunks homeward also works with hotels, and it was only a short time later that Harvey, grimacing with the effort of simply staying upright, found his way into the revolving door of the Atlantic Rollers. Revolving doors are difficult things at the best of times and this one seemed designed to confuse. First it wouldn't go at all, then it went very quickly and Harvey found his nose pressed to the glass paneling. Trying to right himself only made it go faster and as it completed its journey Harvey shot out of it, as if finishing a running race. As a bolt of light he flew into the foyer, across the polished wood floor, and collided, pinball-like, with the counter.

"Ow. Fuck." He put both hands on the top and gasped for air. "Shit."

"Mr. Briscow?" The voice made him jump so high that he almost cleared the counter, then, in terror, he peered over it to find a small, bald, disapproving man sitting behind it holding his key.

"Er, yeah, thanks." Harvey took it in trembling fingers and prepared to push himself off from the counter in the direction of the stairs.

"There was a message left for you earlier, sir." The man said "sir" as he might say "bastard" and Harvey bristled.

"Yes, what is it?" He spoke not unlike James Bond: Sean Connery or Pierce Brosnan definitely. Without a word, the man held out a piece of paper and Harvey took it with the air of one who often receives messages in hotels. He might have said "Ah, this will be from M" or he might not; afterward he couldn't remember. What he did do was make it to the stairs and up them out of sight before he tore the folded paper open and read the message.

Dear Harvey,

I have had a very long think about things and I have decided I must go to Jeff. Everything Mr. Simes and Charles Odd have said only makes me think that I may have completely misunderstood so much that has happened to him—and to you. I need to talk it through with Jeff and find out how this affects us. So much has happened. So much seems different from how it was in London. I don't know what happened in the past. I don't know, but you do and you must work it through with Charles. I would stay with you if I could and try to help, but I really need to think too. The last few days have been amazing. Everything about them feels unreal, dreamlike. I think you must go and talk to the police now. Jarvin will listen to you and he will believe you as I believe you. I will ring you soon: back at your shop perhaps. Please don't think too harshly of me, I'm just so confused. I'll speak to you very soon, my dear.

Love Maisie.

It was a long time that Harvey stood in the dim light of the hallway staring at the neat swirls of girlish script in his hand, grunting audibly to himself, before stumbling, half blind, up into the massing intestines of the hotel to his room and falling into a dead and painful rest.

He read the note again in the morning, but still it made no sort of sense. He'd told her what happened in the past. And what had he done since? What had Charles said? Harvey lingered over a breakfast, identical to the one the day before in all but his companion. It somehow didn't taste as good, nor when he patted the drum of his belly did it feel nearly as satisfying. She had gone to Jeff. That was the only salient point as far as he could see; it was certainly the one that he could most immediately understand. She had gone to Jeff.

Did that mean that she had gone back to Jeff? Or did it mean she was meeting him for a coffee and a chat about old times: "I hear you got whipped," "Yeah," "Right, see you later" sort of thing. Harvey tried this on in his mind but was unhappy with it. Why go right now? Why not wait so they could leave together today? Why not do it by phone? Why do it at all? He shook his head over the coffee and observed specks of dandruff settle on its surface. His hair was growing; he hadn't had time to get it shaved for two weeks. He needed to consider his position. It would mean him paying for the room, of course, and he'd sort of hoped they'd go dutch. But that, he insisted firmly to himself, was the least of the issues. It was seventy pounds a night, mind, but that was unimportant. He did the sigh. Maybe she'd be sitting swinging her legs on the counter of his shop when he got home. Maybe she'd be standing outside Inaction Comix waiting in the rain, her eyes filled with tears of remorse. Maybe. He took himself out onto the headland for a breath of fresh air and smoked a cigarette while he did it. His mind ran over the events of yesterday. Had something changed? How had a completely spontaneous shag on the rocks transformed into that note? For all the thinking he did he could not find the point of change, the moment of reverse alchemy that turned gold into base rubbish. With heavy heart he returned to his room—that had been their room—packed his bags, and paid the extortionate bill: more than he'd anticipated because he'd forgotten that breakfast wasn't included. On the walk to the station he was just passing Sainsbury's when his mother came out carrying two plastic bags of shopping and it was only by dropping to his knees behind a parked car and lying on his side in the public thoroughfare that he avoided being seen. Then stealthily—shocked into vivid attention by the closeness of this encounter—he slunk to the station and boarded the 10:47 to Penzance and from there a direct connection back to London.

CHAPTER THIRTY-SIX

Maisie stood outside the house she had lived in for eight years, and looked at it for the first time. Often, in the past, her sight had been edged with a bitterness that she saw now as having a reddish hue. But the redness was gone and she was almost surprised to find that it was actually a rather pretty blond house, built of the local white stone. She did know it: It had so much of her in it, yet she was looking for the first time with the option of not entering, of turning and walking away. She thought for a moment of the mole in *The Wind in the Willows* hearing the call of home and his whole body trembling with the awareness of it. This was her home, and she felt it recognize her and send out its tendrils of welcome. Turning would be hard now, the betrayal greater than it had been before. With a sigh that Harvey would have admired, she hoisted her neat travel case and walked up to the front door. How odd to ring this bell, how odd not to know if anyone was home, and, if they were, how they might receive this particular guest. Her finger paused for a moment over the button and then with an almost impetuous flourish gave two sharp rings.

The pause was the worst bit. She could still run. If he was upstairs, or down in the kitchen, she would be away behind the bushes before he got to the door; he probably wouldn't come out down the front garden and into the street. He would think it was a joke or an error and she would be away, off to London, off to anonymity and limitless potential and strange new boyfriends and weird shop assistants and all the little encounters with all the lives she could have lived, and could still if she ran. She heard a movement inside; still time, still time. But then the latch was turning with a sound that she hadn't known she knew in her soul, until she heard it again. The way this door opened, the squeaky Yale and the way you had to sort of yank it a bit so it scraped away from the jamb. That sound was as familiar to her as her own name. And as the door opened to a crack another face equally familiar gazed out at her.

"Oh." Jeff stood for a long moment in complete surprise. "Maisie." And his voice was so known and yet so strange that she needed suddenly and unexpectedly to reestablish contact at once. She dropped her bag on the ground and stepping forward took his face in her hands and he, as if instantly and irresistibly galvanized, pulled her to him so together they stumbled backward into the generous embrace of the house.

"Yes, well, that is interesting. Yes, it interests us very much. No, I think you have done exactly the right thing, sir. No, I don't; these things have a habit of coming out at some point in my experience, sir. I would see it as your duty really, sir, as simple as that. Yes, we'll come at once." Inspector Allen watched his superior officer's face as he responded to the caller's concerns. Jarvin put the telephone down with a look of great unease and Allen put down the pad on which he had been writing.

"We must go at once to Old Street," Jarvin said slowly in just the sort of voice you wouldn't use if you had to go somewhere at once. "Something has come up. I am unsure about this. As unsure as I have been for a very long time." He let his eyes rest on his desk and the scribbled notes he had taken of the call. "I can't believe I am going down the road that seems to beckon me . . ." He looked up and caught Allen's eye. "Well, we must do what we must do. A road can only lead where it leads. Come along, Allen, let us go to see what we can do. I think that warrant you've been preparing may be unnecessary, but bring it along anyway, there's a good chap; you can never be too sure, can you?"

"No, sir." Allen, unfazed by the riddles in which his superior spoke, picked up the envelope that lay on the very top of the pile of papers on his desk and then followed Jarvin to the car.

"It was just there." Josh was hopping from foot to foot as if needing the toilet. "I saw it on Monday, before Harvey left, but I had bought some *Pokémon* cards and I didn't want to make him any angrier so I didn't mention it. He chased me out of the shop, you know. He can be quite violent, actually."

"Really?" Jarvin nodded without raising his eyes from the *Superman One* that lay before him on the desk in Harvey's office.

"Well, not violent as in a killer, yeah? I mean, not a murderer or anything like that, but rough. He had a fight in Cornwall, actually, and he threw me on the ground the other day for no reason: just for a laugh. I'm sure he wouldn't kill anyone, but there it is, there's the comic. When you rang me yesterday to ask about the meeting you arranged with Harvey and why he hadn't come I just had a long think about what I should do, you know? And, like you said, I saw it as my duty."

"Yes. Thank you, Mr. Wylde. You have handled this, I presume?" Jarvin indicated the plastic sleeve.

"Er, yes, a bit, and I took the comic out. I mean, I had a look at it. It's the genuine article, actually. Really rare, total privilege even to see one. Total thrill, yeah? So I had a look. So fingerprints, yeah? That's what you're thinking. So mine are there, too, don't get confused and lock me up." Josh giggled and fidgeted the more.

"Do you have any idea how this came to be here? Was it wrapped in anything or in an envelope?"

"Er, yes, it was in that white envelope on the desk, no address or anything. I'm not sure Harvey was going to send it anywhere, I think he just put it in there to keep it safe and stop me finding it."

Jarvin, thinking briefly that the force hadn't suffered too great a loss when Josh ignored the possibilities of a career in the police, nodded and said: "But you did find it."

"Well, I needed to get some money out to pay the Pokémon man and there was nothing to show that it was private."

"No, no indeed. But you see there is an issue here. If it was brought here by Mr. Briscow, then that points in one direction. But if it arrived by post, then that points in another. But you don't know of any other envelope of any kind apart from the blank white one we found with it?"

"Nope. I haven't seen anything like that." Josh's voice took on a slightly sulky tone. He hadn't thought to look for another envelope.

"Well, we will need to search these premises to check for that and to ensure that there is nothing else that might be considered material evidence in the case. Do you have any problem with that, Mr. Wylde?"

"Shit, yes, I do." Josh looked genuinely alarmed for the first time since they had arrived. "Harvey will kill me if I let you mess up the shop."

"We do have a warrant, sir." Allen, who had been standing quietly in the office doorway, reached into his pocket and extracted the paper. "But we will do everything we can to avoid any mess or disturbance. I do think it might be better if you close the shop though, sir. It would be unhelpful to have members of the public intruding on the search."

"Close the shop?" Josh's concern was multiplied. "I can't close the shop, not without Harvey's permission. It's all right, we never get any customers."

But Allen was insistent and Josh was forced, complaining bitterly as he went, to go to the front door and turn the picture of Thor around. He timed this motion perfectly so that he could also let in the four uniformed officers that Allen had summoned to the shop and who would provide the manual labor in the search. He led them back into the office and offered them to Jarvin, who was looking at Allen with sadness.

"We do now need to find Mr. Briscow," he said.

There was a telephone on the train. This struck Harvey as extraordinary but also potentially sinister. He had bought a mobile phone when they first appeared, but, after a long bank holiday weekend when he watched all the episodes of *The Prisoner* back-to-back, he had decided that they were the work of a totalitarian system and that they inhibited the essential liberty of the individual; also he was concerned he didn't know enough people to put in his address book. In an act of reckless radicalism he had put his Nokia at the bottom of his sock drawer and forgotten about it. Now it seemed that even after taking this revolutionary stand he was still not free of the potential oppression of monitorable communications. These thoughts crossed his mind as he sipped his third can of Watneys and fumbled for a pound coin. When he had put it in the slot he dialed—not an easy thing to do on a train moving at 120 miles an hour with a full can of beer in your hand—but he did it and then waited for Maisie or Jeff to answer. The number he had found in his old address book—Jeff Cooper, alongside all those dear old friends, just like he was one of them. He had spent most of the journey as far as Exeter planning the dialogue with Maisie. If Jeff answered it would be less difficult as it just involved slamming the phone down so hard that it might hurt Jeff's ear a little bit. Harvey wasn't sure which he would prefer.

He got Maisie. "Hello?" And didn't she sound like the lady

of the house? Surely her voice should sound a little less sure and comfortable on her first morning back. What if it was Jeff's mother or someone?

"Er, yeah, all right, Mais?" Off-script already, Harvey gave himself a shake.

"Harvey!" He was rather thrilled to hear her voice drop to a sort of husky whisper.

"Yeah. I just wondered if you were OK? Didn't see you this morning sort of thing and I got your note but it didn't make a lot of sense to be honest, but hey, not a problem."

"Oh, Harvey, you shouldn't be ringing me. I need time to think, remember? I need time away just to think. I ran away from here to try and make sense of things and now I've had to run back for the same reason. You shouldn't be ringing me. I really think I said everything I could say in my note."

"No, right. Fair enough. But I need to talk to you, actually. A lot's happened, yeah?"

"Oh, God, I know. What Simes said, and then Charles . . . it just made me feel as if perhaps I'd misread everything. I don't think I understand anything that has happened really. Jeff and I sat up most of last night talking. He's asleep now, but we said more to each other than I think we've ever said. He told me everything, about the past, about that terrible day at the Odds' house. I know everything about that now, Harvey. Charles told me the facts and Jeff has filled in the details. It is so terrible. What happened to you—it could make you . . . Well, I just wonder . . . I do understand, I really do."

"Er, OK. But look, I need to see you. Bleeder had a lot of interesting information to pass on, and I mean a lot. I mean job done. Mission accomplished. We went down there to sleuth and we sleuthed, you know what I mean? So look, I need to talk to you today, before I go to Jarvin; I need to talk it through with you. In fact, you should come with me to see Jarvin, I mean, you are as much a part of this as I am." Credit where credit's due.

"Oh, Christ, Harvey, I've just come home. If this is my home. Well, I'm here, and I've just got here. I need to think about what I'm going to do. Maybe I'll go back to Croydon. Maybe I'll just go away for a bit. I feel like I'm in limbo, like I'm cut off and floating. Did you ever feel that, Harvey, like you are just drifting?"

"Yeah, tricky. But I need to see you now." Harvey was watching the little screen on the telephone telling him how much money he had used. It seemed to be reducing at an extraordinary rate. "I need to, Maisie, I need your help." He heard his voice getting plaintive and pleading, which was one of the things he'd decided wasn't going to happen.

"I know you do. I do understand that." There was a long silence and Harvey watched the little screen with horror before fumbling for more change.

"All right." She spoke as the screen reached critical point and he unhappily fed in another pound. "I'll come. I can't leave you to do that on your own. I'll come and be with you. We'll go to Jarvin together. Just so long as everything we say is the truth. No more secrets, OK, Harvey? Whatever you did: the cleaning up, hoping to steal the comic . . . well, anything that you did . . . you need to tell him. He'll listen, Harvey. He'll understand, all right? But you must tell him everything."

"Um, right, yeah, nice one. But I need you there, Mais; I can't do it on my own." Even to Harvey that sounded a tad melodramatic; obviously, he could take all the credit if he wanted to, but hey, his moment of moral goodness on the cliff top had opened up a new and better Harvey, that's how it felt. "I need to see you tonight. I'm on the train to London; I'll be at the shop by about five. I need to check on Josh—you could come and meet me and we could have a talk and then we could go and see Jarvin, yeah? We could get it all done today. And then it will be over, Maisie. I also have something else I need to show you at the shop. I think I will call it our future."

The line was silent for a moment and Harvey wondered if

they had been cut off. Rising righteous indignation concerning his lost money was replaced by the consideration that perhaps the phone didn't work in tunnels. If it didn't this might be vital information in the battle between free men and the system that he had always felt was somehow one day inevitable. But they weren't in a tunnel and she came back on the line after a moment.

"All right, I'll come, Harvey. I'll come because you ask me to. But I don't know about this, and I don't know what you want to show me and I don't know about the future. You must understand that I am only coming now, at this moment, because I feel it is perhaps a duty I should perform."

"Er, yeah, OK then, see you at five." He put the phone down with a sigh of satisfaction. No problem. He returned to the Watneys and a seat within easy reach of the bar.

CHAPTER THIRTY-SEVEN

Paddington looks different when you're rich. The possibilities, always inherent in any railway station, are expanded and brought closer. Yes, you could go home to your small, anonymous flat in Deptford, or to your one-assistant comic shop in Old Street. But you could also go to Mayfair and find the prettiest prostitute in Shepherd's Market and rent a room at the Ritz, or go to Heathrow and fly to Bangkok. Harvey found he had sex on his mind since the incident in the rocks. Another option was to slump in a pathetic and slightly malodorous heap on a bench, nurse an insipid erection, and gaze up at the arches of the roof as if they were the very buttresses of heaven. Harvey selected the last of these choices and lay for a while, breathing heavily and letting salacious thoughts about Maisie drift across his inner vision. She was gone but she might be back. That still seemed, in his mildly inebriated state, a better position to be in than many. And it was the end of this strange journey he had been on. It seemed to have been going on for weeks, although, in fact, it was only a few short days since he found Mrs. Odd in the basement. Most of it seemed to have been spent on trains, experienced through the haze of warm ale. Through that same haze he now considered his immediate future. He would talk to Maisie and make her see that Jeff was the past, and he was the future; and they would go to Jarvin and tell him everything Bleeder had said, and Jarvin would smile that slightly unnerving smile that never really went away; and Harvey would sell the *Superman One* for a world-record price at the Toronto comic fair in August; and they would go and live in New York, maybe after a few weeks on an island somewhere. Was Maisie ready to see his stomach in broad daylight? Maybe straight to New York, but the point was that everything was going to be fabulous. It would be hard in some ways to leave his little shop forever. That was Harvey's thought as he rolled off the bench and fell heavily on the cold tiles of the floor. And Josh, of course; he'd miss Josh, he thought as he got up, rubbing his elbow. But he'd survive. He staggered a little as he made his way toward the tube. He'd go to the shop this time, but from now on the magical possibilities that stations held were going to be explored. The easy options of poverty were coming to an end.

"Of course I'm going to come in with you. But I promise I'll say nothing, do nothing." Jeff Cooper glanced across at his wife as he drove, and smiled. "I'll try just to observe."

"Well, you better." Maisie had been unsure about letting him come with her, but somehow she knew they were involved in this together. "But you need to let the anger go, Jeff. Just stop being angry for a while."

"I know." Jeff overtook a lorry. "That's what men are supposed to be: strong and merciless and angry. I learned that from Dad. Then Mrs. Odd died and I knew that someone else had done what I'd been thinking about for twenty years. I'd always wanted to kill her. Sounds bad, doesn't it? But she would come into my head at the strangest moments, usually when I was driving like this. I'd be going along and I'd think, I'll turn the car round and drive to St. Ives and smash in her skull. I must have had that thought a thousand times. But I never did it. I hope you are aware that that did take a certain sort of courage, too, Maisie."

"Yes." She considered this thoughtfully. "I am aware of that,

Jeff. And I'm aware that if you'd told me just a little bit of this twelve years ago maybe we would be different now, maybe we would have a future together . . ."

He glanced across, quickly this time, and the car wiggled in its lane.

"You mean we don't?"

"I don't know." Maisie stared straight ahead and looked at the approaching lights of Hammersmith. "I don't know. Until yesterday I would have been pretty certain. But now I can't answer that question at all. I suppose it's what I've been saying for a while now—and not just to you: I really do need time to think."

"I didn't know we had that." Josh picked up a copy of *Wonder Woman* with interest from where the constable had carefully placed it. "Heaven knows what it was doing in with the *Vampirellas*. Must have just slipped down there. Well, well."

"Mr. Wylde, please don't touch anything, I have asked you more than once." Jarvin, who was standing like a minor deity in the midst of the careful ruination of the shop, spoke with severity.

"Sorry, sorry." Josh put the *Wonder Woman* down and wandered over to the graphic novels pile to perch on the edge of a now empty rack. "But it's about time we had a spring clean. The last time we did this was . . . what am I saying? We've never done this."

"We are not here to clean, Mr. Wylde." Jarvin did not really want conversation, there was a lot to think through.

"No, no." Josh, on the other hand, was eager to chat. "Harvey might even like this; he might walk in and thank us . . . He might not, of course." His face fell slightly.

"But where is he, Mr. Wylde? Where is Harvey Briscow? You say he went to Cornwall, but his parents have not seen him and are now in a state of some concern. His mother is considering organizing a search for him through St. Ives. Why did he arrange to come to a meeting and then disappear to the other end of the country? Do you know, Mr. Wylde? Do you realize how important this is?"

Josh, unnerved slightly by these confidences and questions, shook his head. "I dunno," he said earnestly, "but he'll be here in the morning. Harvey's always here in the mornings in case I buy porn. Not that I ever do," he added quickly, "but you know, just in case. Porn or Pokémon. I'm not meant to get those. And he doesn't like boxed sets cause they're hard to shift. I got a box set of *Batman Returns* tie-ins once and he hit me with a pencil."

"Yes." Jarvin realized that he was now involved in a conversation that was entirely unnecessary to him; he began to move away when there was a knock at the shop door. Being the only policeman unemployed, he sprang forward and opened it.

"Hello, Mrs. Cooper, how do you do? And Mr. Cooper? Come inside, please." As if he had summoned them himself, as if they were expected guests and he a good host at a casual drinks party, Jarvin let the surprised and potentially querulous new arrivals into the shop, carefully relocked the front door, and then took them back into Harvey's office, where the search had now been completed. "We are searching the premises, as you can see, but I would not wish you to read too much into that." He waved his hand at Harvey's unsanitary sofa and the couple perched awkwardly on the edge of it. "We have not yet completed our investigations. We are trying to make contact with Mr. Briscow, Mrs. Cooper, and my understanding was that he was with you."

This was so forthright and to the point that after a moment's shocked silence Jeff Cooper burst into a guffaw of laughter. "Well, there you are, Maisie, no point in disguising things, is there? Yes, I believe my wife was with Mr. Briscow, Chief Inspector. In what sense she was with him needs as yet to be clarified, but she was with him, but is with him no longer. As you can see, she is at present with me."

"Yes." Jarvin frowned and nodded slowly, as though trying to follow a map committed to memory. "But I wonder if you know where he is, Mrs. Cooper? I understood, from Mr. Wylde . . . Josh Wylde . . . the shop assistant, yes, from him"—Jarvin waved vaguely in the direction of the shop where Josh had retrieved the *Wonder Woman* and was reading excerpts aloud to the busy constables—"that you were traveling to Cornwall together, and yet he had arranged to come to have a blood test performed on Monday afternoon and to have a meeting with me. His nonappearance is troubling to me. I really do need to contact him, Mrs. Cooper."

"Why?" Maisie unexpectedly went on the cautious offensive. "I mean, I'm sure he could perform the test another time. Yet here you are searching his shop as if you suspect him of more than missing a blood test."

"Yes, we do have something more." Jarvin had remained standing and he now walked to a plastic evidence box that had been placed on the desk. Opening it, he extracted the *Superman One*, still in its wrapper, and held it up carefully between the palms of his hands. "This was found here by Mr. Wylde. I wonder if either of you recognize it?"

"Only by reputation." Jeff Cooper leaned forward with interest. "This is the legendary *Superman One*, eh?"

Maisie too was leaning forward but her expression was more shock than interest. "He had the comic? How could he have the comic? That doesn't make any sense. If he had the comic, then . . . it wouldn't add up. It's not right. Where did he get it from?"

"That," said Jarvin, "is why we'd rather like to see Mr. Briscow, to ask him. But I suppose I am wondering why you feel it doesn't add up, Mrs. Cooper." Maisie was suddenly aware that the green eyes were upon her; like green rays from a laser gun she felt them opening her up. She shook her head, her own eyes closing for a moment.

"I don't know," she said. "He told me he didn't have it, that it wasn't there . . . Why would he lie?" She frowned in real uncertainty. "But if he has the comic he can't have killed her, can he? Not that I ever thought he did, but when Charles Odd told me about him getting caught by the mother, I wondered, I really began to wonder . . ."

"But he must have killed her!" Jeff almost shouted it. "He got caught too, you just said so. Mrs. Odd caught him and she beat him, beat the skin off his back if it was anything like my encounter with her. He carried that around, just like I did. Carried the scars and the bitterness, that terrible dull rage. He carried it and then he cracked. He cracked and God knows I don't blame him." He turned his face away and Maisie, almost automatically, put her hand on his arm.

She was clearly thinking hard and Jarvin let her think, watching her face, watching her try to work it through. "But why . . . ?" It was as if Maisie was trying to open a jam jar with her mind, her head twisting from side to side, as though loosening something with the motion. "Why the comic? If he went for revenge . . . if he went to kill her . . . then he didn't go to steal. And if he went to steal he wouldn't kill. He wouldn't kill if he has this. He can't have done. Unless . . ." She stopped and looked at Jarvin. "I will tell you everything I know, Inspector. And I will tell you the truth. But I need to believe that you will listen with sympathy."

Jarvin nodded slowly. "Everything about this case has made me require that quality, Mrs. Cooper," he said softly. "I think perhaps I will feel it for Mr. Briscow without needing to try." And then, again slowly, he moved to the door and called Allen, who came and sat neatly on his unstable chair with every appearance of the living rock, apart from his right hand, which crossed and recrossed his notepad.

———

"In the Liverpool slums. In the Liverpool slums. They look in the dustbin for something to eat, they find a dead rat and they think it's a treat. In the Liverpool slums," Harvey sang as he walked from the tube. The train had been full of Scousers down for a midweek evening game with Arsenal, and Harvey was happy to sing one of his favorites in their honor. It was past six and he knew that Josh would have gone, and this only improved his mood. He was late, so Maisie would be waiting outside the shop, looking a little bit forlorn possibly, a bit lost and small in the big roaring quiet of the closing city. But he would warm her with a hug. Not too much kissing—his breath must smell like Oliver Reed, after he died—but a nice long sexy hug. And then he'd take her inside and sit her on the sofa and tell her everything and she would be so impressed and then he'd open the drawer and show her the comic and she would be so thrilled that there was a future for them both that she'd roll back on the sofa and he'd climb aboard and . . . shit. He stopped for a moment and took a few deep breaths and then tried walking again—yes, that was better. Perhaps keep the thinking to a minimum. So he sang another chorus or two and peered ahead of him to see if he could see her.

When he arrived outside Inaction Comix two things struck him. First, she wasn't there and that meant he hadn't kept her waiting, which he'd kind of hoped he would so as to give her a little punishment for leaving him behind in Cornwall. And second, the shutters were up and the lights still on, which meant that Josh was here. Bugger. He stepped back from the window, not wishing to be seen. Perhaps he'd just wait outside for her; she wouldn't be long. But that would mean that she kept him waiting, even though he was meant to be punishing her. Was that fair? What if Josh had let her in? Maybe she was inside. What would Josh be doing to entertain her? Hurriedly Harvey fumbled for his keys and with unprecedented speed found the right one, opened the shop door, and stepped inside.

"Um." He looked round with interest. "Ah." Jarvin and the Coopers were just emerging from his office, so nine faces simultaneously turned to look at him. "Right." He shut the door carefully behind him and came rather slowly into his shop. "So, er . . . how's it going?" he asked.

CHAPTER THIRTY-EIGHT

There was a long silence, long enough for Harvey to wonder if this was pregnant. He felt fairly sure that it was. Pregnant with twins and ready to drop was how he had characterized it before Jarvin spoke.

"Mr. Briscow" is what he said. Harvey wasn't sure this really added anything much to the silence, not containing any real information that wasn't obvious to everyone present. Except perhaps the four uniformed policemen who stood watching silently from around the room. Perhaps Jarvin said it to sort of introduce him to them. He wondered what their names were. But something else was niggling at him, something he couldn't place.

"We have been trying to find you, Mr. Briscow," Jarvin added and Harvey was aware of Allen going off into the office, presumably to call off a search party. Had they really been hunting for him? Was there an APB out? He felt rather thrilled and also very slightly amused, as well as shitting his pants, of course.

"Er, well, here I am." Again this didn't really seem to bring much to the occasion but Harvey felt it right to speak. "I went to Cornwall, but now I'm back."

"You had a blood test booked, Mr. Briscow." Jarvin spoke gently, sounding like a Harley Street specialist.

"Yeah, sorry. Bad one that. I just kind of got mixed up and stuff." Harvey was taking in the room more now, rather than just the faces. It was almost bare. He'd never realized how small it was before. Really it might be better if they turned the comic stands the other way and then had aisles running across...He caught Josh's eye and Josh looked instantly hangdog. Harvey wondered what he'd done. He looked round hastily to check for new purchases but there were piles of comics and boxes everywhere and it was hard to tell if he'd bought anything. He gave Josh a long frown, but still felt that niggling feeling: Something was amiss. Apart from all the obvious things, of course.

"We have been searching your shop, Mr. Briscow, as you can see," Jarvin continued. "Of course, we would rather have done so with your permission and in your presence but unfortunately we could not contact you."

"No. Never liked mobiles—fascist," Harvey muttered. But his attention was elsewhere. He'd worked out what had been niggling him: What the fuck was Jeff Cooper doing here? Why wasn't Maisie jumping into his arms and what in fuck was Jeff doing with her? When you invite your lover for a rendezvous prior to running away to New York to start a new life together you don't expect her to bring her husband. What the fuck?

"Er, hi, Maisie," he said.

"Hello, Harvey." Shit. Her voice was low and sad, like his mother's that time he swore at the vicar.

"You all right?"

"Yes, I'm all right. Are you all right, Harvey?"

"Er, yeah, yeah, no problem. All right, Jeff?"

"Hello, Harvey, how are you?"

"Good, ta. Yeah. Nice one. Right, so...you OK, Inspector?"

"The reason we are seaching your shop, Mr. Briscow"—Jarvin refused to enter into the spirit of the reunion—"is that something was found here that we are having trouble explaining." He turned and pointed. Moving with eerie silence, Allen had returned from the office, unnoticed by Harvey, and was standing behind the counter. Like an auctioneer's assistant he was holding a *Superman One* in a gloved hand, its plastic slipcase still smudged with Mrs. Odd's blood.

Harvey nodded. He felt very relieved, actually. That must be what Josh was looking guilty about: squealing on him to the pigs. While a dubious thing for a shop assistant to do, it was at least better than more *Pokémon*, or for that matter the *Whip Dancers Trilogy*.

"Yeah, the *Superman One*." He tried to sound airy, although in fact he could feel his bowels tightening to the point where he badly needed the toilet. "You found that, yeah?"

"Yes, we did, and of course we don't know this, but we are assuming it is the same one that Charles Odd owned and that was missing from the house in St. Ives after his mother was murdered."

"Right, yeah, good call." Harvey nodded.

"Now, Mrs. Cooper has told us an interesting story, Mr. Briscow, about you visiting the house after the murder was committed, intending to steal this comic. However, since then it has been suggested that perhaps you had a motive for murder; that you carried a grudge against Mrs. Odd; that you killed her and then returned later to steal the comic and to clean up your tracks. I wonder what you think about that, Mr. Briscow."

What Harvey thought was that it was a bit of a public place for such a deeply humiliating statement to be made. Couldn't they do this in private somewhere? He was aware of Maisie trying to catch his eye with what he feared was a look of deepest concern. But for some reason he was thinking about Josh. All the showing off he'd done about having a girlfriend and now this. He did the sigh, which involved closing his eyes for a moment. When he opened them he became aware that two of the uniformed constables had quietly moved behind him to block the door. He shook his head hard to clear the Watneys a bit. If ever there was a moment for clarity, this was it.

"Look," he said, "let's get this straight. I did go to the house, yeah? I saw the body; I did a bit of cleaning up; OK, I admit that. But I didn't steal the comic—I just happen to sort of have it and I'll explain that in a minute, and I didn't kill Mrs. Odd, for reasons that I will go into. And I don't have a motive— Maisie, you can't really believe that." He looked at her; did she believe that? She was sort of shaking her head, but in a way that seemed dangerously noncommittal under the circumstances. He shook his in return. "Look, honestly, everything is OK."

Harvey noticed two things at once. One was that Allen's radio had crackled and he had repaired to the back office once more. The other was that Jeff Cooper was moving toward him. He tried to step backward but trod on the toe of one of the policemen who was standing rather too close behind him.

"Um, sorry." He stepped forward again, but Jeff was still approaching. Were all these policemen just going to let him be assaulted? He began to panic; Jeff was looking bigger than ever in a threatening pink polo shirt. "No, no." Harvey put his hands up to his face as Jeff moved in. Then he felt Jeff's arms go round his neck. He was going to throw him. Harvey braced himself and waited to be wrestled to the ground. But instead he was simply squeezed.

"Let it out, Harvey. Let it go." Jeff was speaking.

"Um, OK." Harvey nodded hard and peered over Jeff's shoulder, looking for assistance.

"It's over. Don't hold it in anymore. Just be free of it, free forever." Jeff pulled back and looked Harvey full in the face. "Just let it be, Harvey."

"Er, right you are, Jeff." Jesus, what the fuck was going on? He was being handled by a maniac and the police were just standing around watching—in Jarvin's case with the hint of an indulgent smile on his face. Jeff stood for a moment and Harvey saw to his horror that tears were beginning to streak down his face, until with a wrench of his head he turned away and was folded in what looked like a deeply erotic embrace by

Maisie. Had the world gone mad? Jeff Cooper, the Jeff Cooper, had just burst into tears and was now being caressed by Harvey's girlfriend. His shop was a ruin and he was being patronized by a policeman who looked like a dolphin. He shook his head again and looked at Jarvin with desperation in his eyes.

"Look, I don't know what the fuck is going on," he said, "but I can tell you everything, and everything is going to be fine. I didn't kill anyone, honest. I just broke a window, that's it. And the comic is mine. It really is. I can tell you who did it: It was Bleeder—I mean Charles Odd, sorry. It was him. He killed his mum and then he sent the comic to me as a present. So it belongs to me, for real. After all these years it is finally mine and we can go off to New York and open a coffee shop." He looked uncertainly at the continued embrace of the Coopers and frowned. "Well, I can anyway. You can ask Charles—oh, sod it, Bleeder; that's what he's called. You can ask Bleeder Odd, he'll tell you everything."

Harvey had hoped to have the attention of the room at this point: It was, after all, rather momentous information that he was imparting, and while he had never been terribly good at storytelling or anecodotage, preferring the sardonic rejoinder to holding the floor, he did rather expect everyone to pay attention on this occasion. However, Allen had come to the door of the office and was signaling to Jarvin, and that man, while not actually stopping Harvey, was moving away and leaning over the counter to listen to what Allen had to say. Harvey paused and waited and tried to prevent his heart from pounding in a way that felt dangerous to his health. He was fine, he told his heart. He was A-OK. He had taken the risk and he had saved the heroine from certain death and he was back in Metropolis, back in civilian clothes. The cape was off. Taking deep breaths he felt himself slowly relax. He even shut his eyes again for a moment, but the Watneys was still swirling, making him feel sick, and he had to open them again. Jarvin was returning to stand in the middle of the shop—Harvey's shop, as it happened—as if he owned the place. But Harvey didn't complain. He just listened.

"I have very sad news," said Jarvin, and Harvey wondered vaguely about other people being sad. It seemed hard to believe really; surely all the sadness in the world was pretty much saved for him. "My colleague in Cornwall has just contacted us to say that Mr. Charles Odd was found dead at the bottom of the cliffs in St. Ives just moments ago. It is believed that he took his own life by throwing himself from the rocks at the end of Porthminster Point." He looked round at the assembled company, at the shocked faces of the Coopers, who had both come up for air.

"Dead?" It was Jeff who spoke. "Charles is dead?" He shook his head and began to pant very hard, as if he couldn't breathe. "She did that. It's still happening . . . Jesus, we did that. Oh, shit, this has gone further . . . I can't stand this, I just can't . . . It needs to stop!" And then he was back with Maisie.

"Bad one." Josh, forgotten until now, had been surreptitiously flicking through the *Wonder Woman*, but now felt moved to speech. But Jarvin did not turn to him, for his eyes were fixed on Harvey. That man's eyes had moved up to the ceiling and his lips were moving as if he was reading from the peeling, nicotine-colored paintwork.

"He's dead." Harvey's eyes came down with a bump and collided with Jarvin's. The chief inspector nodded.

"Yes, I'm afraid he is."

"No. But hang on . . ." Harvey put his hand up as if about to make a rhetorical point but then it fell by his side. "If he's dead . . ." He stopped again, gazing round wildly. Maisie surfaced over Jeff's shoulder and looked at him.

"It's all right, Harvey," she said. "Just tell the truth, whatever that is. It's time to tell the truth."

"Oh, fuck!" Harvey stepped forward with both hands up. "But look, I didn't, honestly I didn't, it was Bleeder, he told me, he told me! It was Bleeder fucking Odd!" And then he spun and dived for the door but was enfolded in the arms of the waiting policemen.

Acknowledgments

This book would have been impossible without the hard work and generous input of Sophie Hicks and James Gurbutt. My thanks to both of them.

About the Author

ANTONY MOORE was born in Cornwall and now lives in London with his family.